UP IN FLAMES

UP IN FLAMES

A FLIRTING WITH FIRE NOVEL

JENNIFER BLACKWOOD

Montlake
Romance

Published by Montlake Romance, Seattle

www.apub.com

Amazon, the Amazon logo, and Montlake Romance are trademarks of Amazon.com, Inc., or its affiliates.

ISBN-13: 9781503903487
ISBN-10: 1503903486

Cover design by Letitia Hasser

Printed in the United States of America

To the women in my life. You are beautiful, strong, and an inspiration.

Time: 0815
15 minutes into B shift
Dispatcher notes: 1432 Butternut Lane. Male, late twenties,
attempting suicide. Needs medical attention.

Reece tore down Butternut Lane, sirens silent, red light swirling against the unlit houses. His team had barely even had a chance to do their daily check of the engine and their gear before they were called out here.

"Ready to bring this man out alive, brothers?" Reece said into the intercom.

His fellow firefighters, Jake Bennett and Cole Gibson (a.k.a. Hollywood), gave a resounding "Hell yes" as Reece parked the engine across from the house they'd been dispatched to.

They hopped down onto the sleepy street nestled on the edge of the West Hills. For a Sunday, it was especially deserted. Nobody walking their dogs. Nobody shuffling out in their robes and slippers to the front of their driveways to grab newspapers. That could be attributed to the early winter chill. Two weeks till Thanksgiving, and Jack Frost had taken downtown Portland into the single digits. Reece's ears stung as he exited the engine and hooked around to the other side to grab his airway bag.

Jake and Hollywood had lugged their kits over their shoulders and were making their way up the driveway.

"Should we wait for the PD to get here?" Jake asked.

It was protocol to wait for police presence if there was a remote possibility of a threat. One that Reece was willing to look past if a man's life was at stake.

"There wasn't any message about weapons. I say we go in. Don't know if we're already too late," Hollywood said.

Reece examined the exterior of the house. Little reddish flecks Reece didn't even want to begin to imagine the origins of peppered the walkway. A light was on in the bedroom on the top level, but other than that, it was dark in the house. Paint peeled from the mottled wooden door. The siding wasn't much better off. In its prime, the house appeared to have been painted some type of dark blue or brown. Now it was the color of a grease stain. Peeking into a window, he saw stacks of newspapers and trash littering the front room. Not a single person in sight.

He looked over to Jake and wasn't surprised that his friend seemed unsure. Jake had been overly cautious these past few months, especially with Erin in his life. It was still weird to think of his best friend and his sister together, but they were happy, and that was all that mattered.

Jake and Hollywood both looked to him. They'd been on hundreds of calls just like this. Nothing new here. So Reece made the final decision.

Reece moved to one side of the entryway and pounded on the door. "Portland Fire Department. Open up."

He went to reach for the doorknob to see if it was unlocked when a loud bang rang in Reece's ears, and he stumbled backward as debris from the door exploded. His foot caught on the cracked pavement, and he fell to the ground. Everything went to static and moved in slow motion as something dark in the corner of his vision caught his attention. Blood. Everywhere. And that's when all hell broke loose.

Concrete dug into Reece's back as he lay there, momentarily stunned. He moved to sit up, to make sense of where the loud sound had come from, when a searing pain burned in his shoulder, forcing him to suck in a sharp breath.

Jake kicked in the door and disappeared into the house as Hollywood hovered over Reece. He was saying something to him, but Reece couldn't make out the words, Hollywood's voice sounding like he was talking underwater.

Four cops rushed past them into the house, guns drawn.

His hearing finally regained clarity, and several voices boomed from the house's entryway. Hollywood's voice cut through the ringing in his ears. "Are you okay, man?"

"Yeah." Reece tried to get up again, and Hollywood put a hand to his chest to stop him. "We should be in there with Jake."

"Are you serious right now? You just got shot. Save the heroics for the cops." Hollywood grabbed gauze out of his med kit and looked at him uneasily. "You wanna take off your shirt, or do you need me to?"

"You'll need to buy me a few drinks before I show skin," Reece said.

Hollywood shook his head and sat back on his haunches while Reece unbuttoned his shirt with one hand, hissing out a breath as he slid it over his shoulder. From what he could see, it was a graze.

Hollywood pressed a wad of gauze against the wound, and sparks of pain jolted through Reece. He glanced to his shoulder, the white material staining red beneath Hollywood's hands. "What the—?" Where had he gone wrong? He always made sure to stand to the side when knocking, but had he forgotten this time? Was he getting too comfortable in the job?

As if Hollywood could read his thoughts, he said, "Gunshot came through the door. A hell of a shot, since you were standing pretty far to the side."

Just then, two cops, Watkins and Juarez, exited the house with a handcuffed guy in between them. The guy glanced over at Reece and smirked.

Fucker.

Chapter One

Time: 0830
30 minutes into B shift
Status: On call

"I'm fine. Will everyone cut the shit and stop fussing?" Reece gripped his shoulder, the bandage beneath it already staining with his blood.

The initial shock of getting shot had worn off, and everything around Reece was sharp and irritating. So maybe it wasn't the smartest idea to go into a suicide call without the PD. Lesson learned. Luckily, he was the only person to pay the price for his stupidity. Jake and the PD had been quick to disarm the man.

His shoulder ached, and all he wanted to do was kick back a cold one and a few aspirin. Instead, he was sitting in an ambulance with two overly concerned EMTs, Emma and Brice. Really, it was just a graze. He was lucky—he knew that. He didn't even want to think about all the ways it could have gone south. A bit of broken skin was the least of his worries.

"Maybe next time try not to get in front of someone's bullet?" Emma said while she applied fresh gauze and bandages to his wound. She was new to Portland Metro. He'd seen her on a few calls in the past month, and he liked her laid-back personality. "You'll need to go down to the hospital and get stitched up."

"I'll get around to it. Thanks." Reece hopped down from the back of the ambulance and pulled a fresh shirt Jake had found for him over his shoulder. He winced as he carefully guided the fabric over the bandage. "Soon."

He walked over to Jake, who was pacing in the driveway. His friend stopped abruptly when he saw Reece.

"What did Emma say?" Jake asked.

"That I needed to stay on people's good sides."

Jake shot him a look. Guess he wasn't up for joking around. Usually he was the one to bring some levity to a situation, but instead, Jake's face pulled into a tight expression.

"Said I need stitches," Reece said.

"Then go down to the hospital, idiot. I'll ride in the ambulance with you, and Hollywood can take the engine back to the station."

"I'm willing to take my time." He'd pissed off enough nurses. He had to be strategic about who stitched up his arm.

"Your reluctance has nothing to do with Susan or Ellie, does it?"

"Brittany."

So he went on dates. Sue him. He was always up-front about what that entailed. Which meant that there'd be no seconds. Or thirds. No phone calls or texts. Reece kept it simple and liked it that way. No need to add complications to his life.

They walked back to the ambulance, giving a few nods to the crowd of onlookers who stood behind a barrier the PD had set up, aiming their phones at the scene. A local news van pulled up just as Reece hoisted himself into the back.

Emma and Brice marked their unit as "on a call" in the system and drove down to the hospital.

Twenty minutes later, they arrived at the entrance to Portland General. For the past twelve years, Reece had been on the other end of hospital visits; he'd been the one wheeling the patient into a room. He prided himself on taking care of others. Now Jake walked beside him, bypassing the main entrance and instead going through the doors reserved for emergency personnel and up to the nurses' station in the ER.

Tina, one of the nurses who'd been working at Portland General since before Reece had been born, smiled up at them. He mentally blew out a sigh of relief at the fact that this was one nurse he hadn't managed to piss off.

"What's up, guys?" Tina asked.

Jake propped an elbow on the counter and jutted his chin toward Reece. "Reece is having a rough start to the day."

"I told you. Lay off the nurses, Jenkins." Tina gave him a pointed look. After a moment, her gaze settled on Reece's shoulder. His wound was already starting to bleed through the new shirt. "What happened?"

"Just a graze to the shoulder."

Jake shook his head. "He's downplaying it. He got shot, Tina. Can we get someone to stitch him up?"

Her eyebrows rose. "Room three is empty. All the docs are swamped right now, but I'll send our nurse practitioner to take care of that."

"You're an angel," Jake said.

Reece and Jake made their way to the room on the opposite side of the nurses' station and shut the door behind them. Jake slumped into the seat next to the hospital bed. The last thing Reece wanted to do was sit. That would give him the opportunity to stew over what had happened. He didn't need that right now. So instead, he paced the room, his eyes scanning over the **HAVE YOU GOTTEN YOUR FLU SHOT?** poster.

"What are the chances you've pissed off this nurse practitioner?" Jake said while he played a game on his phone.

"Not very high." He wasn't even on a first-name basis with any of the NPs. Which was good, because he wasn't in the mood for regretting any more life choices today. "Why are you smiling?" Reece's adrenaline had bottomed out, and a headache pulsed at his temples.

"Because I think I know who's on shift today, and this should be good," Jake said, barely able to hide his amusement.

Reece turned to tell him to screw off, but the movement pulled at his bandage, sending a hiss of breath through his gritted teeth. "You're really going to mess with a man who just got shot?"

"Like you said, it was a shoulder graze." Jake raised his brow at him.

Before Reece could say anything else, the one woman who'd hated him for the better part of a year walked into the fluorescent-lit hospital room. Shit. He'd take the jilted one-date wonders over this woman any day.

"Well, look what the cat dragged in," Sloane said. He'd grown up with her. She'd been best friends with his younger sister, Erin, since they were kids. She was his friend by proxy. Until about a year ago, that is.

"Hi, Sloane." The painkillers weren't doing nearly a good enough job pacifying the biting pain of the wound, and Reece gritted his teeth.

"Guess it's my lucky day to be on the ER floor. What brings you in? Sprain your wrist playing Xbox or whatever you boys do over at the station?"

"I got shot."

Her brows knit together in concern and then smoothed out as she did a once-over of Reece. Obviously deciding he wasn't in any imminent danger, she put her hands on her hips. "Go ahead—show me."

Out of all the nurses to walk through the hospital-room door, Sloane was by far the last pick he had in mind. Not that she wasn't a great nurse. She'd managed to stay at the same hospital for seven years. No, the merits of her skills had nothing to do with it. It was more that she'd be the most likely candidate to leave him in a ditch for naught, which he was sure violated the whole Nightingale Pledge. To say their relationship was rocky was putting it mildly. Still, he wasn't going to piss her off any further.

He gingerly gripped the bottom of his shirt and slid it off.

She let out a low whistle. "Lucky. How did this happen, anyway? I thought the only people you pissed off were nurses."

"Your bedside manner leaves much to be desired." Reece winced as the shirt descended his arm. He could really use something stronger than Tylenol at the moment.

Sloane grinned and moved to the sink, lathering up and washing her hands. After grabbing a pair of gloves from the bin on the wall, she slipped them on and pulled out antiseptic, bandages, and thread. "Just for you, Reece."

He eyed the needle that she extracted from another drawer and swallowed hard. He'd never been shy of them—his whole body was covered in tattoos—but the thought of a needle in *Sloane's* hand? That was enough to make him second-guess his decision to get stitched up. If there wasn't a good half-inch gap in his skin, he'd hop down from the table and sprint out of there, pride be damned.

"Is now too late to say I adore you and you're the best nurse ever?" he asked.

"You're a year late to that party, man," Jake muttered, and shot him a sympathetic look. Like he wouldn't want to be in Reece's situation either.

Reece and Sloane . . . well, they'd had an incident a year back. One in which he'd acted like a complete moron and for which he was continually paying the price.

Sloane focused on the tools on her metal tray, placing them each an equal distance apart. "Don't be a whiny baby. I'm not going to hurt you." Although he could have sworn the word *much* was said under her breath.

Jake pushed up from the chair in the corner and strode over to the door. "On that note, I'll just wait outside. Don't want to see poor Reece cry."

"Thanks a lot, man." So much for his fellow firefighter and best friend always having his back.

But Jake was already out the door, and it was just him and Sloane.

"Sit still and this'll be over before you know it," she said as she sterilized the wound.

He sucked in a breath as the antiseptic stung his skin. "Is that what you say to your boyfriend?"

Last he knew, she was on-again, off-again with that complete tool she'd dumped the year prior. Right before *the incident*. Brandon? Byron? Whatever the guy's name, Reece didn't like him. Didn't give him a good vibe with the way he looked at every other woman in the room except Sloane.

"Really want to say those types of things when I have a needle in my hand?"

"Isn't a doctor supposed to do this?"

"Lucky you, I'm now a certified nurse practitioner. I get to do all the fun stuff." After administering a shot of lidocaine, she tore open a plastic case and took out the supplies for stitching him up. The skin barely had time to numb before Sloane threaded the string through.

"Yes, lucky me."

She paused for a second, examining her work. "You really should be more careful out there."

"Aw, Smurfette, would you miss me?"

Sloane glared at him. She hated the nickname he used for her. But when she had blue hair and wore Smurf scrubs, was there really any other option?

"Smurfette has blonde hair. Get it right. As for missing you? If I wasn't on the clock, I'd tell you exactly how I'd feel," she said, not missing a beat. Sloane's hand worked steadily—up, down, in, out.

"Noted. I'll make sure you're in charge of the eulogy if it comes to that."

"I think it'd go something like this: *Reece Jenkins, loving brother, son, and absolute prick of a human being who thinks of no one but himself. Does that sum it up okay?" She finished the final stitch, dropped her tools back on the cart, and plastered a bandage to the neatly stitched wound. Then with a fluid grace, she spun around, tore off her gloves, and disposed of them in the waste bin.

Cold shoulder didn't even begin to describe what she'd given him since their run-in one night at a bar. Ever since they were teens, Reece had had a thing for Sloane. He'd never told her because she was Erin's friend, and he'd been dating his high school sweetheart, Amber, at the time. He'd been engaged to Amber, but when he had left to train for the hotshot fire crew in Bend, he'd come back to nothing. After that, his faith in dating hadn't been salvageable.

Fast-forward to last year when he'd seen Sloane sitting alone on a barstool at Henry's. She'd been drunk out of her mind. He hadn't thought much of it—just that he'd give her a ride home because he didn't want some dickhole to take advantage of her. And then when he'd dropped her off, she'd made a pass at him. And he'd responded in what was probably the worst way possible: by lying and saying she was the furthest thing from his type. He had never regretted passing up a drunken chance with her, but when he'd tried apologizing the next day, the damage had already been done. As evidenced by the drink she'd thrown in his face.

"Hey, you forgot to add that I care about a cold beer and Sunday football," he retorted. Her claim was ridiculous, of course. He cared about his family and friends. That didn't matter to Sloane, though.

She ignored him and washed her hands in the sink. "You're all set. I'll prescribe something for the pain." After drying her hands, she scribbled on a medication pad, tore off the paper, and handed it to him.

"Thanks. And can you do me a favor?"

"Besides stitching you up?"

"Don't deny you liked jabbing me with a needle."

Her lips twitched in response. "What do you want?"

"Can you not mention this to Erin? It'll just freak her out." Tell his sister and it was sure to get back to his mom. And the last thing he wanted to do was put his family into a full-on panic. His mom was especially on his case about safety, and he'd be hearing an earful from her if and when she found out.

She didn't bother to answer his question, just smiled sweetly and said, "Have a good day, Reece." And with that, she breezed out of the room.

That didn't bode well.

Sloane Garcia made her way to the nurses' station. Reece Jenkins. In the emergency room as a patient. The thought made her hands tremble, because even though she couldn't stand the man, she'd never want to see him actually hurt. She sat down in the rolling chair and typed notes into her computer, documenting the visit.

Out of the corner of her eye, a pair of dark blue scrubs moved her way. Sloane glanced up from the computer to find Keisha. A Cheshire-cat grin spread across Keisha's face when she peeked around Sloane to see who was buttoning his shirt in triage room three. "Is that Reece Jenkins?"

"The one and only." She stared at the computer, finishing up her paperwork.

"Please tell me you caused him pain and agony."

"Only a little." Okay, so she'd been a little rougher than necessary with a couple of stitches, but she'd kept it on lockdown. She was a professional. Even if the sight of Reece's face made her want to throat-punch something (preferably him), he still deserved quality care, even if he was repulsed by her.

Ugh. A year later and she still couldn't get his words out of her head. Add that to the fact that he'd made the rounds through her entire nursing unit, and it didn't do much for the good ol' ego.

"I don't know how you did it. I would have slipped a little with my needle. Maybe gone straight for the carotid."

Sloane shook her head and laughed. Keisha was one of the many women who'd fallen victim to Reece Jenkins. He had a type—women. Or really anything with a pulse. And he'd made his way through her nursing unit with surprising efficiency. Except for her, that was. She wasn't jealous, of course, because she'd grown up with the dude. She knew all his nasty habits. Like the fact that he chewed chips abominably loud, and he *always* had to be in control of the remote. A man who needed that much control over stuff would not last one minute in her apartment.

Whatever. No need to let this mess with the good day she'd been having. Even if it did skyrocket her blood pressure to think that he'd been shot. A few inches lower, and he'd be going to a different part of the hospital. One that patients didn't return from. The thought made her blood pound in her ears.

But thoughts of Reece soon slipped to the recesses of her mind, because she had bigger things to worry about, like the next trauma victim currently being wheeled into the ER.

Chapter Two

Two hours later, Reece made his way back to the station. By now, word would have traveled about his injury. But when he arrived, he was relieved to see that everyone was going about their business. Hollywood was cooking chicken in a skillet—God help them all. Jake, who had escorted Reece back to the station, busied himself with helping to make sure Hollywood didn't burn down the station. Collins, another firefighter who was usually on A shift, was sitting at the kitchen table, filling out some sort of paperwork. Reece assumed he'd been called in after the incident.

"Heard you had a rough morning," Collins said, looking up from his papers.

"Just another Sunday." One that he would like to never repeat. Reece pulled out one of the rolling chairs at the table and sank into it stiffly. He'd been in fistfights before and had his ass kicked in training, and even that didn't compare to the sharp sting in his shoulder. As soon as he found a somewhat comfortable position, heavy footsteps sounded from deep inside the station.

"Jenkins. Get in my office," Chief Richards bellowed from down the hall. From the sound of it, he was more pissed off than usual. Not a surprise. This close to retirement, everything rankled the guy. Reece breathed in the wrong direction at a morning meeting, and it pissed him off. So the incident this morning was sure to add fuel to the fire.

Reece wasn't one to get reprimanded at work. He did his job, and he did it well. In fact, he could remember only two times in his life when he'd been in deep shit. The first was when he'd forgotten to open his mom's food truck on Black Friday (he'd been out on a date), and the second was two hours ago when he'd messed up on that call.

He prided himself on keeping it together while he was on the job. That was the one time when he felt capable, when he had a handle on life. An unblemished record in his ten years of service proved as much. Well, not now. He was sure this was going straight into whatever file Chief kept on him.

He strode down the hall to the battalion chief's office. Most people who had an office at the station decorated their desks with photos of family, kids' artwork, and achievement awards. Chief Richards prided himself on zero clutter. Ever since he'd transferred from Station 12 a couple years back, the chief kept his desk completely bare, except for his computer and a tumbler of coffee. Although Reece would be hard-pressed to say that the cup didn't contain a little something else.

Reece clasped his hands together as he stared at Chief Richards, who glared at him from across his desk. Didn't even give him a chance to clean himself up after their engine parked in the bay. Instead, the chief had called him into his office like he was a delinquent kid being sent to the principal's office.

The chief squinted at him, looking like he was trying to x-ray him for damage. "You okay?"

Reece nodded. "Just grazed my shoulder. No muscle damage." His scorpion tattoo might look a little crooked after the skin healed, but nothing he couldn't get touched up. So lucky.

Seeming pleased with that answer, Richards launched into the tirade Reece had steeled himself for. "What the hell was that, Jenkins?"

"You're going to have to specify, sir." There was a lot that had gone wrong. Starting with his piss-poor decision, the PD taking forever to show up, and the fact that he hadn't bothered with the proper protocol by making sure the place was safe to enter first. It was a circus act of a call. And he'd paid the price for it—luckily, not the ultimate price.

"I expect this from a rookie. You're our engineer. You're supposed to make good judgment calls, keep your men safe."

Reece didn't bother to argue with him. The man was right—he'd made a crap call. And he'd keep his trap shut since the chief's vein was throbbing in his forehead. Reece felt like a piece of shit for putting his brothers in danger with his actions. The whole thing shook him up. People said that their whole lives flashed before them when faced with a life-or-death situation, but all Reece had experienced was splintered wood and the regret that he hadn't snagged a Krispy Kreme doughnut from the kitchen that morning. He pushed those thoughts away. He didn't need to be spooked on the job. If there was one thing he couldn't afford, it was to hesitate. Seconds were the difference between bringing out a person alive or waiting till the ME arrived.

"It won't happen again," Reece said.

"You're damn right it won't. You're up for a review, and I can make a recommendation to send you to another station. Seems you're too comfortable here."

Reece's gaze shot up to the chief's. Richards stared at him, irritation clear in his brown eyes. Reece had worked at this station for almost a decade. The thought of going anywhere else, away from his men—well, that just wasn't an option he was willing to consider.

"Chief." Reece would like to say he was surprised by this, but that'd be a lie. The chief had had it out for him since day one, always nitpicking everything he'd offered during their morning shift meetings and criticizing the way he wrote up his reports. He didn't know any other person who was that specific about comma splices.

"You may have had it easy before I came to this station, but your free ride is over. Either put in the hard work, or you're free to transfer. I'll be watching your performance. Closely. Take the rest of the day off. I've brought Collins to fill in for you."

Reece didn't expect to work the rest of his shift. Especially when he was hopped up on painkillers. But being dismissed by the chief was the cherry on top of this day.

"Yes, sir." That was all he could say, because telling him to screw off probably wasn't the best choice. So instead, he nodded and stood.

"Jenkins?" the chief called as Reece was about to exit his office.

"Yeah, sir?"

"With your little stunt, I think it's wise to get in as many hours as possible, maybe do a little community building."

He took a calming breath before turning around. He didn't bother to tell the chief he already volunteered his time outside of the station. Richards didn't care about what he did on his off time. "What would you suggest?"

"Were you going to participate in Four for Four?"

Reece shrugged and winced. He'd need to take another aspirin when he got to his locker. "Wasn't planning on it."

The annual firefighter auction, where the community came together to bid on firefighters like they were slabs of meat, was saved for the rookies. The highest bidders had a firefighter by the balls for a month, or until they completed four tasks from their honey-do list. Hence the name Four for Four. Although most chores were finished within a couple days. He'd never heard of anyone's sentence being drawn out the entire thirty days. Reece didn't want anything to do with the auction. The department had more than enough Portland firefighters sign up, so they'd stopped asking for volunteers weeks ago.

"Clear your schedule. You're going."

Reece gritted his teeth. There was a time and place to put a foot down. This was not one of them—not when the chief was dangling his job in front of him like this. "Looking forward to it," he said.

"That's the spirit."

Whatever Chief Richards was getting at, there was no way he'd run Reece out of his own station. He'd earned his place here. Worked with his best friends. He'd rather run himself into the ground than put in for a lateral transfer.

Reece made his way out of the chief's office and went to the bathroom to splash water on his face and finally get a chance to scrub off the dirt the hand sanitizer in the rig hadn't cleaned off. He kept his hands under the scalding water and breathed deeply through his nose.

The door swung open a few seconds later, and Jake appeared in the doorway. "How many days of detention do you have?"

He chuckled and shut off the water. "Asshole." It might as well have been detention. Putting him in the bachelor auction? He hadn't done that in years. Didn't want to be subjected to some bored housewife who wanted to inconspicuously snap pics while he washed her car. He'd been a good sport about it when he was a rookie, but he was well over that phase.

"What'd he want?"

"I have to work a special event this weekend."

"Four for Four?"

Reece only nodded.

Jake let out a low whistle. "Damn, he really does have it in for you. Make sure to put on some extra cologne. I hear the ladies love that."

"Why are we friends again?"

"You're just jealous because I'll be in the audience instead of up on the stage." Jake went to clap him on the back and stopped in the air, seeming to remember Reece's injury.

"You're actually going?" Reece asked. On Reece's days off, he wouldn't be caught dead at the station or doing anything work related. He loved his job but also needed distance in the form of *SportsCenter* and his PlayStation.

"Erin wants to go. Says it'd be fun to donate to a good cause."

Good. Maybe he could convince his sister to bid on him so he wasn't at the mercy of some stranger.

"Enjoy your day off," Jake said, striding back into the kitchen as the smell of something burning on the stove filled the air. "Damn it, Hollywood. Get liberal with the olive oil before you smoke us out," came Jake's muffled voice down the hall.

"I swear I just stepped away for a second," Hollywood responded. But everyone knew that even if he hadn't stepped away, the chicken would have burned. Hollywood would be a great candidate for that *Worst Cook Ever* show. Reece always thought those people were faking it, but then he'd met Hollywood, who could burn water.

Reece chuckled under his breath. The last place he wanted to go was home. So he took his time with changing and then reluctantly grabbed his jacket and keys from his locker, making his way out of the station.

Chapter Three

There were two things Sloane loved about Portland: that her two best friends lived here and that her weird little city had the best coffee in the world. So what if she'd never traveled outside the continental United States? She'd still make this claim no matter where she went. Currently, she was gulping mouthfuls in between checking on patients.

"You need to head home, Sloane. It's thirty minutes past your shift," Tina, her shift supervisor, said. Tina was the resident mom, always making sure that her nurses were taken care of. It was one of the many reasons Sloane loved Portland General. She'd been fortunate enough to be hired on after nursing school, and they'd even paid for her to become a nurse practitioner.

She nodded to Tina, bone-weary. After the day she'd had, all she wanted to do was snuggle under a bunch of blankets and read a good book. "I will. I just want to check in once more on a couple of patients."

Changeover was the most dangerous time for patients. They ran a tight ship here, but Sloane didn't like to take any chances. She popped her head in on Zachary, the twelve-year-old who was receiving fluids after severe dehydration from the flu. She stared at the monitor. All his vitals were stable. Then she moved to the next room, where there was a four-year-old who'd had the misfortune of taking a spill out of a second-story window.

Her patients were stable and as comfortable as they could manage. She'd done her job.

"Girl, go home," Tina said, shooing her down the hall and to the nurses' station near the front of the building.

"Fine. I'm leaving." She grabbed her coat and made a show of putting it on. "I'll see you on Wednesday."

"Sounds good."

Sloane wrapped her scarf around her neck and disappeared through the sliding doors out into the chilly November night. The trees had long since shed their leaves, and the bare branches reminded her of fractured bones as they were backlit by the full moon.

It'd been snowing earlier that day when she'd stepped outside on her lunch break, but it had melted off by the time her shift ended. Not surprising. Rarely did snow stick in the Portland area, but when it did, it made for a glorious winter wonderland, and also the busiest times at the hospital.

She made her way to her car in the staff parking lot, and once inside, she blasted the heat until feeling came back into her chilled fingers. Instead of driving across town to her apartment, she headed down the 405 to catch Front Street to take her to the Northwest District. She was meeting up with her best friends, Erin, Madison, and Jake, tonight at Brodie's Tavern. It was a new brewery downtown that early reviews touted to have beer rivaling some of the big names in the area. She didn't think many could match a Deschutes IPA, but she'd be willing to try it. Plus, after the day she'd had, she could use one . . . or four . . . right about now.

She still couldn't believe she'd stitched up Reece, of all people. She'd been mulling it over for hours. Even though her fingers itched to text Erin what had happened to her brother, she took HIPAA laws seriously.

Plus, Jake was a tattletale. He'd totally spill the beans to his girlfriend. So she saw that as a win-win.

Sloane managed to find a parking space on a side street a few blocks from her destination. Even with Thanksgiving a couple weeks away, the whole town was in Christmas mode, wreaths hanging from storefront windows, garlands winding up lampposts. Salvation Army bells rang in the near distance. Sloane took a deep breath, and a white puff of smoke erupted from her lips on her exhale. She loved winter. Loved the feel of the cold air against her skin. The luxury of a cashmere scarf bundled against her neck.

Brodie's was in an old brick building that used to house the local newspaper. It'd been abandoned for the past few years since the newspaper had gone out of business. She could still make out the faint *Portland Press* logo sun-stained into the brick. Portland had a habit of doing this—refurbishing buildings, breathing new life into otherwise deteriorating subsets of the community.

The old ramshackle press stoop that used to be the target of spit wads by the nearby middle schoolers and drunks sleeping off their rough nights was now replaced with a heavy oak door with a long, spindly iron handle. The kind she'd expect to see in a castle or a cozy tavern in the Scottish isles.

As she pulled open the door, the smell of hops and fried food enveloped her, and the heaviness of her day melted away as she made her way to the back table. The place was packed. Which wasn't all that surprising, since it had just opened this past weekend. Every seat at the bar and the surrounding tables was taken. She scanned the room for her friends and finally landed on them, sitting in a corner booth.

Sloane slid into the empty seat next to Madison. Across from her sat Erin and Jake, who were currently staring at each other like maybe they should get a room. They'd been doing that since they first got together. Every relationship tended to lose that shiny, new relationship glow after about week three. Nearly six months, and they glowed more than the models in a face-wash commercial.

Sloane ignored the two lovebirds and pulled Madison into a hug. "Have they been like that all night?"

"Heard that," Erin said. "And I was just grilling Jake about today's events with Reece. Where was my text?"

"I figured he'd tell you." Sloane motioned toward Jake. "My job is complete."

Sloane gave a wry smile to Jake, who just shrugged in response.

"How was your shift—besides stitching up my brother?" Erin asked, taking a sip from her pint glass.

Sloane let out a long sigh and settled farther into the plush cushion lining the booth. "Long."

"We already ordered mozzarella sticks and crab wontons. They should be here any second."

Madison pushed a beer in front of her. "And this is their signature IPA. Although I don't know how it can be a signature item when you've been open only two days, but who am I to judge?"

Madison was always thinking of others. If Sloane was good for a quick comeback, Madison was the mom of the group. She bet if she peeked into Madison's purse, she'd find wet wipes, tissues, and probably a box of Band-Aids. Sloane didn't even own a first-aid kit. Which was sad, considering the fact that she worked at a hospital.

"You're a goddess," Sloane said. She smoothed her thumb over the condensation that had built up on the outside of the pint glass and then grabbed the glass and took a long drink. The liquid hit her lips, and the bitterness of the hops exploded on her tongue. She'd need a few more sips to see if it would make her favorites list, but it was off to a good start.

"So just to give you a heads-up . . . ," Erin started, but trailed off when she looked past Sloane.

"Smurfette. I didn't realize you were going to be here tonight."

Sloane steadied herself and managed not to choke on her beer. It would be a waste if it had sprayed in his face, because the beer was actually pretty good.

"Shouldn't you be home healing? Or, I don't know, not getting shot by people?" Sloane asked. She caught Erin eyeing her brother protectively.

Everyone had the nerve to look a little sheepish. Except for Jake, who merely nodded at Reece and went about sipping his beer. For the past six months or so, Sloane had managed to avoid most of the events where she knew Reece would be in attendance. At first because she was so mortified about the whole drunken exchange she'd had with him. And then it had slowly built to a simmer of resentment. Because he'd confirmed her worst fear—that her ex was right, and she was in fact disgusting and undatable. Or, as Brian had so lovingly told her, *You've let yourself go, babe.* After ten years with someone, maybe she'd been lax about hauling her butt to the gym, but she'd brushed it off as him being an angry ex. And then when Reece had basically said he was repulsed by her? Well, Brian's theory didn't seem so far-fetched. "Is this why you guys bought me a drink? A preemptive sorry?"

Madison and Erin groaned. She loved her friends, but damn it, they knew how much she loathed Reece. As far as she was concerned, he was on the same level as black licorice and candy corn. Maybe a step lower, and that was saying something, because she wouldn't feed that to trick-or-treaters, not even the high school punks who arrived way past the appropriate door-ringing hour. And seeing him twice in one day was definitely pushing it.

"You guys used to be fine. Can't we go back to the good old days?" Erin asked. She had recently moved up from California after she'd been terminated from her teaching job due to budget cuts. Now she was a teacher in Portland and sickeningly in love with Jake.

Sloane took another sip of her beer. Normally, she held the mantra of "Give as few craps as possible." Jerk patient at work? She let it slide off her back before she made it to the exit at the end of her shift. Doctor trying to mansplain something that Sloane already knew? Yep, she let that slide too. But something about Reece's words still haunted her, and she resented the fact that she couldn't just let it slide. *Ew, Sloane. I wouldn't get with you if you were the last woman on earth.* And then he had gone on to date several nurses around her. So yeah, she was saltier than a McDonald's french fry.

"You mean when Reece used to keep it in his pants around the people I work with?"

He raised a brow. "I haven't heard any complaints."

"You just did."

"Unfair bias. You have to actually experience it before judging."

She let out a snort. Yeah, that wasn't happening. She was way too tired to be dealing with this crap. If she had known he'd be here tonight, she would have skipped and opted for her couch and some much-needed cross-stitching time. She'd finished up a dozen or so projects in the past few weeks, and she was proud of the one she'd just made that said DOWN WITH THE PATRIARCHY, with Rosie the Riveter on it. In fact, that was exactly how she felt about Reece. She wanted to roll up her sleeves and Hulk-smash that disgustingly masculine face.

"Not in a million years," she said, throwing his words back at him.

He mashed his lips together and had the decency to look like he felt a little bad.

"On that happy note, I'd like to make a toast," Erin said. "Thank you, guys, for showing me that coming home was the right choice to make. I've just learned I'm being invited back next year and get to keep my position teaching science." Erin beamed. The charter school she worked at seemed to be treating her well, and she loved the administration and the kids.

Jake kissed her forehead.

"So proud of you," Sloane said.

"Only took you ten years, but we're glad you came to your senses," Madison said.

They liked to give her a hard time. She'd been so reluctant to come back to Portland, but once she and Jake started dating, there was no chance of her leaving.

Erin raised her glass again. "And here's to my brother, who scared the living shit out of all of us but lives to annoy us for another day."

"To friendship, and Reece annoying the women in his life," Jake said. He eyed Erin with an intensity that even made Sloane blush. If a man looked at her the way he did her best friend, she might believe that love still existed. As it was, she had a perfect setup with a body pillow, a boyfriend of the rechargeable variety, and a subscription to the Hallmark Channel. By her standards, she was doing just fine, thank you very much.

"Glad you decided to stick around. We're all pretty fond of you," Erin said.

"Some more than others," Madison snickered.

Jake turned to Reece. "Did you ever end up hearing back from the Craigslist person about the part for your car?"

He frowned. "Gertie is still without a radiator."

Reece had this annoying habit of naming his cars. His first car in high school had been Prudence. After that was a Shelby Cobra named Alice. There were a couple of other junkers he'd fixed up and sold throughout the years, but Sloane hadn't bothered to learn their names.

To be fair, she probably wouldn't have an issue with anyone else who named a car. It was a Reece-specific pet peeve. Just like the way he chewed gum and his jaw would pop. And the fact that nine times out of ten, he wore a plaid button-up. Like a mountain man. By his size, he definitely fit the criteria, the big oaf. As evidenced by his wardrobe at the moment. A red-plaid flannel and dark jeans. A few women from the bar kept glancing his way as he kicked back his beer.

Yeah, good luck, ladies. Not one you want to waste your time on.

"Do you ever name your cars male names?" Sloane asked, moving her finger through the condensation on her pint glass.

Reece chuffed. "Why would I do that?"

"Because it seems a little desperate that the only women in your life are of the mechanical variety."

"Funny, I'd put money on mechanical objects being your only form of entertainment these days." He raised a brow, challenging.

Sloane's cheeks heated. Oh, the nerve of this man. Didn't matter if it was true.

"Who wants beer? I love beer," Erin chimed in a little too brightly. She hated conflict, especially when it came to her brother and Sloane.

"We should just set them in a room and let them duke it out," Madison said. "It'd be safer for us all. Plus, I put fifty bucks on Sloane winning."

Jake laughed. "Of course Sloane would win. She'd make poor Reece cry like a baby. But Erin's right. I'm dying for a beer. Mind helping me, Reece?"

Sloane liked Jake. He was calm, levelheaded, and made her best friend go all heart eyes, which she'd never seen Erin do before.

Reece's gaze cut to hers. Cold, distant. Much more so than when he'd landed on her hospital bed this morning. The shock from being shot must have worn off.

He gave her one last once-over and then slid out of the booth, not seeming at all affected by the stitches in his shoulder. He and Jake made their way to the bar as Erin scooted over in the booth to sit directly across from Sloane.

Sloane knew what was coming. Especially when she felt Madison's stare coming from next to her. Instead, she focused on scanning the bar. This early time of evening saw patrons who were well on their way to getting buzzed but still a few hours away from the complete fiasco that this part of Portland exhibited once the bars started closing up for the night.

Sloane was thankful that she'd moved to the day shift again. Anything was better than being on the night shift in the ER, which saw the worst of the bar fights, the fraternity-brother dares, stupidity in general.

"What is with you? Can't you be nice for one night?" Erin hissed. Her fingers raked down the condensation of her glass, leaving a set of vertical lines from top to bottom.

Yeah, Sloane felt like a jerk. No, she would not admit this to Erin. "He started it." Okay, maybe she had this time. She wasn't keeping tally.

"What are you, three?"

"We all know I have the mentality of a thirteen-year-old boy, but thanks."

Erin gesticulated with her hands. "I know he was an asshole to you. And dated a couple of women from the hospital, but can't you try to be nice?"

"Eight women."

"Right. He was an ass to eight women, but dear God, can we save the torturing for another night? The man's been shot. I feel like this should at least give him a few hours of you two not fighting like cats and dogs."

Her best friend was right, of course. "Fine."

"Plus"—Erin's lips curved into a wicked grin—"I have a much better way that you can get back at him."

Sloane took a sip of beer. "I'm all ears."

Chapter Four

"When you said getting back at your brother, I didn't think it'd require spending money. Seriously, why are we going to the auction?" Sloane asked. She groaned as she buckled her seat belt and turned to face her best friend. When Erin had told her to meet her at her apartment the following Saturday, she hadn't known what to expect, but it definitely wasn't going to a charity event. To be honest, she'd become sort of a recluse on the weekends. And if Erin hadn't coaxed her out of her apartment, there was a 110 percent chance Sloane would be in sweatpants and cross-stitching right now. Basically, she was living her best cat-lady life, minus the cats.

She'd prided herself on fostering rescue pups from the shelter, which kept her busy most of the time, but her apartment building had recently changed their policy on animals, which meant that she wasn't able to foster any until she found a new place.

"It's for a good cause. What's better than watching hot firefighters up on a stage getting bid on like cattle?"

Sloane could think of a lot of things better than this, but she didn't want to rain on her best friend's gung-ho attitude.

"Plus, I got some insider info." Erin tapped her fingers along the steering wheel and practically bounced in her seat. "Reece is apparently going to be a fetch boy with the champagne."

Champagne. Now she could get behind that. If she was going to pay to come to the event, she might as well enjoy the commodities of the alcoholic kind.

"I almost feel bad for your brother for having to dress up."

"Knowing him, he'll be in his turnouts," Erin said.

Reece had two types of dress: plaid flannels and work gear. There was no in between. Both held no appeal to her, especially the latter of the two.

As a rule, Sloane had no interest in firefighters. A certain type of person went into that field of work. Overconfident, overly masculine, just too much man in general. She'd much rather date the quiet, bookish type who hung out in coffee shops while filling out crossword puzzles. Yes, apparently she was ninety. The only other thing to complete the look would be to plant her in front of the TV with the evening news and *Jeopardy*.

Erin's boyfriend, Jake, remained the one and only exception to the rule. He was a decent guy who treated her best friend like a queen—just how she deserved to be treated. The firefighters Sloane dealt with while at the hospital were a different story. Okay, maybe one in particular clouded her judgment. He oozed enough macho-hero vibe to compensate for the rest of them. She'd dated that type. Been there, done that . . . had the emotional scarring as a souvenir. A year on her own and she liked her newfound control—of the remote *and* the number of covers on her bed—so she'd come to the conclusion that that type of personality would never mesh with hers.

Erin slipped an arm around Sloane's shoulder. "Just relax. It's a night of fun. You don't even have to bid if you don't want to."

"Oh, trust me, I won't." Every penny went straight into the bank. She'd had her eye on a house right off Mississippi Avenue. It was a bungalow with a white picket fence and a purple door, and it had enough room in the backyard to start a garden. And the best part was that it had plenty of room for foster animals. She passed it on her running route, always admiring the handcrafted shutters with hearts etched into the wood. She'd heard through the grapevine that the owner was looking to sell soon, and she'd be ready to strike the day it went on the market.

As Erin pulled her Prius into the event-center parking lot, Sloane stared at the swarm of people moving toward the entrance. They were in all styles of dress—casual, formal, somewhere in between. Sloane lumped herself into the latter of the three options, with her black dress and candy-cane leggings. The holidays were just around the corner, and she'd already busted out her Christmas wardrobe. Tomorrow she'd wear her Grinch scrubs. Patients always loved those.

A parking attendant swiveled his arms toward an open space in the lot, and Erin parked the car.

They both slid out of Erin's car and made their way to the auditorium. If there was a silver lining for the night—because Sloane always liked to look for one—it was that the event raised money for local charities.

"Who knows? Maybe someone will catch your eye," Erin said.

"Told you, I'm not looking for anything right now. Plus, I'm up to my eyeballs in dating apps." One night while angsting over the empty left side of her bed, she'd signed up for a dating site. She still had yet to meet up with anyone, but she had come close a few times. It just never felt like the right timing. Either she'd had to work several days in a row when the guy had shown interest—and then by the time she *had been* available, the guy had ghosted her—or she'd come up with some excuse to put off meeting up. She had to take care of a foster dog. Vet appointments. Volunteering at the Humane Society.

Putting those apps on her phone was more stressful than the fact that she was still single. Consensus: Fielding weirdos was more trouble than it was worth.

"Just haven't found the right guy yet." Her best friend smiled brightly. Sloane had made the distinct observation that the only people who expressed this sentiment were the ones who were already happily in relationships.

Sloane wasn't in any hurry to commit. She liked being single. Had come to terms that she very well might be for a long time, and she was okay with that. But that didn't mean she didn't occasionally miss human contact, to be wrapped in the warmth of a man's touch. "Where's Jake?" she asked.

"He's meeting us there. He had a few things he had to do with Bailey beforehand."

"Sounds ominous." Erin and Jake had been dating for almost six months now and were living together. Sloane figured he'd be popping the question anytime, given how serious her friends had gotten over the past four weeks or so.

"No, just something with computer coding." Bailey, Jake's daughter, was a computer whiz. Bailey had even set up Sloane with a new computer. Did Sloane understand half of Bailey's explanation in code-speak? No. But the computer ran Netflix and Facebook just fine, so that was all she could ask for.

They made their way into the event center, and Sloane paused to take everything in. A layer of hay was scattered over the concrete floor, hay bales were stacked up against the walls, and country music blared through the speakers.

A banner reading **47TH ANNUAL FOUR FOR FOUR FIREFIGHTER AUCTION** in bright red letters stretched overhead. Underneath it said **FOUR WEEKS, FOUR FAVORS**.

Good thing Sloane hadn't opted for complete formal wear tonight. They made their way inside the building, and Erin texted Jake the spot they'd secured toward the back of the room.

Erin glanced down at her phone and smiled. "He says he'll be here in a few minutes."

"How did Madison get out of this?"

Erin dropped her purse on the table and glanced around the room. "She *is* here. She's doing her photography wizardry."

Sloane slumped into her seat and drummed her nails along the white linen table runner. She wasn't usually this bitter. In fact, she loved going out. Loved girls' night. But she'd been in a funk lately. One bad shift in particular still haunted her. Compartmentalization came with the nursing territory, but she'd had a patient who'd coded in the middle of the night and hadn't made it. The girl was six.

She could still see the little girl's pale blue eyes lose their light. Could still hear her parents' wails as they cradled her.

Sloane swallowed past that thought. This was supposed to be a fun night out.

Jake slid into the seat beside Erin and kissed her on the forehead. "Sorry I'm late, babe." Erin melted into his touch, closing her eyes and leaning into him. A pang hit Sloane straight in the chest. She was so incredibly happy for her friend. And so incredibly aware of how much she felt like a third wheel at the moment.

She pushed that thought away.

"Hey, Sloane. Good to see you. Thanks for coming," Jake said.

"I'd say *You're welcome*, but when it comes to Erin, I don't think I had an actual choice in the matter."

He grinned down at her. "She is pretty persuasive when she wants to be."

"She used her teacher glare." She shot her best friend a look, but Erin just shrugged and smiled in response.

"Ah yes. That works every time. I come bearing gifts, though, so hopefully that makes it better?" He slid two wineglasses in front of them.

"Now why didn't you start with that? It'd be much more persuasive."

Sloane took a long pull from the glass. A nice rosé that lightly bubbled across her tongue.

"Where's your bestie?" Usually him and Reece were attached at the hip.

"He's out there somewhere." He motioned to the packed banquet hall. There had to be at least five hundred people in attendance, and each of the circular tables was filled to capacity.

"How unfortunate," Sloane said drily. Probably using that perfectly straight smile of his to get extra donations for the charity.

"Ladies and gentlemen, welcome to the forty-seventh annual Four for Four Firefighter Auction."

A round of cheers erupted from the audience.

"See those paddles in the center of the table? Those are your bidding sticks. Once you see a firefighter that tickles your fancy, raise 'em high in the air to claim your prize." The auctioneer spoke quickly, rattling off something that Sloane didn't quite catch.

"Tickle your fancy? What is this, the fifties?" Sloane murmured.

Erin swatted her arm. "It's for charity."

"If you win, the firefighter of your choice owes you four favors that expire in thirty days. So get that honey-do list ready. Our men are great at washing cars, mowing lawns. They even do laundry."

Another bout of cheers erupted.

Maybe Sloane had reached a herculean level of self-sufficiency over the past year, but she couldn't think of anything that she'd need someone else to do for her. Unless they wanted to rob a bank for her or save her a spot in line at that southern-food joint across town that always had an hour-long wait.

"Without further ado, let's get this party started."

And with that, the lights dimmed, and a big spotlight shone on the stage that was in the shape of a catwalk. Something Sloane could only describe as porn-techno music blasted, the deep bass pulsing in her chest.

This time, even Sloane found herself cheering along. Maybe it was the glass of wine. Maybe the energy was just infectious.

"First firefighter up is Eli. He's been at Station Twelve for a year and loves walking his golden retriever and hiking on the weekends."

Eli walked out onto the stage in full gear, touting the complete package of broad shoulders, sandy brown hair, blue eyes, and high cheekbones. A table of overly raucous women cheered. Eli's smile widened, and he looped his thumbs in the waist of his pants, managing to look both shy and tantalizing at the same time. Albeit young. Way too young for what Sloane would consider acceptable ogling age, let alone dating. Someone in the front row tossed a feather boa onto the stage, and Eli picked it up and wrapped it around his neck, the crowd going wild.

"What is he, twelve?" Erin asked.

"At least fourteen. I see a chin hair," Sloane replied.

"I thought that was glitter from the boa."

"At least they had the decency to make him look wholesome," Sloane whispered in Erin's ear. Much better than the dick pics some of the guys on her dating apps sent two minutes into a conversation. In what world did guys think, *Hey, I said hello; now it's time to show them the goods before my lacking conversation scares them away.*

"We'll start the bid at twenty dollars. Do I hear a twenty?" the auctioneer called.

Not to Sloane's surprise, several paddles raised in the air.

"Fifty dollars!" a woman toward the front shouted.

"Seventy dollars. Do we hear a seventy for the fine young firefighter?"

Eli moved the boa between his legs like something out of a *Magic Mike* movie, and the room was a tidal wave of paddles. Well, there went the wholesome vibe he'd had going for him.

The bid ended at four hundred and went to a little old lady in the front of the room.

"Holy crap. That's a hundred dollars per chore," Sloane said. She could think of a lot better uses for that money. Such as buying dog food for the Humane Society, new decorations for her apartment, or at the very least, a few pairs of new shoes online. She drained the rest of her wine, everything going softer around the edges.

Erin leaned in and murmured, "Think she'll make him wear the boa while he does them?"

"For sure."

A new song blared over the system, and the auctioneer started back up again. "Next is Bart from Station Six. He enjoys rock climbing, Cherry Garcia ice cream, and stargazing."

This guy was another young one of the muscle-upon-muscle variety. He had on the blue uniform that firefighters wore when they weren't in full gear, whatever those were called. Bart had man bangs that were far better managed than Sloane's last attempt at them seven years ago. Veins corded down his forearms, and even from her spot toward the back of the room, she could tell the guy had *large* hands. Like, whoa. Although she did enjoy looking at large, well, everything, she had a rule about dating guys who looked like they took more time getting ready in the morning than she did.

Sloane grabbed another glass of wine from a waiter's tray and took a sip. Okay, maybe she'd underestimated this event. It was pretty fun. Mr. Stargazer went for three hundred bucks and was currently shuffled off the stage. A loud round of applause erupted as the winner—a woman around the same age as Sloane—jumped up and down at her win.

"So are you going to tell me how this is going to get back at your brother?"

But before Erin could answer, the auctioneer started the next bid.

"Next up, we have Reece from Station Eleven. He loves vintage Jeeps and ketchup on his scrambled eggs, and is every bit as sweet as his namesake candy, ladies."

A stream of rosé dribbled out of Sloane's open mouth, down to her candy-cane leggings. She couldn't have heard the man right, could she have? There was no way Reece, of all people, would offer up something so generous. No, not the man who grumbled over adding money to the group tip pile when they went out for drinks. She quickly grabbed a cocktail napkin off the table and did her best to dry the dark spot staining her tights and turned to Erin, whose wide eyes looked like they might dislodge from her head. When Erin had said that Reece was working tonight, she thought he'd been roped into handing out wine to patrons. This was better. So much better.

He stood there, looking grumpy and rugged compared to the last two fresh-faced firefighters. His beard was a couple of days past scruffy, and his scowl was barely contained. Even if he looked pissed off to be there, his shoulders were pushed back, and he stood to his towering six-foot-three height. He was in full gear, his suspenders stretching across his broad chest. The reflective strip across his helmet gleamed in the light, flashing straight into Sloane's eyes. She blinked back spots and folded her arms, waiting for this to take a disastrous turn.

"Do we have twenty dollars to start the bid?" the auctioneer began, but even Sloane could tell that there was a bit of hesitation in his voice. Like he knew this package was defective goods.

Sloane sat back and waited for Reece to crash and burn. She'd be surprised if he made it past the fifty-dollar mark.

A paddle shot up. "Twenty!" a woman cried out.

The auctioneer's tight expression softened into what Sloane could only assume was relief. "Twenty dollars. Twenty dollars. Do I hear thirty?"

Reece squinted as his face tracked across the ballroom, but Sloane doubted he could see anything with the stage lights in his eyes. He'd have no clue who bid on him.

Four more paddles went into the air.

For real? People wanted grumpy mountain-man firefighter?

His thumbs were hooked around the straps of his turnouts, and a grin splashed across his face. Some woman was going to have the biggest disappointment of her life when she realized he'd peace out after his favors were done. Most women didn't even get that much, according to some of her coworkers.

And then it hit Sloane. Four chores? Four chores where Reece was on the receiving end of someone's mercy? Oh, she could put Reece to work. In fact, this seemed like a positively excellent idea. This was completely evil and sinister, and if she'd been in a movie, this would be the part where her hair would have twirled straight up like the Grinch when he'd solidified his diabolical plan to ruin Whoville's Christmas.

She looked over at Erin and shot her a small grin. But Erin was still staring, slack-jawed, at Reece on the stage.

"Do I hear forty dollars?" the auctioneer asked.

Sloane's paddle shot up.

"What are you doing?" Erin asked, her brows slanting until a small groove formed on the skin between them.

"You wanted me to donate my money to a good cause. Well, here I am."

Erin shook her head and smiled. "You are so evil, and I love it."

"It's taken years of work to achieve this level of evil genius." Erin would be too nice to put someone through the gamut. Same with Madison. Sloane never claimed to be a saint. And now she'd go straight from Santa's *naughty* list to his *rotten as shit* list after what she had planned.

Jake leaned in and said, "Don't seem too eager. Those ladies in the front row bid big every year." He pointed at the group of ladies who were around her grandmother's age.

She turned to them and grinned. "Don't you worry. I'm getting my money's worth."

A sea of paddles raised in response.

"Fifty dollars."

Sloane held her paddle high.

Paddles continued to drop the higher the bid went. Finally the auctioneer rattled off, "One hundred dollars."

There were only four people bidding now. Sloane guessed there weren't that many women on the market for a firefighter who looked like he'd rather chew on a rusted nail than complete four favors.

Sloane glanced around the room. Two women were enthusiastically waving their bid cards, the women around them tittering and slurping back more wine. Move over, ladies, because this was hers.

"Two hundred dollars!" Sloane shouted.

"Two fifty!" a granny yelled from the front row.

Oh, Grandma. Not today, girlfriend.

Sloane was ready to go to bat for this. She'd committed, and she'd see it through that Reece Jenkins would owe her a solid. Four, to be exact.

"Two sixty. Do I hear a two sixty?" the auctioneer asked incredulously. He was clearly shocked that the bidding had gone this high.

"Three hundred!" Sloane found herself yelling. The tiny voice in the back of her mind was saying, *Guuuurl, aren't you trying to save your money?*

That voice took a hike as soon as the last paddle went down.

Victory.

"Going once, twice. Sold to the lady with paddle two eleven. She wins for three hundred dollars."

Erin stared at Sloane with wide eyes. If she were a cartoon character, her eyes would bug out of her head. "I can't believe you just spent three hundred dollars on my brother. Is any man worth that?"

She raised a brow at Erin. Sure, that was a pretty penny to drop on him. But it was for charity, she reminded herself, and, oh, she'd make it worth it. "Is that any way to talk about your brother? I thought you'd say something like he's priceless." She patted Erin's hand.

Erin snorted and took another sip of wine. "You do you, Sloane Garcia."

"Don't worry. I won't be too awful to him." That was a lie, of course. Oh, she'd make him squirm. She didn't know where this new masochistic streak had come from, but she'd run with it.

Jake let out a loud guffaw. "I can't wait to see his face when he finds out who bid on him."

"Looks like it'll be happening sooner than later," Erin muttered under her breath. "Oh, hi, Reece. Fancy seeing you here."

Reece walked up to the group. He still looked like he'd rather be anywhere else, but his features eased as he got closer to the table.

"Guess I'd better go pay so I can claim my prize." Sloane pushed away from the table and made her way to the back of the event room, to the cashier table. She made sure to keep her paddle hidden from sight as she passed Reece. Let his mind be at ease for another few minutes.

"I pity the man who owes you favors," Reece said.

"Me too." She smiled up at him sweetly and brushed past him.

She wound her way around the bustling ballroom and took her spot in line at the collection table. Thumbing through her wallet, she extracted her credit card and clutched it in her shaking hand. It still hadn't fully registered that she'd basically lost her mind and spent hundreds of dollars on Reece Jenkins, of all people. If anyone asked, she'd chalk it up to temporary insanity. Less than a minute later, she found herself at the front, an older man working a tablet with a credit-card reader attached.

Sloane recognized the man as Chief Richards. She'd met him at a local fund-raiser for the food trucks downtown. "I'm here to pay for my firefighter." She handed the man her paddle, then handed him her credit card.

RIP, dear money—guess that end table from Pottery Barn will have to wait.

Seriously, what had she been thinking?

Chief Richards thumbed through the ledger, and then his brows furrowed. "Reece's girlfriend?"

Her head tilted back, and then she let out a loud cackle and smacked her hand against the table. Oh, this guy was funny. The chief's eyes widened, and did he just scoot back in his chair? Okay, maybe she'd kicked back a little too much wine. "God, no."

His brows knit together. "Interesting someone would pay so much for someone they didn't know." He said this to himself more than to her. Which was odd, because wasn't this whole event about spending the most money possible to raise money for charity?

He ran her card and then handed it back to her along with the tablet. She signed with her finger, finished the transaction, and handed it back to him.

"Oh, I know him." She'd spare the chief the nitty-gritty details. "We're acquaintances." Of about twenty years, give or take. But as of recently, she couldn't even say she knew a thing about him. He'd changed so much from when he was that sweet high school guy who made sure his sister always had a ride home from school and cooked them mac and cheese when their mom was working the food truck.

"Do me a favor, will you? Please let me know that he has fulfilled all obligations." Chief Richards handed her his card. "It's important to know."

"I'll do my best." Odd. Why was the fire chief so invested in Reece's abilities to complete a bunch of stupid favors? She'd email the guy, but still.

After paying him, she hung out within earshot for the next person to pay. The woman, probably in her midforties, was collecting on a firefighter named Morgan. The chief handed her a receipt and thanked her for her contribution. No mention of contacting. No card given. *Huh.* Sloane must have stumbled on the jackpot, and it was going to have a sweet, juicy reward. Maybe, just maybe, Reece would finally have one big karma pill to swallow.

Reece paced in the lobby, staring at the red and tan blocks in the carpet design. The event had been over for twenty minutes, and the winners had been instructed to come out and claim their prizes. Like he was a piece of meat to be claimed. *Ridiculous.* He hated the auction. Would rather spend his time helping others in more useful ways, like he did every few weeks at the soup kitchen. Even if all the proceeds did go to charity, he didn't like that this time around, the fate of his job was tied to someone he owed a stupid favor to. Or four.

Who was this number 211? Was it an ex? Who in their right mind would bid so high? He'd done the bare minimum to prep for tonight. He'd showered, run his hands through his hair, and thrown on his turnouts. At most, he'd expected a fifty-dollar pity donation from his sister.

A throat cleared behind him, tearing him out of his thoughts. "Such a perfect night to auction off firefighters. Wouldn't you say?"

Sloane. The muscles in his jaw tensed. He turned to find her looking up at him with hands on perfectly rounded hips. Even in her heels, she barely came up to his chest, but she was every bit as menacing as someone three times her size. He usually saw her in crazy patterned scrubs, but tonight she wore a dress that clung to her curves. The candy-cane stockings were a bit much, but that was Sloane. The definition of over-the-top. Over-the-top enthusiasm for boy bands when they were kids. Over-the-top wardrobe choices. Over-the-top amount of love for Barry's Bakery, where she and his sister and Madison met up every week. And keeping with that trend, over-the-top hate for him.

"What are you still doing here?" he asked. She should have been long gone by now, since the event had ended.

"Erin's my ride. She's still off somewhere with Jake, so here I am." She rocked back on her heels and looked like she was enjoying his discomfort.

Damn it. Where's the chick who bid on me? He scanned the lobby and didn't see anyone wandering around, just the rest of the firefighters from the auction talking to their bidders. "If you don't mind, I'm waiting for my bidder. It's always a pleasure seeing you, though." He gritted his teeth. He was at a public event, with the chief around. He'd be nothing but cordial.

"Looks like we'll be seeing a lot more of each other." She held up a pay stub.

He ripped it from her hand and scanned the ticket. There in big letters was Reece's name. His stomach dropped, and it took everything in him not to crumple up the receipt and chuck it to the ground.

What the hell?

"You bid on me?" He took back all the sour thoughts he'd had about lonely housewives. He'd offer twenty favors to them in exchange for getting out of the four he owed Sloane.

"I wasn't going to, and then I thought, oh, what an excellent contribution to the Muscular Dystrophy Fund."

"And you just had to bid on me."

"Of course. It's going to be a fun few weeks." She winked.

He didn't think it was possible, but his piss-poor mood turned down an even darker road.

And to think at one time, he'd thought Sloane was hot. With curves for days, light-brown skin, full red lips, and honey-brown eyes, she still was. He liked that she wasn't a stick. He liked having something to grab on to. But when there was zero chemistry there, it wasn't worth even thinking about.

To put the cherry on top of this ridiculous situation, the chief decided to walk over. "Ah, Jenkins, I see you've met your winner. I told her that you would treat her especially nice."

"Of course, sir. Wouldn't have it any other way." He forced his lips to pull into something that might be considered polite. At the very least, like he wasn't chewing on glass.

Sloane smiled over at him with such a sugary grin, it probably pained her face.

"I'll let you two kids get to it, then. Have a great night." The chief nodded to himself, clearly pleased at Reece's discomfort.

"You too, Chief," Sloane said.

His pulse hammered as he watched the two of them exchange a pleasant smile. What did she have planned for him?

Reece flexed his fingers, fighting to stay calm. Sloane had no idea that his career was in her hands, and he wasn't about to tell her. It was information too powerful for this one woman to have.

"So about my favors." She tapped a bright blue nail to her lips. It matched the color of her hair. Ever since high school, she'd forgone her brown hair and had moved from one shade of the rainbow to the next. He'd seen her with fire-engine red, neon green, purple, but it'd remained blue for the past year. Out of all the colors, he liked this one the most. Ice-cold, like her soul.

"What do you want, Sloane?"

Her teeth raked over her full bottom lip like she was thinking hard about what she wanted. She wasn't contemplating, though. Sloane didn't contemplate. She schemed. And he had no doubt that she'd take her sweet time finding ways to make Reece squirm. "I have to think on it. I'll give you a list of my demands in the morning."

"You don't have anything that comes to mind? Not one thing?" It was pointless to argue with her. They'd just go around in circles until both of them left pissed off. That was how it usually went. A year ago, the day after the incident where this whole feud had started, she'd declared he was scum on the bottom of her shoe and then poured her entire cran vodka in his lap. It hadn't improved since then.

"Oh, I want so much." Her tongue glided over her lip as she locked eyes with him. "But I've always heard delayed gratification has a much better payoff."

His dick twitched in response, thinking about what that tongue could do in other places. *Damn it.* No, this would not be happening. Not while staring at Sloane's lips, of all things.

She pushed up on her tiptoes and whispered into his ear, "I'm going to give you everything you deserve."

Reece swallowed hard. He knew that it was wrong to find that sentiment hot as hell, because the woman wanted him taken down like big game with a bazooka, but tell that to his hammering pulse.

"Just send me a text. You know my number," he said.

"Have a good night, Reece. Rest up. It'll be a long few weeks ahead for you." Her lips curved into a smile that promised wicked fulfillment of that threat.

He waved her off. Anyone else, and he might brush it off, but he knew Sloane's wrath. Witnessed it firsthand. He had every reason to be sweating in his turnouts.

Chapter Five

The next morning, Sloane slid into the booth at Barry's. This was her, Erin's, and Madison's go-to place to meet up, share about their day, and sip rich, decadent coffee. Sloane used to work here in high school, to which she attributed her caffeine addiction.

"I got so many good shots last night." Madison plopped into the booth next to Sloane and pulled out her camera. She powered it up and flipped through a few of the pictures. Most of them were of the men in their gear. But there was one of Sloane holding up her paddle. Her mouth was open and her eyes set in concentration. It must have been the exact moment she'd yelled out the winning amount.

"You'll have to print that one out for me. I didn't even see you there last night."

"It's a photographer's job to be a ninja. I shouldn't be noticed. All I need is to get the perfect shot."

Madison had been snapping photos since middle school, when they'd taken a photography class together. She'd since been named the top wedding photographer of Portland two years in a row. The woman had an eye for details and managed to capture a myriad of emotions in a single shot.

"Hear anything back from that show you applied to?"

Madison was hell-bent on making it onto *Professional MeetCute*. She claimed it would be a good career builder, that it would give her international reach. Sloane didn't watch a lot of reality TV, but most of the nurses in her unit were glued to the show. The premise was simple— people of all walks of life and different professions were brought together to complete physical and mental challenges. Madison's parents had both passed within the last year, and it was something her mother had always loved. Sloane guessed that this was a way to pay respects to her mom. That was the only reason she could think of for why her shy best friend would want to be in the spotlight of millions of viewers.

Madison shook her head. "They said that selected people would be notified in the New Year."

"Not too much longer, then."

"I'm busy, anyway. I'm completely booked with Christmas weddings."

"I thought you were going to do Christmas with me this year?"

Sloane's parents had decided that they'd spend the holidays down in Florida in their new time-share. Missing Thanksgiving *and* Christmas was a first for them. They'd invited Sloane to come, but she couldn't get that much time off to make the trip. Plus, she'd peeked at the December extended forecast, and there was snow predicted for the entire week of Christmas. Sloane had experienced a rainy holiday. Even an icy one. But never a white one. There was no way she'd miss this opportunity.

"I'll be there in the evening. Just have a couple of shoots in the morning," Madison said.

Moments later, Erin slid into the booth across from Sloane and Madison, bearing a latte and a plate with three cherry tarts. They were Erin's favorite. Sloane was more of a lemon fan, but her philosophy was a free tart was her favorite kind of tart. "Sorry I'm late. I got caught up in traffic."

Sloane snagged a tart. "Traffic made you late . . . by foot?" She lived five blocks from here.

"Okay, fine. I was with Jake, and we had a late start to the morning."

"At least someone in our group is getting some."

Erin smiled but didn't deny Sloane's comment.

"So you never did tell me. How did last night go? I tried to find you two after the auction, but you were both miraculously gone," Madison said.

"You didn't actually kill my brother and then hide his body, did you? Because that might be a breach of the friendship code."

"Before you drove me home? Not enough time. I did manage to kick some dirt on the fresh grave, though." She bit into the cherry tart, and the flaky, buttery crust melted on her tongue.

"I still can't believe you dropped three hundred bucks on Reece, of all people," Madison said, wide-eyed. Her red hair was pulled into a messy bun, and she leaned over the table, grabbing a sugar packet from the tiny bin in the corner of the table. She opened it and dumped it into her coffee. "There were much better-looking guys there that I wouldn't mind washing my car."

"Yeah, but none as special as Erin's brother." She'd gone to bed last night contemplating if this was really a smart choice. She'd landed on the opinion that *maybe* it'd been a rash decision. But not much she could do about it now. She'd see it through, because now she was getting her money's worth. The only plus side was that this was tax deductible.

"I wouldn't want to spend any more time with him, especially with how he treated you," Madison said.

"I still can't believe he said those things to you. It makes me want to punch him in the face," Erin said.

"Line up," Sloane said.

"Man, how come I never have opportunities like this fall in my lap? I've had plenty of ex-boyfriends who needed to be put in their place. You're a genius, by the way," Madison said.

Let's be real here. Madison could barely manage an evil glance, let alone sabotage. Sloane clapped her hand on Madison's shoulder. "Don't worry. You'll get to my level one day, Padawan."

A piece of tart dangled from Erin's lip, and she swiped at it with the pad of her thumb. "So what do you have planned? Besides total annihilation, of course."

It wouldn't be a complete and utter takedown. She wasn't *that* cruel. Also, she didn't have enough time on her hands to really get into the whole ruining-someone's-life thing. But she did want to make him squirm a bit. "I don't know."

She thought back to last night and her odd interaction with the chief. She clutched her cup of coffee between her palms, savoring the warmth of the mug in her chilled hands. "The weird thing is, the fire chief wants me to report back to him. Is Reece in some kind of trouble at work?"

Erin shrugged. "Beats me. He always seems happy after a shift."

She still couldn't shake the interaction they'd had. How he'd eyed Reece with suspicion. Like he truly didn't like him. *Welcome to the club, Chief. There's a line out the door.*

So Reece would get a taste of his own medicine, just a little harmless fun to put him in his place. Then she'd be on her merry way.

"What if you made him paint your toes?" Erin offered.

Sloane grimaced. "First, I don't want anyone touching my feet. Second, that's too nice."

"What if you made him eat something really gross," Madison chimed in. "Like cow tongue or Rocky Mountain oysters."

"We're not in middle school. It needs to be something more strategic. Reece is all about himself. We need to show him that there's more to the world than him." Maybe she'd make him wait it out till after next weekend. She had a shift at the Humane Society and would come up with something while walking the dogs. Inspiration always seemed to strike her there.

And then it hit her. Reece needed to think of other people. Well, she had an idea.

"Oh, I've got something." She cackled as she pulled out her phone and clicked on her messenger app.

Sloane: I have your first task.

The first message beeped through Reece's phone as he was scrubbing toilets at work. It had been a week since he'd been shot, and his stitches itched and pulled each time he moved. The pain had mostly subsided, but he was more than ready for them to dissolve. The man who'd shot him was in jail awaiting trial. Let him rot in there.

Hollywood and Jake were somewhere in the station performing their daily duties of keeping the station clean and functioning. They'd already met for their morning debriefing, and the chief hadn't even looked in his direction. Which was an upgrade from the tense meeting in his office last week.

He tossed the toilet scrubber into its container and replied to Sloane's message. The faster he got this over with, the better. He'd tried apologizing long ago, but they were far past that now.

Reece: What is it?

Sloane: I'll need you to come with me somewhere this weekend.

Reece: Should I bring a shovel and trash bags?

Sloane: Not this time. But I like your thinking. Wear clothes that you don't mind getting dirty.

"Your face is turning a weird shade of purple, man. Everything okay?" Hollywood asked as he walked into the bathroom. Cole's nickname fit, given his uncanny resemblance to a big-name actor all the women seemed to fawn over. He was a damn good firefighter and had been on Reece's and Jake's engine for a few years.

Reece clicked out of his message app and shoved his phone back into his pocket.

"Just the auction. How did you get out of doing it, anyway?" Hollywood was still new enough to the station that he should have been first pick for last night's event.

"Picked up a shift for Gonzalez. Figured they couldn't make me if I was working."

If he'd had the sense to avoid the chief before the auction, he may have gotten away with it too. "Smart man."

"Has Sloane decided your fate yet? I'd expect her to have a grocery list of items for you by now."

Reece shook his head. Of course Jake had told him. His men gossiped more than a bunch of grannies on a park bench.

But Hollywood was right. That was how it normally worked. Even though bidders technically had four weeks to space out the tasks or chores—which was how the event was created—usually the bidders had the four chores at the ready. Reece could knock them out in a few hours. There was no doubt in his mind Sloane would drag this out to the very last possible minute.

"Apparently I'm needed to escort her somewhere this weekend."

He raised a brow. "Like a date?"

"Doubt it. She told me to wear clothes that could get dirty."

Another text buzzed in his pocket, but he chose to ignore it.

"Should I be worried for your safety?" Hollywood asked.

"I can handle a woman who only comes up to my chest." She might talk a good game, but Sloane wouldn't actually do anything to hurt Reece. Probably.

"We are talking about the same Sloane, right?"

Reece ignored Hollywood's comment. "Don't you have a truck to wash?"

"All right, man. Just let me know if you need me to bail you out. Or delete your browser history before your mom cleans out your apartment after the funeral."

Reece flipped him the bird in response, but Hollywood was already out the door and heading out into the engine bay.

"I can handle her," he grumbled, and then grabbed the toilet brush, finishing up in the bathroom. Unable to ignore the phone in his pocket, he pulled it back out and looked at her message.

Sloane: Might also want to wear shoes that you don't mind getting ruined. See you Saturday. ;-)

Where the hell was she taking him?

Chapter Six

Reece stopped by his mother's house thirty minutes before he needed to pick up Sloane for wherever she was taking him today.

He made it a habit to stop by on his days off to help around the house. Swap out a light bulb for her, fix an appliance that was on the fritz. Today he was changing the filter in her fridge since the light had been on for a few weeks.

He tore open the filter box, extracted the old one from the fridge, and put the new one in its place. He grabbed a glass from the cupboard above the sink and filled it several times, dumping the water into the sink until there were no longer little black beads in the water.

"Thanks, honey." His mom kissed his arm and gave it a squeeze. "What are you up to today?" She sat down at the kitchen table and opened up the ledger she kept for her food truck. She'd owned and operated Butter Me Up since Reece was a kid. He'd grown up helping hand out flyers, cleaning windows, and when he was a teen, helping behind the register in the Airstream. The smell of peanut butter and freshly baked bread would forever be ingrained in his sinuses.

"Just going out with a friend." He didn't bother telling his mom that it was Sloane he was going with. She'd just give him a hard time and start playing matchmaker. She'd kept off his case for the most part after things had gone south with Amber. And now with Erin back in town, it had taken her interest in Reece's life down a notch.

"Well, have fun." She was distracted, hooking the side of her glasses between her teeth as she regarded the papers.

"Anything else I can do for you before I go?"

She shook her head and waved him off. "You go. Love you, sweetie."

"Love you too."

Just as he was about to head out the door, his sister Andie came out of her room, some horrible punk-rock music blaring.

"Can I talk to you for a minute?" she asked quietly, eyeing the kitchen. "In my room."

He walked in, and she shut the door behind him. She turned down the music and flopped down on her bed over a mound of wrinkled clothes and papers. Reece chose to stand. "What's up?"

"I'm, uh . . ." She worried her lip, sucking in her labret. "It's stupid, really."

This was weird. Even for his sister, whose life rode the line of off-beat. Hemp smoothies, Birkenstocks—she'd even gone a couple of years with natty dreads. Thankfully, she'd outgrown that last one.

"Okay. Well, then, I guess I'll just get going." He didn't want to be late picking up Sloane. No need to give her ammunition for writing a scathing email to his chief. He went to turn for the door.

"Wait." There was something desperate in that one word. One that raised the hairs on the back of his neck.

He stopped, his hand resting on the knob. His sister had been acting off for months. Massive mood swings, bouts of reclusiveness. Reece figured it was a phase, but maybe there was something else going on.

"I—I decided to apply for colleges."

His initial worry subsided. He'd automatically gone to worst-case scenario. "That's awesome. And you need my help . . . why?" Out of everyone in his family, Reece was the least qualified to help her. He'd never gone to college. The only courses he took were to further his training.

"I don't want to tell Mom yet. Or Erin. You know how they are."

They shared a look. One they had shared regularly. He understood. He loved his family, but they had a certain knack for bringing the crazy out of people. His mom would set up camp outside Andie's door if she knew she was applying to schools.

"Got it. What do you need me to do?"

"Some of the colleges say they want extracurriculars. I know it's been a couple of years since high school, so I don't really have much. Do you have anything to beef up my résumé?"

At least this was one thing he could actually help out with. "I do. I can take you to the shelter next weekend when I volunteer."

"The shelter . . ." She looked uncertain. He forgot that his youngest sister hadn't worked as much with the community as he and Erin had as teens.

"If you're going to ask for help, we're going to do it right." That was the way Reece did things. Either all the way or not at all. If his sister wanted his help, then she needed to cut the one-foot-out-the-door attitude.

After a moment, she nodded. "Okay." She toyed with the quilt on her bed. "And, Reece?"

"Yeah?"

"Please don't tell Mom. Just in case this doesn't, you know, happen." She shrugged, like it wasn't a big deal. But he knew the look in her eyes. Hope.

"Secret's safe with me, kid." He ruffled her hair. It was nice to see her take some initiative. Hopefully it'd last. "See you next weekend." And with that, he made his way out of the house and to his truck to go who knew where with Sloane.

Reece stared down at the jeans he saved for working on his Jeeps and projects at his mom's house. Knowing Sloane, this was some sick joke, and he'd end up being her wedding date and stuck looking like an idiot. He'd come prepared, though. He had dress slacks and a button-up in his trunk, just in case. Because, if anything, he'd always make sure that he wouldn't be caught off guard, unlike his stupid mistake the other week.

He rolled up to her apartment complex, a couple of blocks from his, pulled into a spot nearest the front entrance, and cut the engine.

He debated texting her and having her meet him downstairs, but his mom had taught him manners and would whomp him over the head with a rolling pin if he did that to Sloane.

Taking the stairs two at a time, he got off on the fourth floor and made his way to Sloane's apartment at the end of the hall. The space outside her door had a festive doormat that read Ho Ho Ho. Christmas lights lined the doorway, and a candy-cane wreath hung from the door.

Even though Thanksgiving was next week, he'd already helped his mom set up her lights on her house. Reece didn't bother putting decorations up at his apartment. A Christmas tree at the station was about as festive as he got.

Reece gave a firm rap on the door, and moments later, Sloane opened it, the smell of peppermint wafting out of the apartment.

Sloane was dressed in faded jeans and a black hoodie, and her hair was pulled back. He could officially cross needing his suit off his list. "Just in time. Let me grab my keys."

"Smells good in here." Through the years, he'd been over here for various reasons. Helped her move her sofa up the stairs, fixed a leaky toilet when the super was worthless. It always smelled like baked goods and never failed to make him hungry.

"Peppermint treats for my friends," she said, scooping them onto a cooling rack.

Reece glanced at the kitchen counter, which had dozens of cookies on racks. They were roped in the shape of candy canes. Not the best-looking things he'd ever seen, but he was sure they more than made up for it in taste. Sloane always did have a knack for baking. When Reece was in high school, Sloane and Erin would bake after school. Reece and Jake would reap the rewards of each baking endeavor. He was especially fond of her peanut butter oatmeal cookies, which were special treats she made during the holidays. "Mind if I have one?"

Sloane looked at him curiously, and then her lips twitched. "By all means, help yourself."

Huh. First his sister came to him for advice, and now Sloane was being nice? Too nice. Something was up. But he wasn't one to pass up free food, so he grabbed one off the rack and shoved it in his mouth. It was a mix of peanut butter and peppermint, and the driest cookie he'd ever tasted. The chalky pieces moved around in his mouth, clumping together, and he forced himself to swallow them. His intestines might regret this choice later when the mixture turned to cement.

"How are they?" she prompted.

The words *worst cookie ever* played at the tip of his tongue, but he decided against voicing this, especially when he wasn't sure what she had planned for him this afternoon. He set the rest of the cookie down on the counter. "Listen, I don't know the best way to say this, but are you sure you want to give these to people that you like?"

Her lips wobbled, and she was on the losing end of a battle to try to hide a smile. "Trust me. I don't think my friends will mind."

He shrugged. So be it. Maybe her friends didn't have taste buds. But Reece could really use a glass of water to wash down the remnants of the cement in his mouth.

Reece shoved his hands in his pockets and glanced around the apartment. Colorful, loaded with art on the walls. It reminded him of the Lisa Frank craze that Erin had gone through when they were younger.

Sloane finished putting the cookies into a plastic bag and then stowed it away in her purse. He watched as she moved around the kitchen, her hips swaying as she walked. The way her jeans clung to her ass. How he'd like to slip his hands in the back pockets, for his fingers to trail under the edge of her jeans . . . and yeah, he needed to stop that train of thought.

Her brows knit together when she caught him staring, and he quickly took interest in the coffee table in the center of the room. "Let's get going before it's too late," she said slowly.

Right. Chore number one. "Works for me." He followed her to the door, ready to get this over with. Whatever it was. He thought about the Seahawks game he was missing and his spot on the couch, just waiting for him when he returned. "So you're not going to tell me where we're going?"

They entered the stairwell, and she walked ahead of him. Her perfume, something roselike, trailed behind her. Reece took a deep breath, inhaling the scent. Damn, she smelled good.

"Where's the fun in that?" she asked. "I thought you liked adventure. Isn't that what all you adrenaline-junkie firefighters like?"

There was a reason why he excelled at his job. He knew what to expect. The proper protocol. Knew every back road, service entrance, and alternate route to get to a call. He knew what to do if a patient was coding. Turned out he was clueless in regard to how to deal with Sloane.

He gritted his teeth as they rounded the corner to the second floor. The stairwell was dimly lit, some of the sconces flickering or burned out altogether. A place that screamed "open invitation" to seedy people. He didn't like the thought of Sloane going through here alone.

Once they hit the last flight of stairs, he focused back on her question. "Not all of us are that way." Although he had to admit that most of his men did like the rush of the call. Even he found himself caught up in the moment from time to time. "That's not why I signed up for the job." The echo of his voice died down as they exited the stairwell.

"Then why did you?" He didn't even have to peer over at her to know she was staring him down with those perfectly arched brows.

Because I want to help people.

When he was seven, Erin was just a toddler at that point. His mom had asked him to watch her for a few minutes while she'd hopped in the shower after a long shift at the food truck. He'd been too transfixed by *Teenage Mutant Ninja Turtles* to notice that she'd managed to unhook the child lock from the slider door and escape out the back. It had taken him almost forty minutes to find her, and she'd broken her foot, falling on something in the backyard. She'd gotten hurt on his watch. From then on, he'd vowed to keep people safe. Sloane didn't need to know that, though. Probably rub it in his face. "What is this, a job interview? Chief put you up to this?"

She held up her hands in response. "Just a curious citizen, that's all."

"You're something, all right," he muttered.

"Sorry, what was that?" They walked past the entryway to the apartment, a small common area off to the side filled with a large TV and a foosball table.

"Just saying I'm so happy to have a concerned citizen in the car." Why couldn't Sloane be like every other bidder and give him a neat and tidy list of four chores? In, out, be done with it.

They climbed into his truck, and he glanced over at Sloane, who had that devilish smirk twisting at her lips. The last time she'd been in his truck had been more than a year ago. He swallowed and tried not to look at her hands splayed across her thighs. How her skin would feel under his touch. How her head would knock back if he was between her legs.

"Why are you looking at me like that?"

Shit. How had he been looking at her? He focused back on the steering wheel, the empty parking lot—anything to get his mind off what he'd like to do to Sloane. Thoughts he had believed were completely evicted from his mind.

"Nothing." He turned the key in the ignition and followed her directions.

Twenty minutes later, they were apparently almost at their destination, according to Sloane.

"Take a right here," Sloane said.

Reece pulled into a large gravel lot and eyed the Portland Humane Society sign. He'd done a few fund-raisers here with the fire department.

"Scooping up dog poop." He nodded. Yep, this seemed right up Sloane's alley. "Nice play, Smurfette."

"Oh, it's much better than that," she said, hopping down from the truck. Her ponytail bobbed as she walked two steps ahead of him to the front entrance, and he made a point to study the exterior of the building and not Sloane's hips.

"What's worse than dog shit?"

She smiled back at him. And that twinkle in her eyes should have tipped him off that he was in deeper trouble than originally anticipated. "We're here to pick out a dog to foster."

"Excuse me? Did you just say *we*, as in plural?" She couldn't mean . . .

"I usually foster a dog or two at a time. But since my apartment has changed their rules on pets, I can't anymore. They're really understaffed and could use the help."

"And you need my opinion?" He wasn't the praying type, but maybe now was a good time to start. "I don't really know much about dogs." He'd never even owned one. His mom had claimed they'd be too much work. And since she was a single parent of three, he didn't bother pushing the subject again.

"Oh, the dog's not for me." She pulled out a tube of ChapStick from her purse and rolled it over her lips, then shoved it back into the bag.

Damn it. He did not like where this conversation was heading. Not one bit. Not when she looked like she'd just won the lottery. "Who's it for, Sloane?"

She toyed with the strap of her purse. "Well, I know how lonely you are in that apartment of yours. Figured you could use a friend."

No.

"You're kidding, right?" Reece worked solo. A lone wolf. No room for a dog in his apartment.

"No. Unless you want to go back on your deal." Sloane shuffled around her purse. "I think I have the chief's card in here somewhere."

Fostering a dog. As a chore. That was a stretch, even for Sloane.

He stared at her.

She stared back.

There was no chance she'd drop this.

"What about when I'm on shift? Who's going to watch the dog?" He had twenty-four-hour shifts. No way a dog could hold it that long. She couldn't argue with that. It might be the one loophole that could get him out of this.

"I've already made arrangements with your mom."

Reece stopped walking and stared at her. Is that why his mother hadn't pushed to ask who he was hanging out with today? Because she already knew? "My *mom* is in on this?" This was a new low. Out of all the people to piss off, he had to get on the bad side of Sloane.

Sloane shrugged. "She was more than happy to help out."

Of course she was.

Four weeks, max. He could deal with a thing that pooped and ate for that long.

He let out a slow, calming breath. "Fine. Lead me to the dog area."

"It'll probably be for only a few weeks. Just until they have an adopter or more room at the shelter." They entered the building, which was painted a sterile white and smelled faintly like wet dog. Each wall showcased professional photos of animals—birds in trees, dogs running through fields, cats on their backs probably ready to rip out someone's throat. On the back wall was the slogan MEET YOUR NEW LIFELONG FRIEND.

Yeah, a lifelong, thirty-day friend.

Sloane waved to the person behind the main desk. "Hi, Jerry."

Jerry's ruddy cheeks bloomed a deeper shade of red, and he straightened when he caught sight of Sloane. His reaction unsettled Reece, though he couldn't pinpoint why. "Well, if it isn't my favorite volunteer. How are your parents enjoying Florida?"

"Having the time of their lives. Getting tanner by the minute." She waved her hand in the air. Sloane was one of those people who talked with her whole body, using bold, emphatic gestures. Stand close enough and someone could lose an eye. "I brought you something." She pulled out a package of brownies that Reece hadn't seen in her kitchen.

Hold the damn phone. Jerry knew Sloane's parents' whereabouts *and* got brownies? This really didn't settle well. For the sole reason that those chocolate squares that were made out of unicorn tears were in the wrong hands. Namely, Jerry's.

Jerry made quick work of the Saran wrap and shoved a brownie in his mouth. Lucky bastard. "You're too good to me." He licked crumbs from his finger and waved her and Reece on. "Have a good shift."

When they got to the dog area, she pulled out the other plastic bag and pulled it open, giving one of the candy-cane cookies to a bullmastiff in one of the pens.

Wait a second.

Realization dawned on him. "You let me eat dog treats?"

"It seemed it was only fitting." She gave him a wink.

If they were keeping score, Reece would have zero points for today, and Sloane would be in the lead with a solid two points. He'd be upset if he wasn't so impressed.

At least that explained why they tasted so dry. No wonder they sucked. "Let's get this over with," he said.

One of the managers came out from a back room to greet them. Another person who knew Sloane by name.

"Kurt, this is my friend, Reece," she said, pointing to him.

Reece raised a brow, surprised by the fact that Sloane would call him any title other than *asshole*. "Reece here is looking to foster a dog. Doing me a favor since I can't foster for a little while."

Kurt smiled at Reece. "Great. Let's get the paperwork started. We have a new arrival that we don't have room for."

His first instinct was to tell the guy he was less than thrilled. He liked his hardwood floors without mud. Preferred not to have his apartment reek of wet dog. Didn't need some mutt dragging in whatever it was they dragged in.

Job. Do whatever she says to keep your position.

He'd seen it before with the chief. A couple of years back, a guy on C shift, Jackson, was in a similar position as Reece was now. Jackson had pissed off the chief because of a bad call he'd made during a routine procedure. He'd been at the station six years, a solid fixture in their tight-knit group. Five months ago, Jackson transferred down to Mount Halo, a station where the most action they saw was a paper cut at the bank. Also the station that happened to have more openings than any other in Portland. Word around the station claimed Jackson had wanted the transfer for a while, but they all knew it was because of the chief. Mount Halo was a place where firefighters went to ride out the rest of their careers, their rigs collecting dust. It'd be a death sentence for Reece. So for the next few weeks, when Sloane said, "Jump," he'd grit his teeth and ask, "How high?"

"Anything to help out a dog," he said, trying to muster up enough enthusiasm to placate Sloane.

Reece wasn't even sure if he liked dogs. But if this made Sloane's evil, sadistic heart happy, then by all means, he *loved* dogs. Would buy one of those stupid bumper stickers that said I LOVE MY BOXER/LAB/1/4 WELSH TERRIER MIX. Because she was the key to ensuring the chief was happy and would have zero reason to run him out of Station 11. He'd just keep reminding himself of that during every task Sloane had for him.

Once they were inside the dog portion of the shelter, he looked into each dog's kennel. Low whines and barks echoed in the cavernous room, bouncing off the concrete floors. Didn't blame them. If he were a dog, he'd whine about being here too.

A boxer stood on his hind legs while looking up at Reece with sad eyes. The golden retriever in the pen next to him whimpered and sighed as he laid his head on his paws. This was like a sad ASPCA commercial. All it needed was that depressing Sarah McLachlan song playing in the background.

"So which one am I taking home?" The thought of a big dog didn't repulse him too much. A German shepherd. Or maybe a Doberman. He could ride shotgun in the passenger seat with the windows down. That would be badass. Maybe fostering a dog wouldn't be too bad.

"Your foster is right down here," Kurt said as he led Reece and Sloane down the walkway. The shelter was a maze of kennels, rows upon rows of dogs in this cold, sterile environment. Each pen was filled with one dog, sometimes two. Lab mixes, some pits, and a Great Dane with drool slicking the floor.

They finally made their way to the end of the row, and Reece peered into the cage. At first, he didn't see a dog and thought maybe luck was on his side and that someone was in the process of adopting it. But then a small yip came from the far corner.

"Reece, meet Peaches."

Reece stared down at the dog. Could it even be classified as a dog if it weighed less than ten pounds? The brown thing wearing a pink sweater looked more like a rat than anything. Based on the color choice, he assumed the rat-dog-whatever was a girl. She jumped up on her hind legs, and a river of pee coated the floor. Reece took a large step back, making sure to avoid the splash zone of this golden shower.

He glanced at her description tethered to the chain-link kennel. Peaches was a Pomeranian-and-Yorkie mix. Or what the laminated sheet labeled as Yoranian. Sounded like an element on the periodic table.

"There has to be a mistake. This is the only dog that needs fostering right now?"

"Peaches . . . ," Kurt trailed off, looking sheepish. "She has a problem with other dogs. With the newest influx of dogs, we just don't have room to keep her in a kennel all by herself."

Sloane patted Reece's shoulder. "Aw, she's just like you, Reece. Doesn't play well with others."

Kurt looked between Reece and Sloane, probably trying to piece together why Reece was barely holding it together. "If you have other dogs at home, this might not be the right fit."

Reece's jaw clenched. "Won't be a problem."

"I'll go grab the box that came with her. She has a few favorite outfits."

"Outfits," Reece repeated. "She wears . . . clothes?" This had to be a joke.

"Yes, the previous owner said she liked to pick out her own outfit every morning."

"You've got to be kidding me," he said. He was fine with a big dog. A manly dog. But this? A dog that played pretty, pretty princess? This crossed so many lines he was practically in an alternate dimension right now. Reece didn't have time for bows and ribbons and whatever else this high-maintenance *thing* required.

Kurt came back a minute later with a small box full of miniature outfits, most of them sparkly. This was a hard no. The box would be meeting the dumpster as soon as he had a moment alone.

"Is there going to be a problem?" Sloane arched a brow.

Job. Chief Richards. Not getting railroaded into transferring to a zero-action station. Sloane had him by the balls, and they both knew it. *Fine.* He needed to take care of a foo-foo dog with the name of a fruit for a few weeks? *So be it.*

He grabbed the box from Kurt. "No problem at all."

Chapter Seven

Reece called Jake as soon as he dropped off Sloane at her apartment, and then he went directly home. He threw his keys, the box of clothes, and the bag of dog food on the counter and stared down at Peaches. The mutt looked up at him, tail wagging.

"What the hell do I do with you?"

What was he supposed to do?

She barked at him. That tiny face eyed him like he was the biggest screwup foster-dog parent she'd ever known. He most likely was.

"Of course. I'll take that monstrosity of an outfit off you." He reached for the pink abomination Peaches wore. The dog was probably embarrassed to be wearing a sweater. He was embarrassed on her account.

He went to pull it off, but Peaches let out a low growl. Reece didn't know much about dogs, but he did know to back off when a dog growled. She might be tiny, but she did have teeth.

He backed up and put his hands up. If she wanted to look like a fool, so be it. Who was he to judge?

He racked his brain and glanced at the clock. Kurt said Peaches ate at six sharp. He had forty minutes. "You need to go potty?" It sounded like he was talking to a toddler.

He'd tried getting her to do her business for fifteen minutes before they'd entered the apartment, with no luck.

The dog yipped. Which he took as a pretty clear *Screw off*.

"Fine. Go ahead and make yourself at home." He didn't know the first thing about introducing a dog to a house. Was he supposed to give her a tour like she was a houseguest? *Here's the bathroom. Here's the kitchen and the food you're not allowed to touch.*

Peaches took it upon herself to trot around the living room. He let out a deep breath. Nothing left to do but settle into their new arrangement.

"She thinks she won this, but Sloane has another think coming."

Peaches barked in response.

"You're on her side? Really? Come on. The woman is ridiculous."

Peaches decided it was time to stretch her legs, and he winced as her nails scraped along his wood floors.

"Man, you're brutal." He was having a conversation with a dog. Maybe he was starting to crack. He needed to hold it together for at least four more weeks, and then he'd be done with all this mess.

He sank down to the couch and grabbed a *Men's Fitness* magazine from the coffee table, waiting for his reinforcements to show up. Jake and Hollywood would know what to do. He cracked open the magazine while Peaches pranced around the living room. His mom had gotten him a subscription last Christmas, and even if he felt ridiculous reading this magazine, it did have good workout tips. He flipped through a few pages and found an article on building up deltoid muscles. He folded the magazine in half and had just started to read when Peaches let out a sharp yip and began to shake.

"What?"

The dog backed away slowly, looking like she was ready to bolt at any second. Was this a sign she needed to finally relieve herself? He set down the magazine and pulled out his phone to check online to see what dogs could get spooked by. But as soon as Reece set down the magazine, Peaches stopped shaking.

Okay, maybe this was a sign of abuse? Had someone hit her with a rolled-up magazine? The thought made Reece want to deck whoever would do that to an animal.

He lifted it up again, and she let out a high-pitched howl.

"Seriously, you're afraid of magazines?"

He lifted up another magazine from the coffee table, and she didn't react.

Huh.

He picked up the fitness magazine again, unfolded it, and looked at the page. A full spread of Blake Shelton. He turned the magazine around for Peaches to see, and she went frantic again, high-pitched yowls echoing in his apartment.

He chuckled. "Don't worry, girl. I don't see the appeal either."

He closed up the magazine, and Peaches settled down, her shaking subsiding. He'd heard about animals having phobias, had seen the cat with the pickle videos online, but he'd never heard of an animal being terrified of a specific person.

Reece sat down on the couch and grabbed for the remote, and Peaches jumped up next to him.

"That's a hard no, sweetheart. You're stuck on floor duty." He scooped her up and gently set her down on the ground. The last thing he wanted was the dog crapping on his leather couch.

The dog stared at him with those big brown eyes. Damn it, she looked pathetic. He turned his attention to the TV and flipped through the channels, hoping to catch the end of the Seahawks game. He'd missed most of it since he and Sloane had spent the rest of the afternoon cleaning kennels and walking the other dogs at the shelter. He knew that she was mainly happy because she got satisfaction out of seeing him out of his element, but he had to admit it'd been nice to be civil for once. Even at his expense.

The dog barked again.

"Not happening. I have the willpower of a Jedi master. Your snooty little yip does nothing for my resolve." This was it. He might have finally gone crazy because he was talking to her like she understood.

Just as she sat back on her haunches, ready to make another attempt at getting up on the couch, Reece opened the magazine to the picture of Blake. Peaches immediately backed off and hid under the end table on the opposite side of the couch.

Nice. Who needed official dog training when he had a picture of a celebrity?

Just then, the doorbell rang.

He shot the dog a look. "Don't you even think about it." And then he got up from the couch and moved to the door. Finally, the cavalry was here.

Jake and Hollywood stood in his doorway, six-packs of beer in their hands.

Peaches let out a medley of barks and yips, dancing on her hind legs.

"Whoa, man." Hollywood backed up.

"Dude. It's just a dog." Albeit an ugly one currently wearing a tutu-sweater deal, but he didn't need to explain that to the guys.

"One that's peeing all over your floor and Jake's shoes," Hollywood said as he and Jake stepped into the entryway. "And what the hell is she wearing? Did you dress her up?"

Jake let out a low grunt and moved to the kitchen to grab a paper towel. He wiped off his shoe. "Does this mean that Sloane has officially started her favors?"

"Yep." Reece cracked open a beer and took a deep pull. "Apparently I am on babysitting duty until she gets adopted. The dog, not Sloane."

He strode into the kitchen, opened up the cabinet under the sink, and motioned for Jake to drop the dirty paper towels in there.

"Aw, Reece is a dad. Who would have ever thought that would happen?" Hollywood said.

He narrowed his eyes at Hollywood. "Temporary. This is not a long-term arrangement," Reece insisted.

"Sure. Whatever you say, man. We're here to watch the game, not judge," Jake said. He bent down to scratch the dog's head. "Poor Reece doesn't know what he got himself into."

Both Reece and Hollywood stared at Jake.

"What? I like dogs. That's not an abnormal thing," Jake said. "Plus, I find it hilarious that Sloane got the best of you."

"She did not," Reece said.

They both looked at him.

"Fine. She did. I don't even know how to take care of myself, let alone a princess dog."

"What are you going to do with this dog for . . . How long do you have this thing?" Hollywood asked.

"Who knows? They said a typical amount of time is three weeks. I've been given dog food and a leash. I figure it can't be too hard to take care of something that weighs less than a sack of flour."

They both stared.

"What?"

"Have you ever taken care of anything before?" Hollywood asked, cracking open a beer and making his way to the couch. Reece flipped to the game, just in time for kickoff.

"I used to have a pet fish." The fish didn't last long. In fact, Reece could still recall walking into his room after having Michelangelo for only a few days to find the fish belly-up. His mom had told him that he was sleeping.

"A fish. What are you going to do when you're on shift?" Jake asked.

"Sloane already thought of that. Went through my mom and set up an arrangement."

Jake let out a low whistle. "I'm impressed."

"Is it weird I find that incredibly hot?" Hollywood asked.

Reece and Jake both said yes at the same time.

"It's pretty straightforward. You feed it. You take it to the bathroom. You give it love and attention," Jake said. "You'll be fine."

"Plus, that means you have an excuse to call up Sloane if you have an issue," Hollywood said.

"Why would I do that?"

"She might have Smurf hair, but she's bangin'," Hollywood said.

"If one can look past her being a malevolent dictator, then sure."

"Come on. You're telling me she's never been part of your spank-bank material?"

Reece had the sudden urge to deck Hollywood in the face. Sure, Reece had pictured Sloane . . . many times. But his friends didn't need to know about that. "I'm going to ignore that you used that term. What are you, twelve?"

"I'm moving up in the world. Last week you asked if I had a pacifier."

Sloane was a few years younger than Reece. They'd known each other since childhood. In fact, when they were younger, they could even tolerate being in the same room with each other. He'd never told Jake, but when they were in high school, he'd had a thing for Sloane. He'd had a girlfriend at the time, so he could never act on anything, and then by the time his relationship with Amber had crashed and burned, the little faith he'd had in connecting with the opposite sex had evaporated.

And then late last year, they'd happened to meet up at a bar when Sloane's friends had all gone home, and Jake had left to go take care of Bailey. Sloane had been sitting at the bar nursing a drink, wearing red stilettos that matched her lipstick and a black dress that molded to every curve.

"Well, look what the cat dragged in," she'd said.

"Where're your friends?" Normally she was out with her nursing pals or Madison. He hadn't recognized anyone in the near vicinity.

"Madison had to head home early. So I'm partying by myself." She'd frowned into her drink.

"Bad day?"

"Yeah, you could say that." She'd swirled her beer in her pint glass and then had taken a long swallow. Reece hadn't spent much time alone with her over the years. Usually the only time he had was when Erin was around. But he'd felt the sharp prick of awareness of just how sexy she was. How much he'd wanted to take her to the bathroom, shove up that scrap of a dress, and show her just how desperate he was for her.

Instead, he'd said, "Let me drive you home. It's getting late."

She'd drained the rest of her beer, hopped down from the barstool, and slung an arm around him.

"God. You realize you're huge?"

He'd chuckled. Even in the heels, she only came up to his shoulder.

"I bet you'd break someone in bed. Or break their bed," she'd cackled while squeezing his biceps.

Reece didn't realize how drunk she was until then.

"You doing okay, Smurfette?" He'd managed to guide her into the passenger seat of his truck and taken his place in the driver's seat.

"Just peachy." He'd driven the short distance to her apartment and walked her to her door. Even debated staying the night on the couch, making sure she was fine. She'd fumbled with the keys, and after the sixteenth unsuccessful attempt at the lock, he opened the door for her.

He guided her to the bedroom, found a pair of pajamas in her dresser, and left the room to give her some privacy. "I'll just go get you some water."

He'd returned to find her sitting on the comforter. Sloane had one of those rooms with an overabundance of throw pillows. Seriously, what did people do with so many pillows? The room was painted a light shade of teal and had enough candles lining the dresser and nightstand to give Reece the sudden urge to check her smoke detectors.

"You should stay." She'd quirked a brow. "Show me what you can do to my bed."

"Sloane," he'd warned.

He would have loved nothing more than to show her what he could do. To her lips, to the soft breasts pressing against the faded AC/DC T-shirt. He'd worship her body . . . if she was sober.

"Please. I want you to stay the night." She reached out her hands, waiting for him to grab them.

He'd never take advantage of a woman, especially Sloane. He'd shoved his hands into his pockets. "I can't."

Her lips pursed into an adorable pout. "Why not?"

"You're drunk."

Her hands moved up his leg.

He'd had to think fast. "Ew, Sloane. I wouldn't get with you if you were the last woman on earth. You're not my type. The opposite of my type, in fact. Never going to happen. Not in a million years."

That was a bit of overkill. And a lie, but one he was willing to stand by if it meant keeping her from trying to do something stupid while she was drunk.

Her smile had morphed into a look of pure disdain. She chucked the water he'd handed her in his face and then pointed a finger toward the hallway. "Get out."

He held his hands up in response. "Okay."

A hand snapped in front of him, pulling him out of his thoughts.

"Hey, where'd you go, man?"

"Just zoned out for a sec. Sorry." He didn't need to be thinking about that night. It'd do nothing but get him into trouble.

"Come on. Let's watch the game," Jake said as he grabbed his beer and cracked it open.

The Eagles were at the five-yard line, about to get their first touchdown against the 49ers. "You should have seen Sloane's face when I said I'd love to foster Peaches. Especially after the dog pissed everywhere. Multiple times." If this was the best Sloane could come up with, she was going to be severely disappointed. Her plan to seek revenge was going to backfire. She'd have no other option than to send a rave review to his chief. He'd play into her game and come out with his job intact.

"Just like now?" Jake pointed to the dog, who was currently peeing on his rug.

"Damn it. I'll be right back." He grabbed the leash from the counter and took Peaches outside.

"You'd better get me a glowing review, girl," he said to the dog as she sniffed around for fifteen minutes on a strip of grass in front of his apartment.

Five hours later, the guys had cleared out. Reece pulled his shirt over his head and made his way to the bathroom to brush his teeth. He'd already done the Peaches Potty Run, or PPR, as he had started referring to it, and she had somehow made her way onto his bed, curled up near his pillow.

"Nope. You get the floor, princess."

She let out a low grunt.

"Attitude? Seriously? You're ten pounds. Tone it down there, pipsqueak." He doubted she understood him, but somehow talking to her made him feel less crazy.

He went to move her off the bed, and she let out a growl.

"No way. I draw the line here. Nobody but me sleeps in this bed." No one had ever slept in his bed before. Of course, other activities happened here, but he had a policy—no one stayed overnight.

He scooped her up and put her on the floor. She turned back toward him, and he swore she fixed him with a glare. She squinted at him with a demonic rage that had him thinking that maybe he needed to sleep with one eye open tonight.

He reached for the magazine on his nightstand and opened it up to the photo of Blake Shelton again, and Peaches let out a yip and beelined it for the doggy bed in the corner of the room.

He chuckled. He'd have to get creative now that he knew what made Peaches fall into line.

Before Peaches even thought about trying to make another go at the bed, he propped the magazine up on the chest in front of his bed.

Chapter Eight

"You made him foster a dog?" Madison snorted over her coffee mug.

A smile twitched at Sloane's lips. It was comical how big, brutish Reece was walking a Yoranian the size of a loaf of bread. Her dainty little leash fisted in his big, calloused hands. "It'll be fine. I'll do some welfare checks and make sure the dog is being taken care of. You should have seen the look on his face when he saw that the dog came with sweaters and a tiara."

"You are wicked. But that might backfire on you. Nobody can resist a cute dog in a sweater."

Sloane shot Madison a look. Okay, she was right. Because the dog did look pretty cute in her little rhinestone tiara. Even Sloane had squealed and taken a picture of the dog to send to her mom.

Madison's hands flew in response. "Fine. You're right. Reece is naturally repellent."

"Much better." He might fill out firefighter attire nicely, but she knew the man beneath the Under Armour. Or whatever brand of workout gear he usually wore. Knowing Reece, it was some cheapie brand. He'd always been frugal. Except when it came to his beloved cars.

"What do you have planned for your next task?" Madison asked.

Sloane swirled a spoon in her drink, trying to come up with something. "I don't know yet. It has to be something good." She wanted to be smart about it. Nothing too immature. She did value her own time and money, and she didn't want this to escalate into middle-school antics. Just a bit of messing with him. Just enough to show him that he might find Sloane repulsive while the nurses around her and the entire female population were datable, but she more than made up for it with her brain and the sheer will to squash him like a bug.

"I'm sure you'll think of something."

"What are we talking about?" Erin asked, sliding into the booth with a scone and a steaming cup of coffee. "And please tell me it involves caffeine, because it's three weeks till winter break, and I'm ready to lock myself in my room and never come out."

Erin had told them last week that the time between Thanksgiving and winter break was an absolute madhouse at school. As evidenced by the dark circles under her eyes.

"Total annihilation of your brother," Sloane said.

"My favorite subject," Erin said as she took a bite of scone, crumbs dropping from her mouth. "I say you make him dress up in eighties' style for the rest of the week. Maybe make him wear some cutoff shirts."

"I wouldn't want to subject the general public to that."

"True." Erin pulled out her phone and typed something in, smiling. Sloane liked to see Erin this way. Erin was always the sunny one in the group. But she'd been absolutely beaming these past few months.

"Lover boy?" Madison asked.

Erin nodded. "He's on shift right now. Says that Reece is very tired because the dog kept him up all night."

"Good to know he is suffering on my account."

"Your heart of ice brings me such joy," Erin said.

"It took a lot of practice, but I've honed my magic." Truth be told, this was the first time she'd ever given anyone a hard time. Sure, she spoke her mind, wasn't afraid to share her opinions at work, and didn't put up with bullshit from rude patients. But this was different. Quite possibly a little beneath her, but so what? It was kinda fun.

She guzzled her tea and checked the time on her phone. "Crap. I need to get going." She pulled her hair back into a ponytail and scraped the crumbs off her scrubs. "I'll see you guys later."

"Have a good shift," they both called out.

Sloane made her way to her car and, ten minutes later, parked in the hospital garage. She took one last sip of her peppermint tea and steeled herself for her shift. One skill she'd learned over the years was to compartmentalize. She had to, especially during the last few years in the ped unit, where she'd dealt with chronically sick children. If she didn't, she'd be a blubbering mess the rest of the day.

The past six months, she'd made the transition to the ER. It wasn't her favorite area, but as long as she had a steady paycheck, that's all that mattered. Especially with the house on Mississippi potentially going up for sale soon. Then she wouldn't have to live vicariously through Reece. She missed having pets in her home.

She breezed through the sliding doors and greeted Tom and Rebecca, the other two nurses on shift tonight. She liked the night shift because it tended to be quieter than daytime. Gave her more time to plot Reece's demise. Okay, maybe she *was* stooping to middle-school level with him, but hell, it felt good. What were a few weeks of torture?

"How's it going, lady?" Rebecca asked, her elbow resting on the nursing-station counter. Rebecca had worked here almost as long as Sloane had.

"Good. How is Laura Jean?" Rebecca and her wife had just adopted a baby girl earlier this year.

"Almost walking. I found out she's highly motivated by trying to get to Pickles." Pickles was their Lab mix who treated Laura Jean like she was one of the pack. Rebecca posted adorable videos of the two on Facebook all the time.

"Dogs are great motivation." Sloane shimmied out of her coat and put it on the back of her chair. "How many beds are filled?"

"Two. Slow night so far."

"Excellent."

Just as she pinned her ID to her pocket, two firefighters entered through the sliding doors, wheeling in a patient on a gurney.

Sloane gritted her teeth when she saw Reece. Right beside him was the cute one who was way too young for her to be looking at. She liked her men old enough to be able to rent a car.

"Smurfette. Always a pleasure," Reece said in that gravelly voice that both irritated her and sent a lick of heat down her spine. Reece's voice was deeper today, low and scraping like he'd just woken up.

She ignored the nickname. She also ignored the fact that gooseflesh cropped up along her forearms. She attributed it to the chill in the ER.

"What do we have here?" She motioned them into an open room.

"Fall in the driveway. She has a prior amputation on the left leg, possible fracture to the right."

Sloane nodded and gave a quick once-over to the patient while Rebecca started an IV line on the woman's arm. Scrapes covered her hands and face, most likely from trying to catch herself in the fall. One eye was swollen shut, and a large chunk of skin was missing from her cheek. Her leg was at an odd angle, no doubt due to a break. Sloane made a mental checklist of what to order. X-rays, at the very least. The woman was in for a whole world of pain getting the bone reset . . . and a lot of PT in her future.

Reece and Cole gently lifted the woman and moved her from their gurney to the hospital one. The poor lady made a weak grunting sound as the men gently set her down on the bed.

Reece picked up a small black bag from their gurney and handed it to her. "Here's your purse, ma'am. I hope you're able to make it on your vacation to Ireland in March."

"This one." The patient pointed to Reece. "He's a charmer. Gotta watch yourself around him. I'd take him to Dublin with me, but my best friend has the other ticket."

He patted her hand. "Next time, Grace."

Oh, please. Sloane managed to suppress an epic eye roll.

"He's something, all right," Sloane said. So what if he could lay the charm on unsuspecting old ladies. Didn't mean he wasn't full of crap.

Sloane and Reece both walked out of the hospital room, back to the nurses' station, while Cole finished up with Grace. Rebecca was outside the room, filling in the doctor on rotation.

"How's Peaches?" Sloane asked.

He leaned against a gurney and folded his arms, the muscles in his forearms flexing. His fingers rested on his biceps, and Sloane's mouth went dry. Were his hands always so big? Long fingers like those could do delicious things. He was talking. But she couldn't seem to focus on the words.

"Sloane?"

"Huh?"

His brows pinched together. "You okay?"

There was no way she could be thinking like this about Reece, of all people. Sure, he might have an unfairly nice body, but Sloane wasn't *that* shallow. She needed the brains and the personality to go along with it. She waved her hand dismissively. "Just distracted with . . . work stuff. What were you saying?"

His lips pulled into a tight smile. "She's a delight. A very sweet dog. Although, we've had words about her wardrobe choices."

Liar. She could spot his tells from a mile away. If she hadn't known him since they were kids, she might not notice the way he tapped his thumb on his leg every time he tried to BS his way out of something. Or the fact that he only smiled without teeth when he was fibbing.

"I hope her incontinence problems when she gets excited won't be an issue."

Small dogs tended to have an issue with peeing when excited—a curse among those breeds. She could have told Reece he should be well supplied with piddle pads, but she hadn't bothered. He was a quick learner.

"Not at all." He gave her a tight smile. "In fact, I'll be a little heart-broken when she's adopted."

Okay, maybe she was a monster, but the thought of dog pee all over his floor was kind of entertaining.

"Glad you two are getting along so well. I'll have to tell Kurt that you can keep her for longer if needed."

The muscle in his jaw feathered. "Think of the next chore yet?"

She moved closer to him, their bodies inches away. Heat radiated off him, and she had to tilt her head back to look at his face. It made Sloane aware of just how much he towered over her. A flash of the memory from a year ago invaded her thoughts. How she'd told him he'd break her bed. Heck, he probably could. She swallowed hard. "You'll be the first to know when I do."

"Are we going to have a showdown in the ER lobby? Because at least give me a chance to grab the popcorn first," Cole said as he exited the room and walked up next to Reece.

They both quickly stepped away from each other. "Sloane here is just making sure that I uphold my duties to the community," Reece said tightly.

"No popcorn needed. Sorry to disappoint," Sloane said.

He gave her one last glance, shook his head, and sighed. "Have a good night, Smurfette."

She just smiled and turned back to the room with their most recent patient, relieved to have a reprieve from whatever she was feeling when she was so close to Reece.

Sloane made it back to her apartment at six the next morning. The majority of her shift had been uneventful, besides a car-crash victim. But he'd been moved up to the ICU after they triaged him and would probably be in surgery by now for his neck injuries.

Sloane flopped down on her bed and checked her messages before setting down the phone on the nightstand. Just the group chat between her, Erin, and Madison, but she was too tired to read through the ninety-nine-plus messages about how they were obsessed with Richard Armitage narrating some audiobook. And then there was a text from her mother.

Mom: Miss you. Wish you were here.

She'd sent a picture of herself and Sloane's dad. They had taken a trip to Sanibel Island, and they were both sitting in the white sand, beaming at the camera.

Sloane: Miss you too. Pick me up a seashell.

She was honestly surprised that her parents had decided to go down to Florida for an entire two months. They loved family time at Christmas just as much as she did.

She frowned, thinking that this would be the first holiday that she wouldn't spend at her parents' house. She thought about going to their home and celebrating solo, but that just sounded pathetic. So she'd roped Erin and Madison into spending it with her. She'd be the third wheel, or technically a fifth wheel, since Erin would bring Jake and Madison would bring her on-again, off-again boyfriend, Dereck, if he wasn't traveling for work.

It'd be better than last Christmas, though. Even flying solo this time around.

During the weeks leading up to Sloane's dumping him, Brian had been a complete tool. Even though she'd started dating him during college and had been with him for almost a decade, their last year together had gone downhill quickly. Less time spent together, and the times they *had* been together, they'd fought. When she'd caught him in bed with someone else—like a movie cliché—he'd tried to play it off like it wasn't a big deal. And when she'd insisted that it was, he'd blamed *her*. Said she wasn't *interesting* enough. Didn't have enough variety in bed. He was no longer attracted to her. She wasn't the freakin' circus, and she didn't need to entertain. So his ass had been kicked to the curb. And to think she'd been so sure at nineteen that he was *the one*.

Sloane blinked back tears. So silly. She wasn't that naive teenage girl anymore. She'd gone to therapy, sorted out her feelings. Mostly. But there was always that niggling doubt that maybe it *had* been her fault. She told that voice to shove it.

She smoothed her hair into a ponytail and applied some lip balm. Maybe it was time to try dating again.

She grabbed her phone and fired up one of the dating apps she'd neglected for the past few months. Right after Brian, she hadn't been ready. Now, what did she really have to lose?

She looked over her daily matches. Just as she was about to swipe right on a cutie with tattoos, a message buzzed through her phone.

It was Reece taking a selfie with the dog. He was giving a thumbs-up while at the park. There were several women in the background, petting Peaches, who was dressed in an orange sweater today. Sloane rolled her eyes. She should have known Reece would use the dog to get women.

Another message rolled in.

Reece: I'm ready for my next task.

Sloane: Fine. Come to my apartment.

Reece: Be there as soon as the fan club is done with Peaches.

Ugh. If this man could get gaggles of women, Sloane should surely be able to go on one date without freaking out. She turned back to her dating app and took a deep breath.

Reece pocketed his phone. "Peaches and I are going to head out," he said to the last woman who was still crouched down petting the dog. She was stalling, most likely waiting for Reece to make a move. She'd be waiting a long time because it wasn't happening. When Reece didn't say anything further, she stood and tore off a piece of paper from a notebook she was carrying and scrawled something on it.

"Aw. Well, here's my number if you ever need someone to help walk your dog."

"Thanks." The woman was gorgeous. Long legs, silky brown hair, pretty face. Definitely his type. But for whatever reason, Reece wasn't the least bit interested. He didn't know if it was because the dog was throwing him off his game—Peaches snored like a chain-smoker—or the fact that he was steeling himself for impending doom at Sloane's place.

"What do you say, P? Should I go see the tiny dictator?"

Peaches barked.

"Fine. Would you prefer malevolent dictator?"

She wagged her tail.

He shook his head and led her down the path toward the main road. "You women and your vernacular."

He'd had the dog for a couple days now, and it wasn't too bad. Peaches did whine a bit when she didn't get to sit on the couch, but she'd just have to deal. He'd also have to get used to all the Blake Shelton pictures hanging throughout this house. Four surrounding his bed, two near the kitchen counter, and one near his weight-lifting equipment.

He made the five-minute walk back to his apartment. A text came through just as he'd gathered all of the dog's toys into a plastic bag. He'd take Peaches to his mom's while he dealt with whatever Sloane had in store for him.

Sloane: You do know how to fix showers, yes?

Reece: What part of the shower?

Sloane: The drain. It's not working.

Reece: There's this thing called Drano. Works wonders.

Sloane: Yes, smart-ass, I've used that. It's a lost cause.

Reece: I'll give this to you—you're not one to mess around with your requests.

Reece sighed and opened the utility closet, grabbing the tool he used to fish hair out of clogged drains.

Sloane: Are there stipulations now? Should I be going easy on you?

Reece: You know I like it hard.

Yes, he was trying to get a rise out of her.

Sloane: Not even bothering to answer this. C U soon.

"This woman is going to be the end of me, girl," he said to Peaches. At least the sooner he finished up the shower, the closer he'd be to completing all four tasks and going back to his normal life.

Chapter Nine

While waiting for Reece to arrive, Sloane decided to message with one of the guys she'd matched with a while back on her dating app. Even though she hadn't been actively pursuing anything on the apps for a couple months, she still logged in every once in a while to see if anyone new had joined in her area. *Nope.* Pickings were still slim. She'd been in an epic form of phone tag with a guy named Frank. A flurry of messages would be sent over the course of a day, and then complete radio silence for a couple weeks. They'd been in this pattern for a good two months.

Frank: Sorry, sweet cheeks, I can't meet up tonight. I have to stay late at work.

Frank had an affinity for cutesy nicknames and the unfortunate genetics of a receding hairline.

Sloane blew out a sigh of relief. It saved her the trouble of having to come up with an excuse to text him to get out of meeting tonight. Which was what had happened the last four times. What did it say about her that she couldn't seem to make it past the texting stage to go on an actual date?

Sloane sat at the kitchen counter, working on her latest cross-stitch of the phrase MIRROR, MIRROR ON THE WALL, WHAT THE HECK HAPPENED? She'd started cross-stitch as a way to pass the time after her breakup with Brian. Usually they were snarky sayings that made the sting of being freshly single hurt a little less. Lately, she'd turned to cross-stitching when she was stressed. Like now. What had she been thinking buying Reece at the auction? She should just text him and tell him that he was done and email his chief. There were a lot of adjectives in her arsenal to describe her personality. *Petty* and *vindictive* weren't among those. She sighed and pulled up her disastrous dating profile on her phone. A few new matches. None that really piqued her interest.

She was hoping that the book she'd ordered from Prime would get here sooner than later. E-books weren't really her thing—they tended to hurt her eyes—so she'd opted for paperbacks. She'd caved and bought one of those self-help books Madison had raved about. Because after being stood up for the twenty-fifth time (not that she was keeping count or anything), she was beginning to think that it was an issue with her instead of the men. Seriously, was she that pathetic that she couldn't even make it to the first date? Maybe this should be part of her yearly goals, like the ones Erin put in her planner. Sloane wasn't really the planner type. She'd much rather fly by the seat of her pants. But she was willing to try anything at this point, so she grabbed a pencil and a piece of paper off the counter.

She tapped her pencil on the paper, thought for a minute, and then started scrawling.

Goals for Next Year

Go on an actual date and enjoy it.

Have an insanely hot one-night stand.

Have someone make me breakfast in bed.

Fall in love.

She stared at the last one, frowned, and then erased it. The New Year hadn't even started yet, and the last one was just too much pressure. Where was she supposed to find someone to fall in love with? Portland should really work on providing a store at the mall that doled out husbands. *Yes, I'd like one who is tall and tattooed, has a devilish smile, is smart but not overly cocky about it, and can put his wicked mouth to good use.*

Ew, had she just described Reece? She shuddered and scrubbed that from her mind.

A knock came from the door, pulling her out of her thoughts. Sloane set down her pencil and made her way to the door.

Instead of the UPS man, Reece stood in the hallway.

"You're here quicker than expected." Not the warmest of welcomes. Then again, being jilted yet another time by Frank didn't exactly put her in a warm and fuzzy mood. She did feel a little bad, since Reece had gotten the brunt of her bad moods twice in the same week. But after three graveyard shifts in a row at the hospital, her well was depleted.

"Can't have you dealing with unclogged pipes." Reece procured a snakelike tool from his toolbox and gave her one of his signature lopsided grins. A single quirk of his lips sent a tingle zipping up her spine. His lips, a dark pink, looked soft. Like they'd feel like silk if they grazed down her body. Holy crap, it was warm in here. She grabbed the bottom of her shirt and pulled it away from her, letting cool air flow across her skin. Seriously, it was not fair that someone who annoyed her so much was so hot.

"Awesome." She led him to the bathroom. She'd thought about all the ways she could torture him just with bathroom supplies. Organize her tampons, clean the hair out of her hairbrushes, alphabetize her cosmetics. But since she didn't exactly like standing in an inch of water while she washed her hair, she'd settled on the practical and asked him for this.

He was dressed in faded jeans, a white T-shirt, and—surprise, surprise—a plaid long-sleeve flannel shirt.

"Where's Peaches?" she asked, perching on the sink area. Her feet dangled, her heels resting on one of the knobs for the drawers. He bent over to unscrew the metal drain thingy from the shower. She really should brush up on her bathroom vernacular.

"She's at my mom's house. Mom says it's like having a grandkid. Lord help us all."

He shucked off his flannel shirt, hung it on the towel rack, and went back to his spot kneeling in front of her shower. His dark jeans stretched across his legs as he squatted down to assess the damage. Sloane's throat went dry. Reece had massive thighs, the kind that pushed the fabric of his jeans to the brink. Ones that her fingers itched to squeeze, to feel the muscles jump under her touch.

She blinked away that last thought.

When they'd been growing up, he had always been a head taller than most of the guys at school. He'd sported broad shoulders by the time he'd hit high school, and when Sloane was a freshman and he was a senior, she remembered seeing all the girls fawn over him in the halls.

He'd been with his girlfriend, Amber, since sophomore year. Sloane remembered how he didn't even look in another girl's direction. High School Reece and Current Day Reece seemed worlds apart. Now, instead of steady girlfriends, he went on dates as often as she changed her underwear.

"I think it's sweet that your mom likes the dog." Reece bent over farther, and the fabric of his shirt rode up, exposing a sliver of tanned skin and two dimples on his lower back. The muscles flexed as he pivoted and grabbed the drain snake. Her fingers curled around the edge of the counter. Holy wow, he was nice to look at.

Reece shoved the tool into the drain and dug around in there. His triceps flexed, along with muscles she swore did not exist in her anatomy and physiology books.

He grunted and reached farther down. "Uh, Sloane. Are you the only person to use your shower?"

"Yes . . . why?"

He pulled out a massive clump of blue gunk. "It looks like you murdered a blue Wookiee and tried to dump the evidence in your shower." Good thing she'd cleaned off her shower wall. It could have been considered a mini crime scene. Like one of those cartoon birds splatting against a window and—poof! Feathers everywhere. But in her case, it was tufts of blue hair.

"I was getting sick of his yeti calls." She made a Chewie sound in the back of her throat.

Reece turned and smiled at her, flashing a dimple.

Her brain turned into a discombobulated mess. There were so many options. Too many neurons firing.

Option 1: Tackle him into the shower, tear his shirt off, and take advantage of all those muscles.

Option 2: Turn on the shower, watch his shirt plaster to his skin, and stare at him while puddles of drool trickled out of her mouth and pooled on the floor.

Option 3: Stay put and continue to have no fun.

The third option was obviously the most stupid of the three.

Stop this. You are being persuaded by pesky hormones.

Her legs crossed in response. At least her body knew that it needed to stay away. Her pervy mind was on another wavelength. Though she had to admit she was sick and tired of her dirty Tumblr feeds being the only form of action in her life. She wanted the real thing, damn it.

"You like something you see, Smurfette?"

She cleared her throat. "Package doesn't matter if the insides are damaged goods."

She expected him to stick her with a good comeback. Instead, he just shook his head and said, "I'm gonna let you in on a little secret." He shifted and stood, his huge frame looking so out of place in her tiny bathroom. "We're all a little damaged on the inside. You're kidding yourself if you think otherwise."

"I—That's not always true." She thought about her friends, her family. Everyone she knew had quirks, sure, but she didn't think they were all broken. But something about the way he said it struck something deep inside her. Because, yeah, maybe she was a little broken. She'd fallen off the wall, and there were a few pieces that didn't quite fit back in place. Did he see that in her? Was she that obvious?

"You don't think so?" he asked. "The Sloane I knew wouldn't waste her time with petty revenge plots on someone who was trying to do the right thing."

He put down the drain tool, walked over to the sink, and brushed past Sloane to wash his hands.

She swallowed hard. "You want a truth bomb?"

He moved to dry his hands on the towel hanging from the rack next to Sloane, and he had somehow managed to slip in between her legs. Her body went on high alert, blood pulsing at the space between her thighs.

He looked down at her, his sandy hair falling over his forehead, his face inches from her. "Hit me with it," he said. His hands moved to rest on either side of her hips, his thumbs brushing along her jeans. She swallowed hard.

Nope. Do not get distracted.

"Of course I'm damaged. I dated a guy for almost a decade who turned out to be a complete waste of time. So I've come to the conclusion that once a dick, always a dick."

"Fair enough. I get you're lumping me into that category. That's your own cross to bear. But I'm here. Disposing of the blue Wookiee crime scene."

A message beeped through her phone, tearing her out of the moment. Probably Frank again, apologizing for not meeting up with her. She'd heard it all at this point. The dude had to walk his dog. He forgot to put gas in his car. Got called into work. She couldn't put all the blame on these men, though. She'd been just as guilty.

She opened it to find a text from him.

Frank: Sorry, I can't meet up tomorrow either. I have to take my friend to the airport.

She closed down her phone quickly and placed it facedown on the counter.

"What was that?" Reece asked.

"Nothing."

"I thought we were past the lying stage, Smurfette."

He grabbed for the phone and turned the screen on.

His lips twisted into something that could be considered a grin. "A dating site? And what's up with this Frank dude?"

"He's just a guy I was thinking of seeing. But apparently not."

Oh God, this was embarrassing. It was one thing to be on the sites, but for people other than Erin and Madison to know? She wasn't ready for that.

"Why the dating site, though?"

Yeah, she didn't exactly want to broadcast to the world that she was putting her hat in the online-dating ring. Especially when she was failing. Quite spectacularly. She snatched the phone away.

"I'm busy with work. Where else am I supposed to meet people?"

"I don't know." He shrugged. "Out and about." He backed up a step, and she hated to admit that she'd liked the warmth of his body brushing against her skin.

"Great idea. Maybe I'll come to your work and start dating everyone there."

Reece's eyes hardened. Not that he had any right to get possessive over his men. He'd done exactly that to her nursing unit.

"In fact, that Cole guy was pretty cute. Maybe I'll get his number the next time we see each other." *Ugh.* She hated that she was getting defensive again. But it was her automatic response. She'd been defending herself for months with her friends, fielding questions about why she wasn't getting back into the dating game. She wasn't even sure she knew *how* to date. She'd gone from a first date with Brian at the Cheesecake Factory to basically living with him for ten years.

"He has a girlfriend," he gritted out.

"Oh darn. Guess I'll just have to find someone else."

He opened his mouth to say something and then shut it. Then he let out a heavy breath through his nose. "Do you want some help with it?" He pointed to her phone.

Dating advice from someone who didn't make it past the first? Not exactly the type of help she needed.

"From you? Yeah, I think I'll pass." She hopped down from the counter but didn't realize how close Reece had been standing. Her body rolled down his, one delicious inch at a time, her lady bits screaming, *YAS, QUEEN, MORE OF THIS*, as she roamed over each morsel of his skin.

Mistake. Big mistake. His hard muscles felt spectacular as they glided across her body.

Oh crap, oh crap, oh crap. Step away from the man candy. She quickly moved out of the bathroom and booked it to the kitchen, Reece trailing behind her.

"I'm serious. What could it hurt for me to take a look?"

He wanted to look at her disaster of a dating life? *Fine.* Not like he could make it any worse. She sighed and handed over the phone.

His eyes scanned the phone, and she kept her hands from fidgeting. This was like someone reading her diary. Her cousin had done that in fifth grade and had read an excruciating passage of how she'd had a crush on Michael Lamont and how he'd liked Fern Anderson. Oh, fifth-grade angst.

He cleared his throat. "I know we don't get along on the best of days, but even I can't let you have an unapproachable online profile."

She crossed her arms. No way her profile was *that* bad. Maybe a little too honest, but since when was honesty a bad thing? "What about it is *unapproachable*?"

"For starters, why are you telling people that you're an ice queen? I mean, I know that is a fact"—he smirked—"but it's not something you want to advertise."

"It was supposed to be a joke." So maybe her brand of sarcasm didn't translate to online dating. Why had she even put that in? Was it because, even though she'd been on these sites for a few months, she had yet to really give anyone a chance? Everyone on here seemed so . . . fake. There was the one guy who'd claimed he was thirty-two and then ended up being nineteen. Then there was the guy who'd hid his criminal record. She wanted to find someone, but the whole online thing just didn't match her style. Then again, where was she supposed to meet someone? She'd never date a doctor. And she didn't work with many male nurses. Basically, it was slim pickings in the eligible-bachelors department. And now, here was Reece ridiculing her pathetic attempt at a dating profile. Seriously, could this get any more embarrassing?

"It doesn't come off as a joke. Not when guys are skimming."

"What is this? A half-assed class assignment?"

He chuckled. "Think of it like a CliffsNotes version of yourself."

She schooled her features and put on a cool front. "Then what would you put?"

"You like that baking show with the British people, and you like wearing those shirts with the horrible Harry Potter puns. Why not start with that?"

Sloane did a double take. This was Reece she was talking to, right? They'd grown up together, but he was always around in the sense that they shared the same space. Went to the same movies because it was convenient. He'd been on the periphery. She never knew he'd actually bothered to notice stuff about her. And here he was, already creating a better online-dating rap sheet than she could come up with on her own.

She snatched the phone from him and pocketed it. "Thanks. I'll consider putting those in."

"Or you could add that you sleep with your mouth open and drool. I'm sure there's a market for that."

Yep. There was the Reece she knew. "You've been so helpful. Thanks again for unclogging my drain. I'll let you know when I have my third chore." She'd blazed through the first two and would make sure to drag out the final two a bit more.

But before she could shoo him out the door, he picked up the piece of paper on the kitchen counter that she'd been scribbling on, the one with her goals.

"What's this?"

A spike of alarm zipped up her spine. That list was for her eyes only. Because, hello, embarrassing. "Reece. Give that to me." She tried to hide the panic in her voice, but the last word caught in her throat.

She went to make a grab for it, but he was taller and held it higher than she could jump.

"Goals for next year, huh?"

"They're stupid."

His playful demeanor shifted. "Why are any of these stupid?" he demanded.

Okay, so she didn't think they were, but she didn't want Reece, of all people, knowing just how badly she wanted these things. She practically ached for them. "They just are. Now will you please put it down?"

He relented and set the list on the counter. "Just putting it out there—I've heard I'm not a bad date."

"I'll take that into consideration. But seeing how the last time with you went, I think I'll pass."

His lips pressed into a hard line. "You know why I turned you down, Sloane. And it had nothing to do with whether I wanted you or not."

"Next time just say that to Drunk Me, okay? Because even while hammered, I still remember, *Ew, Sloane*."

His hands went to her arms, cupping them. He moved into her space again, his huge body towering over her. This was a horrible time to think she needed to take up mountain climbing—she'd need a pickax and rope to scale Mount Reece.

His gaze burned into her, heating her blood until it simmered in her veins. "Trust me when I say the last thing that comes to mind when I think of you is *Ew*. I was stupid and immature, and I'm sorry. And if you were sober that night, I would have taken you back to your bed and fucked you until you couldn't walk the next day. But you weren't."

She swallowed hard. The space between her thighs ached. She should just brush this off. Reece was a serial flirt. He was probably just trying to talk himself out of a sticky situation. But the heat flaring in his eyes told a different story. One that made her brain turn the emergency shutoff valve. "On that note, I need to get some stuff done around the house."

He leaned down, his beard brushing against her cheek. He whispered, "If you ever need help with that list, you know where to find me."

The "Hallelujah Chorus" broke out in her head. Another voice yelled, *Yes, girl, ride that behemoth of a man until you break!* And a third voice was pondering whether everything was anatomically proportionate. Because, whoa. She shoved those thoughts away. She'd entertained it once . . . okay, plus a few more times, and that was enough.

"Cocky oaf." And with that, she pushed him out the door and closed it behind him.

She could hear Reece's deep laugh through the door.

Reece stared at his phone. He'd never been one to sign up for dating sites. Found such frivolous things a waste of time and money. Mostly the money portion. He liked to keep that where it belonged—in his bank account. Much to the chagrin of all his previous dates. His buddies teased him that he was cheap, but really, Reece was economical.

He'd be laughing them to the bank, because his pension was at top tier, and he was set up for retirement. Sure, that made him sound like an old man. But he didn't like surprises. And also he didn't want to be working until he was using a walker.

Jake's name popped onto the screen, and Reece answered.

"What's up?"

"Come out with us tonight. Hollywood and I are meeting at Henry's."

"Sure." *Why not?* He needed to get Sloane off his mind. Something about the dating site didn't sit well with him. It wasn't even the money aspect. He didn't want to think what else it could be besides the fact that Sloane would be subjecting some poor sucker to her glares. Her attitude was enough to scare hardened criminals.

By nine thirty, he had joined his friends at Henry's. People gathered in clumps around the high tops and bar. He threaded his way through the crowd and made it to their table in the back corner. Jake and Hollywood were there, pint glasses in their hands. An empty pint glass sat at the open spot at the table, and Reece slid into the booth and poured beer from the pitcher into the pint.

"Where were you earlier?" Hollywood asked.

"Helping Sloane with something."

Hollywood raised a brow. "Does this something involve shaving her head?"

"Why?"

Hollywood grabbed a clump of blue hair from the back of Reece's shirt and tossed it to the floor. "Just an educated guess."

Reece thought back to this afternoon in her bathroom. Her sitting on the counter watching him. The way her legs parted. How he'd fit between them. He had the fleeting thought of taking her right there, pumping into her while her back banged against the mirror. He swallowed hard. "Unclogged her drain."

Hollywood nodded. "Not the exciting response I was hoping for."

"At least two of the chores are done." Two more and he could go back to ignoring her. Which was probably for the best. Things had gotten too real today. He'd never opened up like that to anyone before. Where had all that shit about being damaged come from? It was much better to keep those thoughts to himself.

"So you mean to say nothing's going to happen between you two? Seems like a missed opportunity, man."

If there was ever a time that proved Hollywood knew nothing about women, this was it. "Not going to go there. Just need to finish the last two tasks and be done with it. Then hopefully I still get to keep my job when this ends."

"Whatever you say, man. But if I had a chance with Sloane, I wouldn't pass it up."

"You need to be tall enough to climb onto the big-kid rides before you begin to throw out judgment like that, man." He didn't like what Hollywood was implying. Not one bit.

Hollywood's phone buzzed on the table, and he peered over, then sent the screen to black without responding.

This happened several more times.

"You going to answer that?" Reece asked.

Hollywood flipped over his phone. "Nope."

"Angry girlfriend?"

"Who said anything about angry? Just not sure things are working out." It looked like there was more to the story, but Reece wasn't one to push. If his friend wanted advice, he knew where to go.

"And you don't want to work it out?" Jake asked.

Hollywood shrugged. "Not sure."

"You should at least text her back. Don't leave her hanging," Jake said.

"Okay, Dad." Hollywood gave a smug grin.

"I say the fewer attachments, the better," Reece said. It'd worked for him so far.

"Yeah, and you can end up like Reece and have an empty apartment," Jake said, shifting in his seat.

The comment caused a spear of anger to slice through Reece.

A smile spread across Hollywood's face, and he picked up his phone. "Maybe you're right."

"Hey. It's called minimalism." Reece liked his life. Work, food, sleep. A woman's company every once in a while. He'd never thought of his life as lacking. But when Jake put it that way, it made it seem like he was doing something wrong.

Jake laughed and took a swig from his pint. "Whatever you want to call it."

"Just because you're sick and in love doesn't mean the rest of us need to drink the Kool-Aid." It went without saying that he was happy for his best friend and his sister. But that wasn't the life he'd planned for himself. Reece didn't need anyone and was completely fine with that.

"Whatever you say. Hollywood, I'd text the girl back. It's worth it," Jake said.

Reece took a deep pull from his beer. He definitely did not have enough alcohol in him for this conversation. Not when he kept sneaking glances at Sloane's dating profile like a bona fide stalker. He noticed that she'd changed her bio, per his suggestion. He didn't know whether that made him happy or made him want to punch himself in the face.

"I need to head out. Erin wants to see a movie." Jake threw down a few bills and stood.

Reece turned to face Hollywood. "What do you say, Hollywood? Want to take some shots?"

Hollywood shook his head and continued to nurse the same beer he'd been nursing when Reece had arrived. "I need to take it easy tonight. Going to do stairs tomorrow and don't want to regret my very existence."

Reece sat at the end of the bar with his phone out. On a normal Friday night, he'd be making the rounds, blowing off steam from his shift, talking to women. Tonight, he just wasn't in the mood. Music blared, and most of the patrons were well into their fourth or fifth drinks at this point.

He scrolled though the dating app. Was he really living a lonely life? He knew Jake didn't mean it as an insult, but it had rankled him. More than he expected.

He stared at the profile page he hadn't bothered to set up yet. He'd downloaded it to . . . what? Spy on Sloane? That didn't make for a great explanation. The profile setup page asked for a picture and a description. He scrolled through his gallery and loaded one of the pics he'd taken while he was hiking at Silver Falls and BSed a few lines.

He looked over the information. This was stupid. He didn't want to have someone depend on him. He liked the quiet of his apartment. The fact that he could do whatever he pleased and didn't have to check in with anyone. To hell with what his friends said. He was going to be an eternal bachelor and would happily live that existence. His finger highlighted the words he'd put in the description, and then he hit the "Delete" button.

Chapter Ten

The next morning was Reece's day off from the station. He made his way across town with Andie on the MAX, and they got off at the last stop before Pioneer Square. Every three or four weeks, he made his way down to the local homeless shelter. He'd been volunteering here since his early teens. Mark, the manager, had been running the place for nearly two decades. The man reminded Reece of his uncle, with his barrel chest and scraggly white beard, and he was always in his signature gray Patagonia hoodie.

When Reece walked into the shelter, he breathed a sigh of relief. With everything going on at the station and getting roped into being Sloane's errand boy, he welcomed a moment of routine. The building was packed with people. Some were around Reece's age with kids in tow, and some were older and looked like they'd been going through a rough time for years. Mark's shelter specialized in not only giving people a place to stay until they could get on their feet, but he and his partner, Gary, also found a lot of work opportunities for people.

"Why are we at a homeless shelter?" Andie asked.

Reece had to remind himself that Andie came from a different generation than he did. Even though he was only twelve years older, it made a whole world of difference when it came to how they were raised by their mom.

His mother had focused a lot on giving back to the community and had hammered it into Erin and Reece as kids. Reece figured that by the time Andie came around, his mom was tired. And he didn't blame her. But now Andie wanted to get into college and had zero to show for the last year.

"You said you needed a way to build that résumé of yours. Well, here you go, kid."

Back when he was younger, their mother had started Reece and Erin out volunteering at soup kitchens. Said that giving back to the community was of the utmost importance. Both Reece and Erin had taken that seriously, and they'd ended up in careers that helped the community.

"I have character. I donate to the Salvation Army during the holidays." She toyed with the thick braid that hung over her shoulder and glanced around the shelter uncertainly.

"Spare change in a red tin isn't going to win you points, Andie." Jesus, his sister had a lot to learn. He was hoping that he could get her set up on a regular schedule down here. It might do her some good.

She released a dragged-out sigh. "Fine."

"I can't believe Mom never made you do this when you were in high school." It hadn't even been an option when *he* was younger. He liked that about their family—that they had been so involved with the community.

"Well, she was busy with you guys, and then once I got to high school, I don't think she cared as much." His sister frowned.

Reece couldn't even begin to contemplate how that must have felt, but she had a chance to break out from that and do some good today.

He didn't know how to respond. Because he'd felt it. How his mom was more worried about the food truck and making ends meet back then.

"We ruined her," he admitted.

"Totally." She smiled. "So what do we do first?"

"We meet with the manager."

Mark caught sight of Reece and moved from the back part of the building, where he was folding blankets, over to him. He clapped a hand on his back and smiled.

"Haven't seen your ugly mug in here lately. Thought you might have disappeared on us."

"Been crazy with the job lately." He shrugged off his coat and hooked it onto the rack in the corner of the volunteer station. The movement felt familiar, something he'd done hundreds of times.

Andie shuffled next to Reece with her thumbs in her pockets, her back hunched as she nervously looked around.

"Mark, this is my sister Andie. She's here to help out a little. Beef up her résumé before she goes off to a big-shot college."

The skin around Mark's eyes crinkled as he beamed at Andie. "Wonderful. Well, we need help in the serving line today. If you could help dish out lasagna, that'd be great. Do you have a food-handler's card?"

Andie looked from Mark to Reece. "Yeah. I work on my mom's food truck, so I know the protocol."

"Great. Where's that other sister of yours? Haven't seen her around in a while."

"She just moved back into the area. Keeping herself busy with a new teaching job," Reece said.

Mark smiled and zipped his hoodie closer to his chin as someone opened up the door to the shelter and a gust of chilly morning air funneled in. "Glad to hear it. She always was a great girl."

Reece nodded. He and his sister may not have gotten along all the time, but he respected her. They were both worried about Andie, who seemed to be spiraling lately. She was working at their mother's food truck, but she seemed angrier than normal. The more any of them pushed, trying to figure out why, the more she closed up.

"What do you need me to do today?" Reece asked, washing his hands in the staff station. The shelter was large compared to others around town, with several rows of sleeping stations, benches upon benches, tables for meals, and an area for job planning and counseling. Mark and Gary had set up an operation that had been highlighted in the national news over the years.

"Lunch is about to be served. You can help your sister out with scooping minestrone to people."

"Works for me." He liked talking with the families and getting to know them. Most were just in a tight spot because they'd lost a job. He pulled on a smock, a hairnet, and gloves.

Once the food station was fully prepped, Mark announced to people that lunch was ready.

A line of about fifty people formed, and Reece started ladling soup. "How are you doing today?" He spooned the minestrone into an older woman's soup cup, and everything he was worried about earlier slipped to the back of his mind.

He looked over at his sister, who was dishing out lasagna to a little kid. His sister may be a little rough around the edges, but he hoped that she could get her act together.

A familiar face moved to the front of the line where Reece was ladling out soup. Eva. She was a regular here at the shelter. Eva had to be in her early fifties, and she camped out on Stark with her husband, who was a military vet.

"I was wondering when I'd see you again," she said.

"Missed seeing your shining face."

Eva blushed. "Always such a charmer."

Andie snorted. "You've really cornered the market on the over-fifty crowd, huh?"

His sister's customer-service skills could use a spit shine. "It's called human decency. You should try it sometime."

Andie shrugged and went back to slopping lasagna onto people's plates.

Once the lunch rush died down, he and Andie helped Gary clean up the area, putting foil over the leftover food and sliding it into the industrial-size fridge.

Andie was folding the final piece of foil over a tin of marinara when she said, "Hey, Reece?"

He glanced up from writing the date on the lasagna tin. "Yeah?"

Her face softened. "Thanks for helping me out. I know Erin gives you a hard time sometimes, but you're a really good brother."

He wrapped his sister into a side hug. At least he was getting something right. He might piss off Erin, Sloane, and his chief, but at least he could help out Andie.

Sloane had become addicted to the stupid dating apps. Self-diagnosed, of course. She was currently in the downward-dog pose at Bikram yoga, sweating in places she didn't think she could sweat, and her eyes kept darting to the pocket of her bag where she'd tucked her phone. Madison had dragged Erin and Sloane to hot yoga since it was Free Guest Saturday at the gym she went to. Yoga wasn't usually in Sloane's repertoire. She'd always been more of the fumble-around-on-a-tread-mill-and-lift-some-free-weights type.

New-age spa music funneled out of the speakers in the boom box next to the instructor on the floor. The woman was in her early thirties, had that slim yoga physique, and not even a splotch of red staining her cheeks. Sloane, on the other hand, had sweat dripping onto her yoga mat like she was a leaky faucet.

"And now we're moving into happy-baby pose." Sloane watched as the instructor lay on her back and then grabbed both of her feet, legs spread wide.

Sloane did the same. She wasn't one to stretch often. If often meant never. She grabbed her feet, and the stretch burned. "Holy crap, I think I broke my vagina," she whispered to Erin, who was on the mat next to her.

She wondered if she'd had a better sex life—or any sex life, for that matter—over the past year, then maybe she wouldn't feel like her body was going to snap like a rubber band.

"Good. And now we are moving into child's pose. Find your inner peace. Let the worries of today flow out your fingertips," the instructor urged.

Sloane didn't know how she was supposed to find her inner peace when blood was rushing to her head and there was a massive wedgie that needed Excalibur-level extraction, but she closed her eyes and tried to channel inner peace.

She glanced over at Erin and Madison, who both looked like they were doing a much better job of finding their inner chi.

The instructor reached for the CD player at the front of the class and turned down the music. "Class is over, my friends. Feel free to take as long as you need to get up from your poses."

Sloane groaned as she scrunched up to a kneeling position. "Do you feel as disgusting as I think I must look right now?"

"Like you've just taken a bath in your own sweat?" Erin asked.

Sloane stood, grabbed the bottle of cleaning product, sprayed down her mat, and then rolled it up. "Is it normal to sweat between your butt cheeks?"

"It's called detoxing. You'll thank your body for this later," Madison said.

"Yes, I'll be thanking it with some Goldfish and a nice red to go along with it," she said.

Sloane fished her phone out of her bag and clicked into her messages. Nothing from any of the guys she'd been messaging.

"Are you guys coming over for Scrabble tonight?" Erin asked while slinging her gym bag over her shoulder. Neither she nor Madison looked nearly as sweaty as Sloane. Maybe she was having hot flashes twenty years early.

Madison dabbed her face with a white towel. "Can't. I have to edit photos from my shoot last week. I'm way behind."

They made their way to the main entrance of the gym and got in line for the smoothie stand. Madison's gym had a steep price tag and the amenities to go along with it. It wasn't the type of place that Sloane could justify putting her hard-earned money toward, but she definitely appreciated it whenever she got a free pass. But right now, with her clothes soaked, Sloane couldn't get home quick enough to take a shower.

"Sure, I'm in," she said to Erin.

Sloane could never pass up Scrabble. It was one of her favorite games. For the sole reason that she could add an *s* onto most words and take the whole table. Plus, she wasn't going to pass up Erin getting supercompetitive over a game. She took her English language seriously.

"Hey, have you seen Jake at the hospital lately?" asked Erin.

"Not since last week. Why, what's up?" The last time she'd even really talked to him was at the firefighter auction. Their paths didn't cross too often at work.

Erin let out a long sigh and glanced at her phone. "Just haven't seen much of him lately. Our schedules are so out of whack with him picking up extra shifts. Doesn't help that I agreed to head the science club after school."

"You guys will get back in sync," Sloane said. Although that was the one perk of being single. She didn't have to worry about anyone else's schedule.

"Relationships go through cycles." They moved up in line, Madison's voice drowned out by the mixer. She waited for the blender to stop and then continued. "Yours is just in the spin cycle at the moment. It'll all smooth out."

Erin shrugged. "You're probably right. It just sucks that we live together, and I barely see him." She shook her head. "I'm just being weird."

"Aren't you always?" said Sloane.

Madison nodded. "You're totally weird, Erin. But that's why we love you. Also, can I rant for a sec?" They moved up until there was only one person ahead of them. Sloane had already decided she was getting the peanut butter banana smoothie.

"I thought you had found your inner chi back in there?" Sloane joked.

"In there, I find peace. Out of the yoga studio, I'm ready to maim someone today."

Madison wasn't usually one to go on rants very often. In fact, the last time she'd gone off, it was about a couple who had made complaints on Yelp about Madison because she hadn't photoshopped them enough.

"What's up?" Erin asked.

"*Professional MeetCute* got back to me." They moved up until the three of them were at the front of the line. "Two strawberry smoothies and a peanut butter banana one," Madison told the barista. The same smoothie orders every single time for the past few months. They each chipped in a few bucks and then waited on the other side of the counter for the drinks.

"What did they say?" Sloane asked.

"They said that I'm in the final round of possible casting, but they need to do an in-person interview."

"That's great!" She noticed Madison's frown. "Isn't it?"

Her lips pursed into a tight frown. "It would be if it wasn't next weekend."

Erin's eyes went wide. "Like, six days from now?"

Madison sighed, and they all grabbed their smoothies from the counter. "Exactly . . . and I have two shoots scheduled. I can't just cancel on my clients."

Erin took a sip of her smoothie. "Ugh. The worst. What are you going to do?"

"I'm going to have to tell them no, I guess. Not really much I can do." She sighed and kept her drink at her side.

Sloane wrapped her in a half hug, trying not to get all her almost-dried sweat on her best friend. "Sorry, babe. Wish there was something we could do."

Madison leaned her head on Sloane's shoulder. "Ew, you really did sweat."

Sloane gave her a playful shove, and Madison smiled, finally taking a sip of her drink. "Oh well. It was a nice thought. But at least I know that I had a chance at making it onto the show. There's something."

That was Madison. Always looking for the bright side. Sloane loved that about her best friend. She was always so positive. Something that Sloane had been lacking lately, she realized.

She looked at her two best friends. These two women got her through all her hard times. And now since Erin was back permanently, she didn't have to see her on a biannual basis.

Sloane took a sip of her smoothie and nearly choked on a chunk of banana when she noticed a certain six-foot-three oaf walking in the door.

"Well, if it isn't my favorite sister and her friends."

"I didn't think they let dogs into this place," Sloane said. She ignored the quickened pace of her heart. And the fact that she had ten layers of sweat cooled onto her skin and had the sudden urge to bolt for the bathroom. No, this was Reece. She shouldn't care what he thought.

"Lucky for me, Hollywood has a membership. I'm just along for the ride. Speaking of dogs, how's it going on your app?"

"Sloane's kicking ass on it, not that it's any of your business," Erin said. "Is there a reason you've taken such an interest in Sloane's affairs?"

Sloane smiled at the arched brow Erin sent Reece's way.

"I thought since Sloane and I are friends now, we're supposed to ask each other about these types of things." He smirked and shoved his hands in the pockets of his gym shorts.

Sloane made an effort to keep her gaze at eye level, but it traveled down, down, down, to the muscles peeking out the sides of his tank top. To the tattoos covering his pecs and biceps. Scorpions, birds, script she couldn't read from this distance. Her gaze traveled to the thick muscles of his thighs, the muscles outlined against the fabric of his shorts. She swallowed hard. Sure, he was sinfully delicious, but she'd also told herself she'd stay away from men like that. Especially *this* certain man. She'd been friends with him in the past, but she didn't think that was possible now.

"Oh, Reece. I have plenty of friends. I'll take that third chore, though."

"Only need me for my services. I feel so used."

Oh, there were so many other things she could think about Reece doing. Things she'd never admit to Erin or Madison. "Just the cold, hard truth."

"I see you're really trying to live up to that self-proclaimed ice-queen moniker."

This was a dangerous game. One Sloane had come to enjoy. She liked the verbal sparring, and Reece seemed to be the only guy who could dish it.

Before Sloane could say anything, Cole stepped in.

"Dude. You guys just have to get all weird and ruin it for the rest of us." Cole smacked Reece on the back of his head. "Sloane, Erin,

Madison, it's a pleasure seeing you guys." He turned to Reece. "Let's go lift."

Reece nodded and said, "Well, *non*friend, I guess I'll see you around." He turned to Madison and Erin. "Nice seeing you ladies as well." And with that, he and Cole disappeared into the gym.

Chapter Eleven

"I'm sorry, but we haven't found an adopter for Peaches yet, Mr. Jenkins."

Reece stopped pacing the length of his apartment and sighed heavily into the phone. "No problem. Just keep me posted." This was the second call he'd put in this week. Both unsuccessful.

"Sure thing," said Kurt, and then he hung up.

"Looks like you live to terrorize me for another day, girl," he said to Peaches. His fingers ran along her back, and a tuft of hair spilled to the floor. The dog shed more than Sloane's shower drain, and there were tiny brown tumbleweeds rolling around on his hardwoods. Even with the foo-foo outfits. Today she'd picked an argyle sweater. Yes, picked. Pointed with her damn paw and everything. The dog clearly had no self-respect, but who was he to deprive the pooch of something that kept her warm? He'd have to find a decent replacement. Like a Seahawks jersey.

He pulled the Roomba out of the storage closet and started it up.

Peaches barked at it when the vacuum moved into the kitchen and hit the Greenie she'd been gnawing on that he'd picked up from the store after he'd worked out with Hollywood. He'd been surprised to see Sloane there. It was impossible to ignore how sexy she looked, flushed from working out, her T-shirt see-through from exertion. That mouth of hers was enough to drive him mad. He'd always managed to put his foot in his own mouth when he was around her. Instead of his words coming off like a joke, they came off assy. Which seemed to be the usual with their interactions. He just couldn't get it right, and damn it, he wanted her to not look at him like she was planning to throw him on a pyre and send him out to sea. At least he'd have a reprieve from her tonight.

He made his way to the door and grabbed his coat from the hook. Peaches looked up at him, hope in her little eyes that he'd take her for another walk.

"Sorry, you're not coming this time. I'll just be a few hours, girl." Reece bent down and gave the dog a few pats on the head and closed the apartment door. Pitiful whimpers came from his apartment, and his heart clenched. It was just a few hours. The dog needed to be able to handle that if she was going to stay with him for an extended period. Any day now Kurt would call and say he found an adopter, so Reece didn't want Peaches to get too used to the idea of going everywhere with him. Not that he was getting attached or anything.

Plus, the dog would be entertained by the Roomba. He'd caught her riding on it earlier this morning. Yoranians weren't supposed to shed that much. His wood floors begged to differ.

He made his way to the Jeep and then drove the fifteen minutes to his mom's house. Since Erin had moved back into town, their mother had insisted that they add on to their weekly dinner together and reinstate game night.

Erin's Prius was already in the driveway when he pulled in beside her. He assumed Jake was with her, since he usually came to their weekly dinners.

Andie paced in the entryway and came to a skidding halt when Reece strode through the door.

"What's up?" he asked.

"They're all in there. Laughing."

Andie looked tired from her shift at the shelter earlier today, but he was proud of her. "At you again?" He ruffled her hair. His youngest sister was never one for large doses of family time. She still lived at home with their mother and had made it known several times that she'd rather have any other living arrangement if her budget allowed. It didn't. He'd offer to let her crash at his place, but his brotherly love only extended so far. Alone time was much needed after his shifts, and he didn't like sharing his space with anyone else. Back in the early days, he'd roomed with Jake. Even their childhood friendship became strained. Reece decided he was just meant to live by himself. He didn't mind it.

"Very funny. Erin's doing that whole Jake's-the-funniest-human-in-existence thing. She's laughing at jokes that aren't even funny."

Reece shrugged. "That's what love does to you."

"Makes you stupid?"

He didn't know if he should be worried or impressed that his sister had come to this conclusion at such a young age. It'd taken him years, ever since he realized that he wasn't going to find anyone that made him feel the way Amber had made him feel.

"Some think it's lucky to find someone that makes you like that," he said.

"Then they're idiots." Andie pressed a beer into his hand.

He unscrewed the cap and pointed it at her. "I'll drink to that."

Andie's shoulders relaxed. She'd had a rough couple of months, but he had no clue why. Reece tried to press a couple of times, but Andie was locked down tighter than the Jaws of Life on a crushed car door.

"Ready to go in there?" he asked.

"Do we have to?"

"If you don't want Mom to have a conniption, then yes."

He put his arm around his sister and led her to the kitchen, where everyone had congregated. And stopped short to find Sloane there.

Sloane was laughing at something, her head tilted back, her eyes crinkling in the corners. The tanned column of her throat was exposed, and he had the sudden urge to run his tongue along the golden-brown skin. Reece momentarily lost his breath as he watched how happy she looked. How her whole face lit up. The laugh died on her lips as soon as she spotted Reece. It was a shame things couldn't go back to before, when they were actually amicable. Especially when she was an honorary sibling in the Jenkins clan.

"Finally! What took you so long?" His mother strode over and wrapped him in a hug. His two sisters might give his mom a hard time, but Reece was never ashamed by his love for her. She'd been there for him when he first applied to be a firefighter. She'd told him to pick himself up and move on when Amber left him for another man. Sure, she had a never-ending to-do list, but he would gladly take care of it to make her life a little simpler.

"Was making sure Peaches was okay to leave."

"You could have brought her. She loves her Grandma Jenkins."

She'd watched Peaches when Reece was on shift this week. He thought a couple of times that she would refuse to give the dog back, but she'd reluctantly handed over the leash. He hated the thought of inconveniencing her, though. Maybe he'd look into someone coming into his apartment to walk the dog a few times during his twenty-four-hour shift. Then again, she'd be adopted soon.

"Trying to get her used to being by herself for a few hours at a time." He sent a look to Sloane. Two more chores. He had this in the bag, as long as she didn't have another trip to the Humane Society planned. Then he'd be done with her and her ridiculous demands.

"I'm sure she's celebrating having the house to herself," Sloane said, smiling sweetly.

"Now that everyone's here, it's game time," his mom cut in. She grabbed the Scrabble box and shook it enthusiastically.

Last week had been Pictionary, so Reece counted this as an upgrade.

They all sat at the table, Andie taking the seat next to him, and Jake on the other side. Across from him sat Sloane. Black storm clouds practically hovered over her since he'd come into the room. He could feel it.

"Sloane, sweetheart, how is work?" his mom asked.

She turned her attention to Reece's mom. "Fine. Been busy since I transferred into the ER."

"I'm sure we'll be bumping into you more, then," Jake said.

"Oh, goodie." Her smile tightened.

"It wouldn't be so bad. You know you enjoy seeing our mugs," Reece said.

She laughed and took a sip of her drink. "I don't know. I can't decide if I like seeing you or stitching you up better. It's a toss-up, really."

"Always were a masochist. You know they have clubs for that?" he retorted.

Erin cleared her throat. "On that note, I think I'm going to start."

"Hey now. We all know that it's the oldest who starts. I've earned this privilege," his mom chimed in.

"It's always the winner of the last round. And"—Erin shuffled through the score papers—"that'd clearly be me."

"That's because you have your fancy teacher vocabulary," Reece said.

"Can't help what gifts I was graced with, Reece. Sad some of us can't be on the same level." She stuck her tongue out at him.

"Hello, I think we need to go with the youngest. Give the weakling a head start," Andie started in.

He bit back a laugh. As much as he grumbled about coming over sometimes, he enjoyed being with his family. To see them all so happy, even when they were bickering. Were they the most functional bunch? Probably not. But life wouldn't be nearly as interesting without them.

After another few minutes, they'd decided that Jake would start because no one in the family could be mad if he did. Reece's mom had rolled out the red carpet like Jake was a guest, even though he was far from that since he'd been another fixture in the Jenkins household for decades.

"Okay, Sloane, your turn," Reece's mom said.

Sloane stared down at her letters, chewing on her bottom lip. Reece found himself staring. They were the lightest shade of red he'd ever seen, almost close to pink.

She grabbed five letters and placed them on the board, spelling out the word *annoy*. Then she made a point to stare Reece down.

"Well, that is quite an interesting word." Reece's mom lifted up the tiles. "You even got a double-word space. Sixteen points." Reece's mom marked it on the score sheet.

Andie added an *ing* onto Sloane's word. When it got to Reece, he put down the word *pesky*.

Erin, of course, went for something science related.

Reece liked a good challenge, and seeing Sloane's eye twitch every single time Reece matched her points was more gratifying than he cared to admit.

He'd been especially proud of his use of the word *frigid*.

Sloane managed to fit in *data* onto the board.

Reece stared at his letters. He saw the word forming and looked at the board, making sure he could find a spot to make it work. Sure enough, there was an opening for it. He placed every single one of his letters down, bracketing her word so that it now formed *undatable*. And then gave his smirk that he'd perfected just for Sloane.

Did he think she was actually a miserable woman who was bound to be by herself for the rest of her life? No. Well, she was miserable to him, but that was a different story.

Her nostrils flared.

The whole table went quiet.

Shit.

"I think we need ice cream. Does anyone want mint chocolate chip?" his mom chimed in.

"What is wrong with you?" Erin asked, staring him down.

"Nothing's wrong with me. It's a word. I used it." If she was going to get her panties in a twist, that was *her* issue.

His sister glared up at him, unconvinced.

"Fine. I'm sorry if my word insulted anyone." His tone could have used some work. In fact, he'd sworn he'd seen something other than annoyance flash across Sloane's face. He'd say that it looked like hurt, but the woman was made of steel and soul-sucking qualities. There was no room for sadness in that mind of hers.

Still, he wasn't going to stick around to see what she was going to put down on the next round.

He pushed back from the table and stood. "I should probably get home to check on Peaches."

"Yeah, it'd be a shame if she peed on those floors of yours," Erin said.

"Always a pleasure. Jake." He nodded to his friend. "Sloane." He went to give her a nod, but she cut him a frosty glare that made his neck tense.

Jake followed him out to his car. "Anything going on between you two?"

"She hates me. I apparently piss her off to no end." He shrugged. "I'd say it's just the usual."

"Not that it's any of my business, but I think maybe you need to smooth things over with her. For the sake of, well, everyone."

He cut a glance to Jake. "You mean because you're with her best friend."

Jake shrugged. "Yeah, exactly."

"She's a big girl. If she can't handle one word, that's on her." Now Reece was sounding like a dick. This was why he liked being at home by himself. He didn't mess up conversations. He didn't make people feel bad about themselves.

"Just think on it. She's more fragile than you think. Karma's a real thing, brother."

To hell with karma. If there really was such a thing, what about all the good people who had devastation rip through their lives? Just last week he'd been on a call where a four-year-old was crushed by a TV. He didn't think that kid had that coming to him. And Sloane? Fragile? He scoffed at that. The Sloane he knew was tougher than any machine he operated. He thought back to that look that had flashed across her face. Maybe there was something more to it.

"Yeah. Will do. See you tomorrow." And with that, he got into his Jeep and turned the ignition.

Twenty minutes later, Reece fumbled with his keys and finally found the one for his apartment. The door swung open, and the pungent aroma of dog crap hit his nose. He recoiled. Peaches must have taken a beast of a dump because Reece was gagging on the fumes. He walked into his apartment, and his foot skidded across the hardwood as he reached for the light.

He choked back a guttural cry as he surveyed his apartment. There was Peaches, at his leg, jumping and prancing, peeing while she did so. The Roomba was making its way around his couch. And every single inch of floor was smeared with dog shit. Every. Single. Inch.

Fuck.

He grabbed a towel from the hall closet, unhooked the leash from the front doorknob, and clipped it onto the dog's collar.

He cleaned her paws off and then led her into the hallway, shutting his apartment door behind him. Without knowing exactly what to do, he dialed Jake's number.

"What's up?"

"That thing you said about karma? Yeah, I believe it now."

Chapter Twelve

A week had passed since the whole Scrabble-night debacle. Thanksgiving had come and gone. The city was in full Christmas mode, with carolers strolling down rain-slicked sidewalks and wreaths decorating storefront doors. Sloane hadn't bothered messaging Reece or asking for a third favor. In fact, she was ready to end this whole thing. It was stupid anyway. She had better things to do with her time, like focus on work and buy a couple of Christmas gifts for Erin and Madison. There'd be no obsessing about how she missed getting texts from Reece. And how she'd gotten used to seeing him over the past few weeks. Sloane needed to get with the program. They were incompatible. Couldn't even get along during a family game night. Even knowing this didn't change the fact that she *did* miss their messed-up, back-and-forth verbal sparring. So much so, that there were only three weeks until Christmas, and she wasn't feeling the spirit of the season. Not even in her tacky Christmas sweater.

She pulled her coat tighter around her as she made her way down the riverfront. Sometimes, before she met the girls for coffee, she'd come down here and walk along the water, staring at the waves. At this hour, it was mostly older couples walking and young business types running with dogs.

Sloane pulled out her phone and called her mom, the one person who could always make her feel better.

Her mother picked up on the third ring. "Hello, sweetheart. How are you doing?"

Sloane's body relaxed. Her mom's voice always had that effect on her. They'd always been close, but ever since she'd graduated college, they'd grown closer. "Good. Just taking a walk before I grab some coffee and go to work. How are you and Dad?" It felt like that was all she was doing nowadays. Working and overloading on caffeine. Maybe she did need a mini vacation.

"We're going to the casino later today and then maybe going to the beach. Sloane, you'd die if you saw just how white the sand is on this one beach. Are you sure you don't want to come out here for New Year's?"

"I wish. I'm just slammed lately." She fingered the cracked piece of plastic on her phone case that had broken when she'd dropped it in the parking lot last week. "Maybe next year."

She had enough PTO accrued that she could take the entire month of January off, but she had no desire to go somewhere hot and humid. She loved Portland. Loved the rain. The cold air that turned her cheeks rosy. She especially loved that there was snow in the forecast. It'd been a mild winter so far, not even that much rain, which was surprising. If snowboarders wanted any chance to carve it up on the mountain, they'd better be praying for the ultimate storm, because half the passes weren't even open yet, and it was the first week of December.

It never felt right, going to another state for the holidays. She'd always associated Christmas with rain and the smell of pine. She didn't even think they sold real Christmas trees in Florida.

"We'll be home in January, so if you change your mind, we'd love to have you come."

"I appreciate it," Sloane said.

She imagined her parents there. They were the lovey-dovey type. The ones who were always touching each other. A hand on the shoulder. A caress to the cheek. With the lackluster streak of guys Sloane had endured in years prior, she didn't think any more good men were out there.

"Are you doing okay, honey? You sound a little sad."

"I'm good." Sloane's throat constricted. At least she thought she was fine. And then Reece had to go and make another BS comment about her being frigid, undatable. It was one thing if she joked about it on a dating profile, but another hearing it from someone else. She knew he wasn't doing it to be mean. That was the game they played. One insult after another. But he'd struck something deep in her. Because she feared that maybe the problem wasn't with the dud guys she'd dated. Maybe the problem was her. And she didn't know how to fix it if that was the case.

"I'm here to talk if you want."

"I know, Mom. Thanks. I just wanted to check in with you, though. I really should be going so I'm not late for work."

"You make us so proud. I know all those patients of yours must love you to pieces."

"Thanks. Love you."

Sloane hung up the phone. What was with her? She had never been too worried about dating before. But now with her best friend in such a great relationship, she suddenly wanted that for herself. To feel that little bit of joy. The weight of a man pressed against her, between her thighs.

She folded her arms and leaned on the rail overlooking the river.

"Rough morning?" a deep voice asked. The voice immediately put her on edge.

She turned to find Reece and Peaches. Peaches stood on her hind legs, dancing in place as Sloane bent down to pet her.

Sweat slicked Reece's skin, and his shirt suctioned to his torso. The wet fabric showcased each muscle of his chest and abs. Her tongue pressed to the roof of her mouth as she fought to keep her eyes on his face.

"Come to throw some more shade at my undatability?"

She *hated* the fact that this bothered her so much. She'd never cared what he thought about her before, and she sure as heck shouldn't care now.

Girl, you are a l-i-a-r.

Seriously, what was with that pesky voice of reason?

"I wanted to talk to you about that. I'm sorry. That was out of line." He stretched his neck and shoved his free hand in his pocket.

"You really think a Scrabble game would rattle me?" Okay, it had, but he didn't need to know that. She didn't like that he was able to home in on the fact that she had, in fact, been hurt. Normally she did a better job of hiding those types of reactions, wrapping them up in a pretty little bow of shiny red lip gloss and sarcasm.

"I saw you, Sloane. I know you like to think I don't know you, but I do. I know that when you suck in your top lip, you're thinking of a good comeback." His eyes searched hers. The type of look that felt like it was digging past the surface to something much deeper. "And when your teeth pull at your bottom lip, you're upset." He pointed to her eyes. "And I know your eyes crease in the corners when you're uncomfortable."

Her gaze settled back on his chest. It was more comfortable to stare at sweaty muscles than to confirm that he had just called out all her tells. It made her feel naked, exposed.

"I don't think you're undatable. Some lucky bastard will date you someday. You just have to show him the real you. Not the one you show me."

"I am completely cordial to you."

"Would you like a Works Cited page of references?"

"Okay, fine. I may have been a bit harsh on you." More than harsh. But what was she supposed to tell him? *Oh hey, I'm really scared about getting back in the dating game after an epically failed relationship.*

"Sloane."

She looked up at him.

"Listen, if we could just put this behind us. We have two friends who are obviously sickeningly in love with each other. They deserve to not have us fighting like a bunch of rabid squirrels."

Peaches barked in response, jumping on her hind legs, the rhinestones on her sweater and collar glinting in the sun. Sloane suppressed a smile at the thought of how Reece must have *hated* dressing Peaches in this outfit.

"Is that why you apologized? Because of Jake and Erin? Or because you had dog crap smeared all over your apartment?" It would make more sense than him coming out and saying all this stuff of his own accord. Although maybe she was wrong about Reece. Maybe there was more to him than the jerk he'd become. She wanted it to be true. But if she'd learned anything from her failed attempt at a relationship, it was that no matter how hard you try to see the best in someone, sometimes it's just not there.

"Don't look so pleased about that one." His lips twitched in the corner. "And to answer your question, no. I was a jackass, and I'm willing to admit when I'm wrong."

"Fine." Really, this grudge had lasted long enough. She was tired of carrying it around. And he did look truly sorry. It was in his softened gaze. "But we're not besties now or anything."

He gave a curt nod. "Fair enough. Hope you have a good rest of your walk. Peaches still has some extra energy to burn through."

Peaches was still on her hind legs, dancing around.

Sloane reached down and scratched Peaches behind the ears. "See ya around."

Once Sloane stood, Reece turned and started in the opposite direction, the pooch's tiny legs keeping pace with him. Sloane smirked at the sight. She'd never pictured Reece as the dog type, especially with a little Yoranian. But it was very cute.

She let out a shaky breath. She had never expected Reece to apologize. And twice in the same calendar year? It was unexpected . . .

and nice. The Reece she'd grown up with shimmered through in that moment. The nice guy, the protective one who made sure everyone was okay. She sighed and pulled out her phone.

Sloane: Apology accepted.

Reece: My services are available if you need any more help with your dating profile.

The thought of Reece trying to delve into her mind and whip up something for her profile was about as appealing as taking her eye to a cheese grater. She didn't doubt Reece was sorry, but she also didn't think he'd do her any favors on her profile description.

Sloane: I can take care of that on my own, thanks. Plus, you'll be too busy with my next task.

Reece: Looking forward to it.

Sloane: You working tonight?

Reece: Off till Friday.

Sloane: I thought you had to work every three days?

Reece: Keeping track of me?

Damn it. Why did she know these things? Never mind the fact that she didn't care which days he had off, but it did make it easier to know when he was available.

Reece: It's my Kelly day.

She'd heard Reece and Jake talk about these types of days before. It apparently was a forced day off to make sure they didn't work overtime. She could definitely use a Kelly day. Or six.

Sloane: Just need to know when to avoid certain firefighters while at work.

Reece: I'm a much better face to see than anyone on A shift.

She smiled. So cocky. Anyone other than Reece and she might actually dislike it, but that was Reece's personality. Sure of himself. Even if sometimes he came off . . . well, like an ass.

Sloane: Looks don't have anything to do with it. I'm more worried about the mouths. Yours tends to open too much.

Reece: I can do plenty of nice things with my mouth.

Sloane: I'm going to ignore that.

But she couldn't. Because now all she was thinking about were his pale pink lips pressing against her own. Moving toward other places . . .

Reece: Missing out.

Sloane: Not according to what my friends have said.

Reece: You wound me.

Sloane: Come by the hospital. I can give you some ice for that burn.

Reece: I thought of another thing you can put on that dating profile.

Sloane: ?

Reece: "I'm a nurse, so I can bandage you up when I give third-degree burns with my very rude mouth."

Sloane: It has a certain ring to it. I might use it.

Reece: Glad I can be of assistance. Does that mean I am done with my chores?

Sloane: Not a chance.

Reece: It was worth a try.

Sloane: I'll be over tomorrow. Be ready.

Reece found himself smiling. Why was he smiling? Maybe because this was the first time he'd really texted something longer than the clipped messages he sent to his buddies telling them he was on his way or running late. And he liked it. He'd been texting her for most of the day, and even though it was well past eleven, he found himself glued to his phone, waiting for her next message to come in. For the first time since this auction, he was excited to see what crazy task Sloane had for him tomorrow. But before he could wonder about that too much, a text came in from his sister.

Andie: Come over here NOW. Emergency.

He grabbed his jacket and was at his mom's house in less than fifteen minutes. Before he could open the door, Andie beat him to it and put her finger over her lips, signaling Reece to shut up. And then she dragged him to her room.

Andie had always been messy. Since day one. When they were younger, Reece and Erin had always picked up their toys and kept their rooms tidy. Andie was the type who had ten glasses of water on her nightstand and trail-mix crumbs crushed into the carpet. It didn't look like twenty years of their mom yelling to keep their rooms clean had done anything to change this.

Reece moved a pile of clothes from Andie's chair, dropped them to the floor that was home to scattered magazines, and sat. "What's up? Why the SOS?"

She took a deep breath and then turned to him. "I'm finally ready to turn in my stuff."

He raised a brow.

"My applications."

"I don't get it, Andie. Why can't we tell Mom about this? And why do you need help at midnight with college apps?"

"You're the only person I can talk to about this. Mom gets all *Game of Thrones* with strategy, and Erin just wants to correct my grammar."

He could tell that Andie's relationship with Erin was still on the mend. The night after Erin had left for California ten years ago, Andie had locked herself in her room for two solid days. Reece had worked a double and had just gotten off his shift when his mother had called him, frantic, not only because one daughter was gone, but because the other was inconsolable. Andie had always looked up to Erin, tried to copy everything she did. When Reece had knocked on his sister's door, she'd surprisingly let him in. They'd eaten gummy bears and watched *Hannah Montana* for five hours straight. Erin had a long road ahead to gain back the relationship she used to have with Andie.

"Are you sure you want my opinion on this portion? I can help with the community service, but maybe you should pick someone who's taken an English course to look over the paperwork."

Andie shook her head. "No, I want your help. I want to start over. I know you've had to do that with . . ." She trailed off, seeming to search for the right words. "Other stuff. I thought you'd be helpful."

She meant in the relationship department. Reece had wondered if this had been the reason she hadn't gone to college in the first place. Who gave up a full ride to a great university? But digging for answers wasn't part of their relationship. She'd cough it up if she wanted to explain.

"I'm here, aren't I? Just tell me what to do."

She pulled up a document on her computer. "This is my essay. Just promise me you won't freak when you read it."

He shot her a look. What was she so worried about? "Isn't that why you picked me?"

Andie pulled her hair back into a ponytail. Her skin was swollen, and it looked like she had a new addition to her ever-growing tattoo list. This one was a bird in flight by her clavicle. "New work done?"

She nodded but didn't explain further. He got it. Tattoos were personal. His own arms were covered from shoulder to elbow with designs he'd accumulated over the years.

She pushed the laptop into his lap, and he settled into her computer chair, rocking back and forth as he read.

The essay itself was good. Reece didn't notice any glaring issues with grammar. The topic, on the other hand, made his chest ache. It was titled "The Invisible Jenkins." Every paragraph detailed how she was so unsure of what she wanted to do with her life. She'd seen her big brother and sister master their careers, and she could barely pick her cereal in the morning.

How could he not have known his sister was floundering? He knew she had more attitude lately, but he thought that was normal, considering she was almost twenty and stuck at home with their mom. He loved his mother, but she was enough to handle once a week at family dinner and a couple of random drop-ins to help her around the house.

He continued looking at the essay, trying to piece together what to do. To come up with something to say that was a cliché that she'd roll her eyes at. But he was out of his depth. This was something that his mom or Erin would handle with grace.

Instead, he said, "Andie . . ." He trailed off. "I had no idea."

She just shrugged. "Do you think this essay is enough? I know I've gone only a couple of times to the shelter to volunteer, but my high school grades were good, and I've held down a steady job."

"It's more than enough." He paused. His sister felt like she'd been living in their shadows for years. Reece had been too busy with his own stuff to even notice, and it killed him. "You're more than enough, kid."

Andie rolled tear-filled eyes, some spilling down her cheeks. She quickly wiped them away. "This is exactly why I didn't want to tell Erin or Mom. Because *they're* the ones who are supposed to be all mushy. Not you."

Too much family time must have been rubbing off on him. "It's not mushy. It's the truth, and you'd best start believing it because no one is ever going to give a bigger shit about whatever you do with your life than you."

His sister was quiet for a moment, her expression softening. "Was that supposed to be like a *Rocky* pep talk?"

"No clue. Did it work?"

She shrugged. "Kinda."

"Good. Show me this college application." He set the computer back on her desk, avoiding the Hershey's wrappers and scribbled-on pieces of paper. From his vantage point, it looked to be a list of pros and cons of the colleges.

She swiveled it to face her, typing in a password, and then positioned it back in front of Reece. For the first time in a while, she looked excited, bouncing on her toes as she waited for him to take a look.

"Have an idea on a major?"

"I'm thinking of going the law-school route. But first I have to take all the prerequisites."

"Always did like to argue."

Andie shoved him. "You're one to talk. I saw you the other week with Sloane."

Not one of his finer moments. Sloane deserved to be treated better than that. Reece decided to ignore her comment and said, "Your application is solid. They'd be stupid not to take you."

"I blew it when I gave up my scholarship."

He'd never been to a four-year university, but he'd like to think they'd be forgiving of mistakes like this. The older Reece got, the more he realized he'd known absolutely nothing in his teens. "You didn't blow it. You know how many kids change their mind about college?"

She shook her head.

"Tons. Just explain to them that you were going through a rough time, and I'm sure they'll be understanding."

Since when was he the go-to for advice? First Sloane, now his sister. "You'll be fine, Andie."

"I just want to get out so bad." Desperation flashed in her eyes. He wished he could help her more, but aside from driving to the university and threatening the dean of admissions—which was a decidedly horrible idea—there wasn't much else to do but wait it out with her.

"I know. And I'm here for you. And so are Mom and Erin. Even if they're both overbearing."

She rolled her eyes. "Ya think?"

"You going to hit 'Submit'?" He looked at the clock. "It's due in five minutes."

She worried her lip. "Yeah. Just freaking out a little."

"I know what you mean. You've got this, though." It seemed like his sister was finally getting her life together. He hoped that she was able to get the opportunity to prove herself. To build on this tiny bit of confidence.

She took a deep breath and hit the "Submit" button. "Guess I'll know if it was enough in a couple of months."

"You are always going to be enough. Doesn't matter what a stupid university says."

Andie gave a watery smile. "Thanks, Reece."

He wrapped his sister in a hug. He had to admit, it felt nice to be the one people turned to in a time of need.

Chapter Thirteen

The next day, Sloane pulled her car into Reece's apartment complex and cut the engine. She took a deep breath and stretched her neck from side to side, working up the nerve to see him. She'd expected to find him on the fifth floor, sitting in that drab place he called home. Really, the place didn't even have a throw blanket. Not a decorative pillow in sight. The thought made her shiver. She'd come from parents who believed in filling the house with trinkets from their travels. Globes bought from their trip to India, intricate carvings from Guatemala, pictures of the two of them with locals. She'd adopted the same sentiment for her own apartment. She'd filled it with plush rugs, rustic frames, and antique end tables salvaged from secondhand stores.

Instead, she found Reece shirtless in the parking lot. It was an uncharacteristically warm day for December, the temperatures touching into the high sixties. He held a garden hose, dousing the Jeep. As far as she knew, Reece had three different cars. He had his truck that he drove around most of the time—at least that was the one parked in the Jenkinses' driveway whenever she'd visited for dinner. Then there was the Jeep that was from this century. And then *this* Jeep, which had seen better days. Pale green, rust in spots, a few dents in the quarter panels. It reminded her of ones that were taken on safaris. When they were kids, she remembered him being obsessed with the brand, even going as far as taking pics with ones they found downtown. *Weird kid.*

Suds slid down the panels of the car and fell to the ground in a steady stream.

But Sloane's attention wasn't focused on the car. Her gaze was glued to Reece's chest. She'd seen it before, when he'd been covered in blood and in need of stitches. But that was at work, and she made a point to never ogle when on a shift. Now, her handiwork was an angry red scar along his clavicle.

Reece was all muscle. His broad shoulders glistened in the afternoon sun, and beads of water dribbled down his pecs, moving toward his abs.

Her tongue pressed against the roof of her mouth. On anyone else, this would be a glorious sight. She'd welcome it. Snap a pic of it to send to her group chat with Madison and Erin to ogle. A powerful body like that taking her from behind, rough fingers gripping her hips as she fought to stay upright, hands clutching her headboard. Yes, she wanted someone to take charge. To make her lose control.

"Gonna stare? Or do you want to help out?" He flung a sponge at Sloane, and it smacked her in the chest with a wet *thwap*. Beads of water pooled on her shirt and drizzled down the inside of her bra. Just lovely.

She chucked the sponge back at him and pulled her shirt away from her skin. "Sorry, was zoned out. I think your innate paleness momentarily blinded me."

He smiled and shook his head, continuing to wash the car. Reece was on the paler side, but by no means worthy of shielding her eyes with sunglasses.

"What's with this car, anyway? It looks like it needs to go in a museum."

"She didn't mean that, girl." He patted the Jeep lovingly. "It's history, Smurfette. Can't compete with good ol' American-made cars."

She moved to the bucket and grabbed another sponge and started wiping down the back quarter panel, to give her hands something to do. Her gaze kept darting to the basketball shorts slung low on Reece's hips. The dusting of hair starting below his belly button and disappearing into the fabric.

She swallowed hard and turned to the very dirty wheel. She scrubbed, harder than she needed to. Anything to get that last thought out of her mind.

Just as she was about to stand, a spray of water hit her back, and she jumped up, shrieking as the cold water crawled down her spine. She straightened, sucking in a coarse breath. Now both her front and back were soaked.

"Oh no you didn't." She pulled her shirt from her back, the material suctioning to her skin as soon as she let go.

"Oops, I guess I missed." And there was that shrug again. His lips twisted into a grin, and he looked like he was ready to take another shot at her.

"You're so full of crap." She charged at him, and just as he jerked the hose back, she grabbed the bucket at his feet and drenched Reece from head to toe.

The material of his shorts molded to his body, leaving no detail untouched. His thick thighs. The V of his torso. The curve of his hips. The massive . . . Oh wow.

Her gaze whipped to Reece's face.

"See something you like?"

Her cheeks heated. Did she like it? Very much so. She just wished that his body was attached to someone else. One that she didn't have such a muddled past with. "I have no idea what you're talking about."

"For future reference, your eyes give you away. Might want to try looking away next time."

She flung her sponge at him, and it hit him square in the face.

He let out a deep laugh that went straight to the space between her thighs, and then he beamed at her, his lips twisting in a smirk that made everything clench.

"You really want to play like this, Sloane?"

She cocked her brow in response. And within the span of a breath, he'd taken aim with the garden hose and pushed on the nozzle. The spray made a direct hit to her stomach, drenching her clothes completely.

The cold water made her skin prickle. Her lungs were suddenly devoid of oxygen. And yet she was smiling like an idiot. If it had been anyone else wielding that hose, she'd admit defeat and retreat for the nearest towel. Somehow, with it being Reece, it had the opposite effect. Made her want to march right in front of him. To do something that would wipe that smug look off his face. "You're going to pay for that!" And with that, she charged him. He grabbed her with both arms and threw her over his shoulder. She landed against his back with a lung-crushing thud, her cheek plastering to his warm skin. From this vantage point, she noted the curve of his spine, the freckles and ink. A tattoo that read *Love will tear us apart.* The one thing she craved was also a warning permanently inked onto his skin.

Blood rushed to her head, and she smacked his back, trying to wiggle free. "Let me down, you oaf."

"Now, is that any way to talk to the person who literally has your life in their hands?"

"Spare me."

A jolt of surprise shot through her as Reece's palm bit into the back of her leg. Sparks of pleasure exploded between her thighs, and everything clenched. A mix of a moan and a cry escaped past her lips before she could hold it back.

His hand stilled on the back of her thigh, the touch warm, heat radiating from his palm. "You like that?" Even though she couldn't see him, she couldn't deny the desire laced in those words.

Did she like it? Yes. Too much.

"Let me down," she said again, her voice shaking.

This time Reece obliged, pulling her over his shoulder. He let her down slowly, inch by inch, her body rolling over his hard muscles. Every speck of skin prickled, her shorts rubbing against her aching center as she slid from Reece's chest, to his stomach, and then to his thickening cock. The last one made her breath hitch, and she was aware of how badly she wanted to be taken here in the middle of a parking lot. She was fully clothed, but everything about this felt so intimate. So intense.

Once her feet were planted on the ground, she chanced a glance his way and found him looking down at her, eyes wide, nostrils flaring.

"Next time you decide to spray someone, make sure they have a change of clothes." She broke eye contact with him and looked down at her soaked T-shirt and shorts. They were plastered to her skin, and everything in her screamed to cover her arms over her torso, to hide every imperfection. Instead, she squared her shoulders. "Fake it until you believe it" was another one of her mantras, and she was sticking to it.

He prowled closer to her, his gaze starting at her eyes and going lower, lower, lower. His pupils dilated, and a grunt escaped from his parted lips. "I can help you out with that."

Those words promised a lot of things.

Yes, Reece, please help me out of these wet clothes. I'm sure your plethora of muscles can act as a sufficient means of keeping me warm.

She took a step back, her back bumping into the Jeep. She was pinned between Reece and the car. Her first thought should have been to give him a slap on the face. Instead, she wanted that face in other places. Spots he had no business being. She swallowed hard. And then he took one final step toward her, closing the gap between them.

"In your dreams, Jenkins."

"Maybe so." Damn him and those cute lines that formed around his mouth when his lips pulled back into a wide grin, which showcased his dimples. "But I meant I have some clothes upstairs you can borrow."

Oh. Maybe they were on two separate wavelengths. "You think anything of yours will actually fit me?" This was basically like asking a Smurf to fit in Dwayne Johnson's clothes. There wasn't enough drawstring or elastic in the world to make that happen.

"I'm sure we can find something." He stepped back, and the sudden rush of air hitting the front of her body sent a shiver rushing through her. She shook it off. This was Reece. She didn't have those types of feelings for him, especially when he did nothing but piss her off. And she couldn't forget the fact that he only ever went on first dates. Her friends and coworkers were living proof.

He quickly squirted off the remaining suds from his Jeep and then grabbed the bucket and motioned for her to follow him upstairs.

Sloane's shoes squeaked as she followed him up the stairs to the fifth story.

Peaches ran to greet her when they opened the door to his apartment. The first thing she noticed was how clean it was. She'd always assumed that he would be messy, the kind of person to leave week-old pizza boxes strewn about. But everything was in perfect order. Her bowl and spoon in her own sink made her look like a slob in comparison.

The second thing she noticed was that it was really clean because . . . there wasn't really anything to clean up. Because just like when she'd visited his apartment last year, the apartment was still bare bones. Like he was ready to move out at any minute. She'd expect to open up the hall closet and find packed boxes.

She gestured to the vertical blinds over the sliding glass door. "An entire year since I've been here and you haven't even managed to buy curtains for the place?"

"I happen to be a fan of clean geometric shapes and the color beige. And what is with everyone hawking me about it?"

She started to shiver and folded her arms over her chest. "Because it doesn't even look lived in."

"I like it this way. It keeps it simple. No cleanup." He rummaged through a linen closet at the end of the hallway and handed her a fluffy black towel.

"Kinda like your relationships." Her teeth chattered as she wrapped the towel around her.

"Exactly."

His smile wavered. Maybe she'd hit a nerve. She reminded herself that this was the same man who'd been a total asshole to her. Right now, all she needed to focus on was getting warm. "Clothes?"

He led her to his bedroom. White walls. Black bedspread. One pillow in the middle of the bed. And . . . holy crap. The *Psycho* shower-scene music played like a soundtrack in her head. Because not one, but—she silently cataloged the number—ten pictures of Blake Shelton surrounded his bed, each one propped up by a chair or a small table.

Oh, this was good. Too good. She pulled out her phone and snapped a pic. Yeah, that photo would be going in her group chat with Erin and Madison.

"Does your mom know you have a thing for Blake?"

"I'm more of a Chris Hemsworth kind of guy."

"Because he's big and broody like you?" The lanky guys of the world were more her type, but something about Reece, in his T-shirt stretched across his chest, each ridge of his muscle clearly defined under the fabric, did things to her.

His lips twitched. "If you must know, Peaches is afraid of Blake Shelton."

She crossed her arms in response. Because, come on. A dog afraid of a celebrity it'd never met?

"There's no shame, Reece. He was voted sexiest man alive."

Reece whistled for Peaches. When she looked to the doorway, Peaches cowered, shaking a little as she eyed one of the pictures of Blake.

Sloane just stared at the dog. What the ever-loving fudge was this?

She'd had dogs with quirks before. One of the huskies she fostered liked to stick his tongue out. Another dog would only eat out of a certain food dish. But this was a new one.

"So let me get this straight. You're using fear tactics on a dog because . . . ?"

"She's a terror and wants to sleep in my bed." He shot her a look like this was normal behavior for a dog owner.

"I see. You've had her almost three weeks, and you can't get her to stay off your bed?"

He shrugged. "This has worked so far."

He disappeared into the closet and came back moments later with another pair of basketball shorts and a Seattle Seahawks shirt.

"Thank you."

"Bathroom is second door on your right."

She nodded and booked it to the bathroom, kicking her shoes onto the checkered black-and-white tile. Her shorts and shirt fell to the floor with a wet *thwop*. She stared at Reece's clothes on the vanity. Dark blue tile and crisp white grout. Toothbrush tucked neatly into a plastic holder. Next to it was a razor, Band-Aids, and mouthwash all in a neat row. She nudged the Band-Aid box just to add a little disorder to the scene. That seemed to be the common urge when it came to dealing with Reece. To create disorder in his perfectly crafted world. And now that she thought of that, it made her feel like an asshole.

She shifted the Band-Aid box to where it originally sat, tugged on the shorts Reece had loaned her, and pulled the shirt over her head. The soft cotton of the shirt brushed past her nose and carried the delicious scent of clean laundry and something she could only describe as Reece. Her eyes fluttered shut. What was it about being in the quiet of his bathroom, wrapped in his clothes, that felt so intimate?

She laughed as she caught her reflection in the mirror because the shirt might as well have been a dress, cutting right above her knees. When she stepped out into the hallway, she was startled to find Reece staring at her with an intensity that made her blood hum in her veins.

Reece swallowed hard and tried to tear his gaze away from Sloane. She looked ridiculous in his shirt and shorts. He was huge compared to her. But she looked cute as hell. Not that he'd tell her that. He wanted to keep his dick attached to his body. And even if they were currently in a momentary truce, he knew her well enough not to push too far.

"Okay, I had an idea for chore number three already, but after seeing your apartment, it's given me new inspiration," she said.

His mind was so far off from his work and what originally had brought them together that it took him a second to realize what she was talking about. "What is it?"

"I want to decorate your place."

He had to be hearing her wrong. "You do know how the chores thing works, right? It's me helping you." A horrific image of Sloane painting every wall bubble-gum pink entered his mind. He didn't doubt she'd throw out her back, maniacal laughter spilling from that pretty little mouth as she coated every inch of surface area until his apartment became reminiscent of a *My Little Pony* episode.

She gave that smile that punched him right in the gut. The one that crinkled her eyes in the corners. "It'd be a favor to all mankind to take this place from model home to respectable thirty-three-year-old dude humble abode."

He shook his head. Sloane hated him, made it a point to bulldoze through his life just to hammer that point in. And now she wanted to go all Martha Stewart on his apartment? "But why?" He had the essentials. His TV, a bed, and a functional bathroom. Add in two first-aid kits, a Costco supply of toilet paper, and enough dish detergent to last until the turn of the next century, and he was set for life.

"I'm feeling altruistic today."

Yeah, he'd believe that when hell froze over. She was scheming, and they both knew it. He also knew that he couldn't say no. Not when it came to her.

"Fine. But you need to stay within a budget. I don't want to go into debt because of you."

"Fair enough. I have a friend who works at a home-furnishing store. I can get a pretty hefty discount. I mean, what do you even do here? Stare at the walls?"

"I play video games. Grill. Watch sports."

She closed her eyes and pretended to snore.

"What? What is wrong with what I do?"

"Nothing, if you're ninety."

"You know, I do have a hose in my sink. It has pretty good range." The image of her drenched in his T-shirt half tempted him to try.

Her lips quirked. "You wouldn't dare."

"To see you wet again, I might." He'd love to make her wet in other ways. To have his fingers press against the hot seam between her thighs. To hear his name on her lips. His cock twitched.

Had that really come out of his mouth? All his control went out the window when it came to Sloane.

"You talk a huge game, Reece. But I don't see a lot of follow-through. I'm beginning to think maybe that's why—"

He couldn't handle it any longer. Before she could continue, he closed the distance between them, pulling Sloane until she was flush with his body. Her body melted into his as he swept her lips into a kiss.

Her lips were so damn soft. She let out a tiny moan as his tongue teased her mouth. Her fingers dug into his hair, pulling him closer, and the kiss deepened. He'd imagined kissing her many times. When they were teens. Even well into his thirties. But with her hot little mouth against his, his imagination wasn't even in the same ballpark.

Her hand slipped between them, rubbing the flat of her palm down his cock. His hands found their way under her shirt and cupped her breasts, his thumbs circling her peaked nipples. He'd thought about this so many times. How he'd kneel in front of her, kiss down her body, taste her. His hand slipped to the waistband of Sloane's shorts, teasing his fingers under her lacy underwear until they dipped beneath, finding the fabric damp. Their kiss turned fevered; then Sloane pulled away, flushed and breathless.

His finger teased her entrance, and she let out a soft moan, moving closer, giving him silent permission to enter her.

"I promise you, Smurfette, I'm not all talk. Is that what you want, for me to fuck you with my finger until you cry out my name?" His lips met hers again as his thumb brushed her clit and her body canted against him. His pace increased, and he added another finger. "I've wanted to do this to you for so long."

As soon as he said it, he knew he'd ruined the moment.

She pulled back with wide eyes. "We need to stop," she said, although the words came out strangled.

Right. He took a step back, breathing hard. What the hell had just happened? One second he was giving her a hard time, the next, her tongue was lashing his in a battle of kisses, and his fingers were inside of her.

"Good idea." His body was evidence enough that he thought that was a terrible idea.

"That can't happen again," she said, a mixture of shock and embarrassment on her face.

Damn it. "I know." But even that was a lie. He'd been ready to take her right there in the middle of his living room.

"I need to get . . . going," she stammered. He'd never seen her so flustered before. "But I'll be over tomorrow to take measurements for all the décor."

"I'm on shift." And he wanted to stall for as long as possible because he didn't exactly like the idea of change in his apartment. He'd had enough of that with the addition of Peaches. But he also didn't want to be one step closer to having Sloane out of his life. He'd put money on her avoiding him like the plague once his auction duties were completed.

"Then I guess I'll need a key to the apartment." She held out her hand. That confidence. He'd never seen anyone with so much. It was sexy.

"Fine. I think I have a spare in the kitchen. Hold on." He went and grabbed the one from the silverware drawer and handed it to her. He knew this could blow up in his face. But to see that smile spread across her face, when it had something to do with him, he honestly didn't care. Just as she was about to grab the key from his hand, he pulled it away. "I just have one condition."

"I didn't think a favor came with conditions." Her cheeks were still flushed with desire. From what they'd been doing a couple of minutes ago. He could barely think straight with lust pulsing through his veins. He fisted his hands, combatting the urge to rake his fingers through her soft blue hair. He'd give anything to bury his face into the curve of her neck and inhale the sweet scent of honey and jasmine.

He realized she was standing there, waiting for an answer. Five more minutes and he'd usher her out the door and finish what he'd started in the hot spray of his shower.

"When it comes to getting access to my apartment, it does."

"Fine. What is your stipulation?" She waved her hand, urging him to continue. "I've already come up with the perfect color scheme."

He cocked a brow. Women really were multitaskers, because the only thought in his head for the past twenty minutes was *Must. Have. Sloane.* "You have?"

Sloane must have seen the confusion written across his face, because those gorgeous lips puckered into a smirk. "Focus, Reece."

He put aside the fantasies of what Sloane could do with that mouth. "You said Peaches could benefit from lessons. Come to obedience school with me." He'd seen obedience-school lessons advertised in the pet store where he'd picked up the dog's food. And maybe he was a glutton for punishment, but he was looking for a way to spend more time with Sloane. "I've tried the basic commands, but she doesn't seem to listen. And since Kurt hasn't gotten back to me . . ."

She rolled her eyes, but he saw the ghost of a smile twitch at her lips. "Why do you want me to come with you?"

"Because you are the technical co–foster parent for Peaches." He didn't mention the real reason, which he was sure she'd never let him live down. That he *liked* her company. Even when she was prickly. Especially when she was prickly.

She let out a deep, throaty laugh. "You drive a hard bargain, but sure, I'm in." And then she grabbed the key from his hand and walked out the door, looking sinfully sexy in his clothes.

He was in so much trouble.

Chapter Fourteen

It was pitch-black when Reece arrived at the station the next morning. Winter was now in full effect, frost glistening from the bare branches of oak trees and puffs of exhaust curling in the air as early-morning commuters drove to work. This time of year always threw him off. If it was dark, he wanted to be sleeping. He dropped his bag in his sleeping quarters and then dressed in his Class Bs.

Hollywood and Jake were already out in the engine bay, making sure everything was properly prepped for their shift.

"Heard you and Sloane are getting serious," Hollywood said as he checked the medical supplies in the engine.

Jake was such a damn gossip queen. He'd texted him last night after Sloane had left, wondering if it'd been a smart idea to give her a key to his apartment. The closest any woman had been to leaving an impression on his apartment was the lipstick mark on his Seahawks coffee mug the morning after.

He looked over at his best friend, who just gave a shrug in response. "What? I'm proud you're finally getting close to someone."

"Do you not remember Sloane has me by the balls for this auction?"

Jake lifted a brow. "You and I both know that this has nothing to do with the auction."

Even if that *were* true—not that Reece was saying this—he'd never admit it to Jake and Hollywood. Truth was, he couldn't stop thinking about Sloane after yesterday. The feel of her body pressed up against him. The flare of her hips under his fingers. Those honey-brown eyes, clouded with lust and desire as her gaze raked over him.

"Reece is growing up." Hollywood sniffed and threw an arm around him.

"Assholes," he muttered, shaking off Hollywood's grip as he grabbed his checklist.

Before he could get to the second item on the list, the tones went off. The operator relayed information about a residential fire, neighbors claiming smoke was billowing out of the windows.

Within a minute, they suited up in full gear and climbed into the rig.

Reece started up the engine, flicked on the siren, and pulled out of the station.

He went through his mental checklist. Wondering if anyone was in there since the operator hadn't indicated. At this time in the morning, it seemed likely. They made it to the scene a few minutes later.

Reece hopped out of the rig and nodded to Hollywood and Jake. Even though they had headsets, they worked together like clockwork, no words needed.

He made his way around the house, the hiss and crack of things burning inside evident. He cased the perimeter, looking at the structure, to see if he needed to create a vent on the roof. It was a small Victorian-style home on the outskirts of downtown. If Reece had to guess, the house had been built early last century. The slope of the gabled roof would make it a pain in the ass to get up there and vent, but it was a possibility if needed. When he returned to the front of the house, a small crowd had formed around the perimeter: people in pajamas, work attire, and kids in school uniforms.

He made his way to the front, where Jake and Hollywood had already entered. The door was hanging on its hinges, smoke ghosting around the frame, spilling out into the frigid air.

Station 10 was already at the scene, gathering the hoses and hooking them up to the hydrant down the street.

"Fire started in the kitchen. Looks like it's coming from a faulty wire," came Hollywood's voice over the headset.

Reece had seen it hundreds of times. People redoing their kitchens, doing the repair work themselves. Not getting anyone to check to see if they were up to code.

In the hallway, an end table was knocked over, along with a potted plant. His boots crunched over broken ceramics and soil as he trudged toward the back of the house. Jake and Hollywood came out of a room to the right, and the three of them entered what Reece assumed was the master bedroom.

Even through the haze, he spotted a figure in bed. As he moved closer, he noticed that blood stained her blonde hair, like she'd been struck with some type of object. Jake made it to her first, shook her, and when she didn't respond, he gathered her in his arms and moved toward the doorway.

While Jake carried the woman to the ambulance waiting outside, Reece checked the rest of the bedroom, under the bed, in the walk-in closet, confirming there weren't any other civilians.

Hollywood's voice boomed over their com, a panicked sound that was clipped short. Reece turned to find Hollywood on the ground. His body was folded over, motionless. Smoke funneled into the room, visibility quickly fading.

"What the—" Something hit Reece against the head. Even though he was wearing his helmet, the force jarred him enough to rattle his teeth. He turned and expected to find a fallen beam, even though nothing about the structure was compromised from what he'd seen. He came face-to-face with a masked man who held a baseball bat. Reece moved out of the way before the man could make contact with him again, and before the guy sprinted out of the room, he nailed Hollywood once more in the ribs as Hollywood tried to get up.

Reece debated going after the guy, but Hollywood was down. He sprinted over to him and helped him to his feet. "Shit, man. You okay?"

Hollywood seemed to have a hard time catching his breath, but he nodded. With a hit like that, it wouldn't be a surprise if he'd broken a couple of ribs. Reece carefully slung Hollywood's arm over his shoulder as they both moved out of the room. Station 10 was inside now, extinguishing the flames.

"We need to clear the rest of the house," Hollywood gritted out, pulling Reece toward the rear of the house instead of the direction of the entrance.

Reece gently guided him to the front door. "You need to see a medic, dude."

"I'm fine." Hollywood looked anything but. His breathing was jagged, and he winced with every step he took.

Two more firefighters from Station 10 ran inside. There were more than enough men to handle this. He needed to get his brother to safety.

Hollywood held up his hand, appearing to give up his protest. "Fine." Once he'd gotten Hollywood out to the front to get checked out by an EMT, he went back into the house.

Reece made his way through the house and didn't find anyone else there. The fire had been contained to the kitchen and most of the living room. A headache pulsed at his temples, and his vision wavered slightly, but he ignored it as he finished scanning the structure.

Once everything was cleared, he walked outside to check on the woman he had found. She lay on a stretcher inside the ambulance, paramedics feeding her oxygen, taking her vitals.

He strode over to Jake, who was helping the paramedics with the woman. "Did you see the guy run out?"

Jake shook his head. "No. I heard you guys over the com, but I couldn't turn back."

The guy had to be long gone by now.

Just then, PD rolled up, and Detective Ross got out of the vehicle. Both Station 11 and the precinct shared a building, and he often ran into Ross on his shift. The guy was in his late thirties. Nice guy, liked to go fishing on the weekends and brought in beer he brewed in his basement. Ross pulled out a pad of paper and a pen from his jacket pocket. "Electrical fire?"

Reece nodded. He was still dazed from the blow to the head, and the pounding had turned from a dull throb to a deep pulse that made the morning light barely tolerable. He was lucky he'd had his helmet on.

Another unmarked police car rolled up. A woman who looked to be in her early thirties dressed in a black pantsuit got out of the driver's side. She was gorgeous, her dark skin and brown eyes shining in the morning light. Her curls were pulled back and swayed to either side of her shoulders as she walked over to Reece and the detective.

"Investigator Betts, you got here fast." Ross gestured to Reece. "This is Reece Jenkins. Reece, this is Emeline Betts, our new arson investigator."

Reece had heard that they'd just filled that position. She stuck out her hand, and Reece shook it. "Nice to meet you," he said.

She nodded and pulled out a pad of paper and a pen. "Can you catch me up to speed?"

Reece relayed what he'd seen. As he finished recapping the events, his vision started to narrow, and he lost his balance, gripping the side of Ross's SUV.

Ross steadied Reece's shoulder. "You okay, man?"

He waved his hand, but another surge of dizziness washed over him. "Just a hit to the helmet. No big deal."

"Head injuries aren't something to mess with," Betts said. Her brows scrunched together. Or at least he was pretty sure they did. Everything was going blurry.

Before he was able to argue, Reece's world darkened around the edges and then faded to black.

Sloane checked her phone in the break room, cursing herself for thinking Reece would actually text. She wasn't the type of person who *needed* attention like that. And yet, here she was, scrolling through her messages. Again.

They were both working today. She'd planned on going over to his apartment after her shift to take the measurements for the new decor.

She wondered what he was up to right now. He was already two hours into his shift. Probably busy annoying his fellow firefighters. But all she could think about was his warm mouth on hers. His soft lips. His fingers slicking over the space that needed him most. *Damn it.* She was in so much trouble.

She turned the corner to the nurses' station, ready to make her rounds with the patients. Mrs. Gonzalez in room 2 probably needed more saline while they waited on the results of her blood tests.

A flash of blue entered the emergency entrance and snagged her attention. Jake's expression was tight, and she tried to peer around him to find Reece. And mentally flogged herself for the way her heartbeat quickened.

When she didn't see him but instead glimpsed Cole, who looked equally as distressed, a wave of goose bumps washed over her arms. Where was Reece?

And then she noticed the yellow uniform on the gurney. Her heart thundered in her chest.

No.

She raced over to the men, and Linda, the other nurse on staff, came flying from the other direction.

Her worst fear was confirmed. Reece lay motionless. The EMTs had already hooked him up to a saline drip. They'd already started a line, which made it easier if she needed to administer any meds.

Oh God. Please let him be okay.

"What happened?" Linda asked in a calm voice.

Sloane didn't even think she could speak.

"Got knocked over the head. Possible concussion. Vitals are stable."

"Get him in for an MRI." Sloane finally found her voice, even if it came out strangled.

Why wasn't he waking up? How hard had he been hit? There was always a risk with firefighting, but two substantial injuries in less than a month?

"Go. Start the paperwork," Linda said, giving her a squeeze on the arm. "Clark and I can take him down for imaging."

Sloane nodded, 90 percent certain that her morning coffee might end up on the linoleum floor. She watched as Reece was wheeled away, her heart in her throat.

She cared about Reece. Like, *cared.* This went way deeper than just thoughts of him being a warm body to fill her bed. Which scared her, because she hadn't felt that in years.

Sloane was glad Dr. Schwartz was in the ER today. He was a nice guy in his early thirties. She liked that he wasn't a dick to the nurses. Treated them like they were capable and important. Forty minutes had passed, and Linda had set Reece up in an empty room. She'd walked by twice as the other nurses tended to him.

Sloane focused back on Dr. Schwartz, tapping her foot, impatiently waiting for the results.

His brows knit together as he studied Reece's MRI images on the computer.

"How's he doing, Doc?" Sloane asked.

Please let him be okay. She'd been mentally chanting this ever since he'd entered the ER. She might very well vomit on his white hospital shoes.

"No damage. Looks like he just has a concussion."

A heavy weight lifted from her chest.

"I'm keeping him overnight for observation."

She nodded. "Good decision." It was what she'd order as well.

Sloane wasn't able to visit Reece again on the sixth floor during her shift. As soon as the clock hit 8:00 p.m., she clocked out and nearly sprinted for the elevator.

Erin and Mrs. Jenkins were sitting in chairs surrounding the hospital bed. Reece was lying down, his skin pale in the florescent lighting. He wore a green-and-white hospital gown. Which was in stark juxtaposition with the tattoos covering his arms. It was all wrong. He wasn't supposed to be a patient. He was strong and capable, and to see him in here with a dark bruise blooming on his cheek made her stomach clench.

She cleared her throat, and all three of them turned to her in unison. "Hi," she said, and gave an awkward wave. Which was ridiculous. She'd been part of the family for years. But right now she felt like an outsider in this intimate moment.

"Sloane, honey. Come on in here," said Mrs. Jenkins. "We were just about to get Reece a little food. Apparently the hospital food isn't agreeing with him, so Andie said she'd make him a double order of sandwiches down at the truck. Would you mind sitting with him while we go?"

"I think I can manage that."

Erin eyed her and mouthed, *Be nice.*

Did her best friend really think she'd kick Reece while he was down?

Okay, maybe she had justification in telling her this. This made her feel even worse. She needed to end this whole charade once he got out of the hospital.

Reece shifted in the bed and winced. "Hey."

"Hi."

She plopped down into the chair Mrs. Jenkins had vacated, right next to the IV hookups. Her gaze quickly scanned the screen. Blood pressure and heart rate appeared normal.

"How are you feeling?" This was so foreign to her. Snarky comebacks? That she could handle. This? With Reece lying in a bed looking so vulnerable? It scared her and sent a shiver straight to the marrow of her bones.

"Fine," he said. "Why does everyone keep asking me that?" He went to push to his elbows and winced.

"Because you got knocked over the head and came in the hospital looking like death warmed over. Lay your ass back on the bed before you hurt yourself."

He lay back. "So bossy."

"You like it." Her fingers traced along the skin outside the radius of his bruise. He closed his eyes and leaned into her touch. He was heartbreakingly gorgeous. "What happened?"

His tongue darted out to wet his lips. "Some jackass. Set fire to the place and left a woman there with her head knocked in."

Whoa. This was so much worse than she'd thought. She hadn't gotten many details from Jake and had assumed a part of a burning building fell on him. "That's horrible."

He nodded and winced. "Yeah." He swallowed hard and regarded her.

"Reece?"

"Yeah?"

She steeled herself. It wasn't often she let her shields down, especially not for someone whom she shared such a complicated past with. But she needed to get this off her chest. Life was too short. "Seeing you wheeled in today scared me."

His lips pressed into a hard line. "It scared me too."

Her hand slid into his, rubbing her thumb across the tops of his knuckles. His hand was big and warm and calloused. A hand she could picture holding a thousand times. What was she doing here? She didn't know. But it felt right. Like this was the place she needed to be.

The machine above her quickened with the beeps, his heart rate shooting up.

"Aw, do I make your heart pound?"

"You make my body do a lot of things." He lifted a brow.

She shook her head and smiled. Even with a concussion, he was still able to be an ass. Typical Reece. Which somehow put her mind at ease. "Try keeping the whole scaring-the-shit-out-of-people thing to a minimum, okay? You're not a cat—you don't have extra lives to spare."

"On it, boss."

She stared at his lips and debated leaning down to kiss him. To show him just how happy she was that he was okay. And then Erin and her mom came into the room.

"Sorry, Reece. I told Andie extra bacon, but she skimped . . . Oh, sorry, are we interrupting something?" said Mrs. Jenkins.

Sloane pulled her hand away and suddenly found her purse very fascinating. "Nope. Was just telling Reece I had to get going. Great timing." She stood and awkwardly fumbled with her bag. "I'm glad you're okay. See you around."

And with that, she said goodbye to everyone and booked it out of the room.

Chapter Fifteen

"Just clarifying—we're here to train Peaches, not you? Because I think you could both benefit from the class," Sloane said.

Smart-ass.

It had been four days since the accident, and he'd had a doctor's appointment this morning confirming he was fine. The doc had emphasized avoiding another knock to the head but had otherwise sent him on his way.

"You must think you're so funny," Reece said, getting out of the driver's side of his Jeep. "Did they teach you that humor in nursing school?" After Reece had been discharged from the hospital, they'd gone back to their usual back-and-forth, the moment they'd shared together never spoken of again. Which was probably for the best. He'd never been that real with a woman before. He didn't need any more complications in his life.

She smiled over at him, and her brown eyes shone with mischief. "Born with it."

Everything about this felt off. He still couldn't piece together why he'd thought it was a good idea to invite her. He needed to focus on his job. One email from her to the chief could screw him over. He had to keep that in mind.

He bent down and gave Peaches a scratch behind the ear—her favorite spot. "Okay, girl, I hope you're ready for this. I sure as hell am not," Reece muttered under his breath.

They all stood outside of the pet store, and Reece took a deep breath.

If he was stuck with this dog for longer than expected, he might as well teach her some manners. Ones that were learned, and not just because he whipped out a picture of Blake Shelton, like the one he kept in his wallet. The next owner would be thankful.

Peaches let out an indignant bark and yanked on the leash, her nails clicking against the tile. If she were a larger dog, this might have been a problem. But Reece was able to just sort of drag her along, and she slid across the floor, her legs spread wide like she was trying to resist.

PetShop was the local pet store that offered classes, vet services, and grooming. Huge banks of lights lined the ceiling, gleaming off the checkered green-and-white floor. They passed the rows of dog food and toys. Peaches beelined it for a squeaky rubber hot dog, but Reece continued to pull her along to the enclosed mini-gladiator arena in the center of the store. The perimeter was made of waist-high white walls and Plexiglas from waist level to about a foot above Reece's head. Posters of dogs on leashes and some chasing tennis balls were plastered to the walls.

A woman wearing a polo with the company logo emblazoned on the front pocket opened the gate to the training area and motioned them to come in. "Are you here for the obedience training?"

"We sure are," Reece said, glancing around. Chairs lined the perimeter on one side, and on the other was a cabinet and two worn dog beds flopped onto the ground.

"Mandy." The woman wore her brown hair slicked back into a ponytail.

"Reece. And this is Peaches."

"What a cute outfit!" Peaches twirled around in her argyle sweater. It was at least a respectable blue and green today. He was sick of the pink frilly things. Mandy pointed to Reece and then the dog. "So we have

Daddy and Peaches. And is this your mommy, Peaches?" the woman used baby talk, which grated on Reece.

"Friend," Reece said at the same time Sloane said, "That'd be a no."

Sloane straightened and said, "I'm Sloane. Here for moral support."

Mandy squatted down to Peaches, and that was her first mistake. Peaches got up on her hind legs and started jumping. It happened in a matter of milliseconds but dragged out like in slow motion. Reece tried his best to yank the leash, to get Peaches out of Mandy's direct path, but he couldn't before Mandy's shoe took a direct hit with Peaches's pee.

"Oh my. We have an excitable girl here." Mandy didn't even blink. Just walked over to the cabinet, extracted a faded white towel, and swiped at her shoe and the dribbles on the floor.

"I'm so sorry. She does that when she's happy to see people. You can fix that, right?" He prayed the answer was a yes, because every time there was a delivery, it had become a problem.

"We can definitely try. It's harder in smaller dogs. This is a very common problem."

Great. He was stuck with a pee-er.

Two other couples walked into the arena. One with a German shepherd puppy and one with a bulldog that sounded like it smoked nine packs a day.

Mandy ushered them both in and took her position at the front of the makeshift classroom. "Welcome, class! You're in Obedience One, which means we will be learning basic commands, like how to heel, and we'll be making sure your puppy is well behaved in public as well as at home."

"Hear that, girl? You're going to be well behaved," he murmured.

Peaches yipped in response.

What was with the women in his life having attitudes?

"First things first. We will work on sitting. Dogs respond best to hand motions along with verbal commands. You'll need a nice firm"—the instructor glanced Reece's way and then cleared her throat—"tone."

"I don't see why you need me here," Sloane said. "Mandy seems more than intent on giving you a one-on-one."

"Jealous?" His gaze raked over Sloane, who'd sunk back in her seat and crossed her arms over her chest.

She scoffed. "Of course not."

"And to answer your question, you're here because you agreed, *and* you got me into this mess in the first place."

Yep. That was what he was going with until he could forge past whatever this was he felt for her.

Mandy continued on, walking around to each dog, giving them a scratch on the head. "You'll need to pick the alpha. This will be the one who the dog listens to."

Sloane leaned in, and Reece's eyes nearly rolled back into his skull at her rose perfume. "I'd nominate myself, but since Peaches is staying at your house, I'll pass that off to you."

"It'd be me, regardless," he said. It was in his blood to take charge. Even if Sloane was bossy, it didn't mean she was in charge.

"Go ahead and tell your dog to sit, alpha man," she mused.

What did Sloane think she was talking about? She wasn't the alpha in this wolf pack. Reece was the one to keep his team together. He called the shots. Kept his cool under life-or-death situations. He could command a foo-foo dog to sit.

"Sit," he said, his voice going an octave lower than normal.

Peaches stared at him defiantly. He stared back. He half expected western showdown music to begin playing over the intercom and a tumbleweed to breeze by.

Seconds ticked by and she was still standing.

"Sit," he repeated.

The instructor walked over, watching him. He'd never experienced performance anxiety before, but having a dog with a teenager attitude give him the shaft in front of the group was definitely pushing him in that direction.

"It might help if you do the hand movement." Mandy showed them the motion of moving the hand up, pinching the thumb and index finger together.

This was stupid. He bet if he pulled out the picture in his wallet, she'd sit right away. But he wanted to do this the right way. He wanted the dog to listen to him for as long as he had to foster her.

So he did the hand motion, even if he felt like an idiot, because Sloane was watching him with that knowing smirk.

"It takes time. Don't worry if you don't get it on the first try," Mandy said.

Reece peered around to the other two dogs that were rolling around. One was lying on his back. Even if Peaches wasn't the only one not listening, he didn't like the fact that this wasn't going as planned. Nothing in the past month had been. Between work, his injuries, and whatever this was with Sloane, he'd never felt so out of control, and he was man enough to admit it scared him.

"Sit." He did the hand motion. Peaches held her ground. "Come on, girl. You know who's boss."

"Yeah, she does," Sloane mumbled as she leaned back against her chair.

"Fine. You want to try it, alpha woman?"

"I thought you'd never ask." She uncrossed her legs and stood. Her breasts bounced in her pale blue sweater, and Reece bit back a groan. Thoughts of ripping her top off and licking every inch of her skin had plagued his thoughts ever since that day at his apartment. They played in a constant loop in his mind.

She put her hands on her hips, unaware of the images flying through his mind. "Peaches, sit."

The dog sat.

"You've got to be kidding me," Reece said.

"I told you. It's an alpha personality. Can't help that I have one."

"I'm calling beginner's luck."

"Says the person who's never had a dog before. And how many have I fostered?" She made a show of tapping her finger to her lips, pretending to contemplate. "Oh, that's right. I've lost count."

Damn it. What was it with this woman? He just couldn't seem to keep his cool. He wanted to shut her up with a kiss. To show her that she might be the ringleader in everyday life, but he'd bet anything he could make her cry out and have her begging for more. The need to do this, to take her, hit him on a visceral level. Pounded in his veins.

Get it together, man.

He was in a pet store trying to teach a Yoranian how to listen without the fear of Blake Shelton. This was the last place he should be thinking about Sloane in that way. He cleared his throat.

He put his hands up in defeat. "Fine. You know dogs. I know nothing."

"I'm glad you can finally admit that. It felt good, didn't it?"

She liked to rub it in when Reece wasn't good at something. He didn't experience failure often. The last time was when Erin had dragged him downtown to a calligraphy pen convention. His writing was chicken scratch, and most of the people around him had looked at it in horror.

"I think you're scared," she said.

"Oh yeah? Of what, oh wise one?"

"To give up control. You don't like the thought of me taking charge."

Reece suspected that Sloane had superpowers, because she'd just read his mind. He didn't think he was that easy to read.

"I don't like the thought of the dog you foisted on me being a total diva."

Sloane motioned to the dog. "She can hear you."

"She's a damn dog," he said louder than intended. His words echoed in the small space, and everyone stopped practicing their commands.

Mandy frowned and made her way back to their spot in the colosseum of dog hell. "I'm going to ask you guys and Peaches to leave."

"What? Why? Is Peaches really that untrainable?"

"Peaches is fine. But you two need to find a spot . . . not here . . . to figure out whatever is going on."

Reece and Sloane looked at each other. He'd never been kicked out of anything in his life.

Sloane quickly grabbed her purse while Reece hooked Peaches back on her leash. He didn't bother to look around at the other people. He could feel their stares. He managed to keep it together during car crashes, severed limbs, and complete bloodbaths, but put him in a room with Sloane for five minutes, and he lost his cool.

A rush of icy wind funneled in through the sliding doors as they opened. Reece, Sloane, and Peaches walked out into the early evening. It was already pitch-black, even though it was a little after five.

"Did we seriously just get kicked out of obedience school?" Sloane asked once they stepped off the sidewalk and into the parking lot.

"I think so." He let out a deep breath and fought for calm. And then he laughed. Because, really, what else could he do? "How am I supposed to get her trained?"

"I'm sure you'll think of a way. You seem to know everything, anyway, Reece."

And there they were. Back at square one. Exactly where he *didn't* want to be. "What is it you want from me, Sloane? To admit that I don't know everything? Well, you're right. I don't. I don't know a thing about my job. Definitely not about women, because the second I think things are cool with you, you tilt my world upside down." Why was he opening up to her? This woman had done nothing but criticize everything when he knew for a fact that she'd never been like this before last year.

"I don't like doing stuff I'm not good at. I acted like an idiot. And now Peaches will remain a hellion because of it."

She looked at him for a long moment, studying him with those light brown eyes. "What is this about your job? Because the Reece I know is an awesome firefighter. Although you could do without getting hurt so much."

He was surprised to hear her admit this. "You don't get it. Chief has a bone to pick with me. To sum it up, we don't exactly mesh too well. And this whole thing with the auction is just the cherry on top of the whole situation."

Sloane opened her mouth to say something, but Reece interrupted.

"And before you say something snide like 'Surprise, surprise,' just know that I've worked my ass off for a decade. I've put my time in, and I don't want to be dicked around by someone who's just biding his time till retirement."

An older woman pushed a cart into the return corral in the parking lot, her cart clattering against other stray ones in the contained area. Reece looked around, realizing he was making an ass out of himself in public again.

Guess he was just hanging it all out there. He didn't like how that put him in a vulnerable spot. There was a reason he didn't open up to people, and it was because there'd be no point. Why share the tough stuff when the relationship wouldn't work out? The only exceptions were his mom, Jake, and Hollywood.

Her gaze softened. "I was just going to say it's his loss. That sucks he's giving you a hard time."

He nodded. This was the Sloane he'd grown up with. Brutal at times, but also kind and compassionate.

"I've had a rough day too." Sloane eyed him, her hands on her hips. "And I won't leave you high and dry. I'll work with her. But you have to be willing to listen to me. And don't complain if I ask you to try something new."

"Fine." They started moving toward his Jeep a few spaces down. He unlocked and opened the door for Sloane and handed Peaches to her after she slid into the seat.

He pulled into one of the spots closest to the entrance of Sloane's apartment. Silence bloomed in the Jeep, and Reece fumbled with what to say to her.

Sloane was the first one to say something. "Since lessons were cut short, you ready to get started?" She unbuckled her seat belt and scratched Peaches behind her ears.

"What about the no-dog rule?" He didn't know how strict her building was or the consequences if they caught a dog in her apartment. The last thing he wanted was to get her in trouble with the super.

She shrugged. "I'm sure we can sneak her in for a few minutes."

He wasn't about to argue with this. He grabbed his coat and the dog's leash and opened the Jeep door.

As soon as they both rounded the back of the vehicle, she said, "First. You need to stop posturing."

He stopped and folded his arms. "I'm not posturing."

She rolled her eyes. "Look, you're trying to be all macho. Just be yourself. No need to sound like Conan the Barbarian. Peaches needs a more delicate touch than that."

"Like the dog cares." He motioned to Peaches, who was a tiny argyle shark circling around them, her nails clicking on the pavement. "She tries to eat her own shit. How complicated could she possibly be?"

Sloane quirked a brow. Reece's hands shot up in response. "Right. I know nothing. You are the Jedi master. Go forth and teach, Dog Yoda."

"It's all about body language. Dogs can sense how you feel, even when you don't say anything." She stood in front of him, her shoulders hunched, her body completely closed off. "This shows them that they can take advantage of you." She straightened, her posture opening up, her breasts pushing out to where they almost brushed against Reece's chest. "This shows you are in charge."

"I stand like that normally."

Sloane laughed, and the sound stroked down Reece like someone was gliding warm fingers down his spine. "Peaches must just think you're an asshole, then. She is a pretty good judge of character," she joked.

They made their way into the stairwell, their voices echoing as they ascended to the fourth floor. "You said you had a bad day at work earlier. What had you so down?" He couldn't help it. The more he wanted to distance himself from Sloane, the more he found his will-power evaporating. He wanted to know about her day. What she was feeling. This was all uncharted waters for him.

"Work was rough."

"Care to expand?" They exited the stairwell and made it down to the end of the hallway to her apartment. It appeared she had added a tiny snowman to the Christmas display outside her door.

"One of my patients didn't make it." She frowned, taking her key out of her pocket and opening the door to her apartment.

He got that. When they lost someone on a call, it put him in a piss-poor mood the rest of the shift. It was one of those things that dug at the crew morale.

"Why don't we take a break?"

She cocked her head, those delicious ruby-red lips pursing together. "We just started."

"I know, but I'm hungry. And I know Peaches is. Let's order a pizza." Because Reece wanted to stay as long as Sloane would let him.

Chapter Sixteen

Sloane stared at Reece, not quite believing what she saw. Why was he being so nice to her? After they'd duked it out in the pet store parking lot, she figured he'd want to hightail it out of there, and yet, he was here. In her apartment. Asking to eat a meal with her.

"Come on. I know you're dying for a slice of pizza," he said. He gave her that crooked grin that discombobulated all her neurons.

She moved across the living room to grab her cell, which she'd tossed on the coffee table when they'd first entered her apartment. Reece unleashed Peaches and set the leash in Sloane's entryway. He moved around her apartment with a fluid grace that sent prickles up her spine. He looked good here. Like he fit.

She shook that last thought from her head. What a stupid thing to entertain. The man drove her up a wall 90 percent of the time. He didn't *need* to look good here. He needed help with his dog. Owed her one more favor. That was it.

"Fine. But I'm only doing this because I'm starving, and I would have gotten something anyway." She mentally slapped her hand against her forehead. What was with her always slamming up the mental shield with him? She couldn't seem to let her guard down.

Food. Focus on something simple. She pulled up the pizza-store app on her phone and placed an order while furtively snagging glances of Reece.

Sloane had been looking for a safe guy to date online. Like a starter boyfriend. She wanted someone who made her feel those little butterflies in the pit of her stomach. Reece was about as unsafe as it came. She didn't get butterflies around him. More like those insects from *Jumanji* that could swallow an entire person whole.

"How's that online-dating thing going?" he asked as he sank down onto the couch. His legs were spread, and he had his arms propped on the back of the couch. Sloane had the sudden urge to crawl into his lap, to grind against the thickness that she'd witnessed the other day when he was soaking wet.

Girl. Get it together. You are better than this.

No, you're not, another voice replied.

She glanced at his lap again. *Nope.* She definitely wasn't.

Right. Sloane should do something besides just stare at him. She pulled out her phone and brought up the dating app. She didn't want to admit that she'd seen Reece's profile on there the other day. Or that it had sparked some weird form of jealousy in her. Instead, she pulled up the picture of Aaron, a guy she'd been chatting with for a week. "I'm going out with this guy on Friday."

He grabbed the phone and grunted. She waited for him to react. To object. To tell her not to go out on the date. Which would be silly, because besides the one time in his apartment, he hadn't shown any interest in her. She didn't count their interaction at the hospital. The man had experienced a concussion, for crying out loud.

His expression tightened for an instant, but then returned to his easy smile. "What do you like about this guy?"

Her stomach bottomed out. Definitely not the reaction she'd been expecting. Truth was, she wasn't even that excited for the date. Not that she'd let Reece know that. She squared her shoulders and lifted her chin. "He seems nice enough. Good hair. An admirable feature. Plus, he likes art."

"Not going to work out, Smurfette." He handed the phone back to her and resituated himself on the couch—a couch that she had no problem lying across length-wise but which seemed so small when he sat on it.

"And why do you say that? Aaron could be *the one.*"

Yeah, no. Aaron was absolutely *not* the right kind of guy for her. His texts were about as entertaining as cleaning the grout in her kitchen. Her stomach growled, and she glanced at her phone. It'd been twenty minutes since she'd placed the pizza order. It should be here any minute.

He let out a guffaw. "I'm one hundred percent certain this guy isn't the one for you. You're picking frivolous things."

"Am not." Was she? She figured that was what online dating was all about. Because she had yet to make any meaningful connections with anyone.

He gave her a look.

"Fine. What would you look for?" She didn't expect to hear anything earth-shattering from Mr. Macho Firefighter.

They'd never had deep conversations before. In high school, there'd been too much of an age gap to hang out and chat. And then when they got older, she saw him only in a work setting and occasional get-togethers with her friends.

He shoved his hands in his pockets and stared down at his shoes. He had forgone his typical flannel and was in jeans and a hoodie. Something about the way the sweatshirt pulled across his broad chest in combination with the scruff of his neatly trimmed beard sent a lick of heat sliding down her spine.

"I'd look for someone who had a good personality. Someone I can just kick it with." The pizza-delivery guy knocked at the door, and Sloane raced to open it. Before she could hand over the proper change, Reece shoved a few bills in the guy's hand and took the pizza boxes.

Sloane stared at him.

Was this really Reece? The one who grumbled about spending his hard-earned money? Maybe that hit to the head had rattled around some of his personality traits.

She went to the kitchen and grabbed a couple of plates and met Reece back in the living room.

"Is that what you were looking for when you made your way through my nursing unit?"

"No," he admitted. "I haven't seriously been looking for a long time."

She'd noticed this. He'd always been so serious about relationships when he was younger. This new Reece, the one she'd known for the past decade, was a far cry from that sweet high school guy. "Why not?"

He dragged out a tense breath.

"Can I be real with you?" he said.

This was apparently a day for truth bombs with Reece. She'd normally tease him mercilessly about this, but she had to admit she liked getting to know him. He was more complicated than she had first assumed. He was like one of those Russian nesting dolls her parents had gifted her from their trips to Europe when she was younger. A new surprise under each layer.

She shrugged. She wasn't sure what he'd say. Sloane remembered his long-term girlfriend in high school. They were one of those sickly sweet couples who were always attached at the hip. When he'd graduated, she hadn't really kept tabs on his relationship status.

"Do you remember Amber?"

"Your girlfriend in high school?" The only thing she remembered was that Amber had this amazing red hair. The kind that couldn't be replicated from a bottle. That paired with freckles and a button nose, and she could see the appeal.

"Yeah. I went to train for the hotshot fire crew the first year I joined Station Eleven. I had plans to propose after I got back. But when I came to surprise her for her birthday, she was seeing someone else. Already engaged and planned to move overseas with him. Wasted five years of my life with her."

Brutal. Sloane never saw a point to cheating in a relationship. If things weren't working out, end it. Why put the other person through all the pain and future trust issues? She mentally side-eyed her ex.

"You really think it was all a waste?" She liked to think that the years she'd spent with Brian weren't completely in the trash. She'd learned something about herself through the process. Like the fact that she was no longer willing to date assholes. Or ones who only put their needs above others. It was good practice for when she finally found someone worth dating.

"All I wanted was to settle down with the love of my life. My mom was always hounding Erin about relationships, about settling down, but I was the one who wanted the kids. I wanted to coach my kids' football teams. Play catch in the yard. I wanted to be a dad and wake up next to the same woman."

Whoa. She'd never expected that from Reece. He'd always seemed so . . . grumpy. Reclusive. Had a sour relationship made him that way? She wondered if this was the Ghost of Christmas Future showing her what it'd be like for her if she didn't find someone.

"Is she still?"

"Still what?" he asked, taking a bite of his slice of pepperoni. The way he chewed—the muscle in his jaw flexing, all those sharp angles in his face focused on what was in his mouth—sent a flick of desire through her. There was something seriously wrong with her if she was getting hot and bothered over pizza.

"The love of your life."

He set his slice on his plate and looked straight at her. "No." His voice was sure, certain. "*The one* would never leave you. I was young and stupid. I didn't know what love was at that point. It took a long time to realize that."

It was nice to know there were men out there who wanted something serious. All the men she'd encountered on the dating sites either wanted a casual hookup or had some unredeemable factor. Like jail time or laughing about little animals being injured. There were some real winners on the internet.

"Then why waste your time now?"

"In regard to what?" He lifted a brow, and she understood her own unintentionally implied meaning. That it was a waste of time to be out with her. It wasn't far from the truth. They were so different, there wasn't a chance in hell they'd be compatible.

She was finally smiling, something Reece had managed to pull out of her, even after an epic fail of a date.

"You know." She waved her hands dismissively. "Dating around." It sounded so flippant to her ears.

"What's the harm in having fun until the right person comes around? As long as both people are on the same page."

That made sense, she supposed. She'd always been a serial monogamist. Going from one long relationship to the next. The thought of actually hooking up with someone just for the fun of it, not looking past tomorrow, was terrifying. This was the exact reason she'd taken the last year off—to finally break the cycle. All it'd left her with was a better bank account and an extreme case of lady blue balls.

Reece grabbed a few pepperonis from his pizza and plopped them on a plate. He set it on the floor, and Peaches went to town, her tail wagging double-time as she chowed down on pizza.

"I guess. Just seems so emotionally taxing." She tore off a piece of crust, tossed it on the dog's plate, and then ate the rest of her slice.

"That's the point of a hookup. No emotions." He shrugged. "I guess if you both decided you wanted something more, that'd work too."

"And how would you know if the person you're hooking up with is the one if you already have one foot out the door?"

He stared at her for a long moment and then swallowed. "I'm guessing you'd just know."

Chapter Seventeen

This was so weird. Never in the past year could he have imagined himself sitting in Sloane's apartment, eating takeout, and talking about *the one*. This was all too deep for him. Stuff he hadn't even told Jake. A, because he would probably give him hell for the next decade. And B, prior to this past year, Jake had battled his own loneliness before he had started dating Reece's sister. Reece didn't need to dump his problems on him.

"It's been a lonely year," Sloane admitted.

Everything in Reece's body tensed. He'd been the target of this woman's anger for a long time. And now she seemed so vulnerable. Fragile. Two words he'd never associate with Sloane. The thought that she'd been deprived of things she'd wanted—*needed*—for that long stirred something deep inside him.

"It doesn't have to be." He looked at her, making sure she caught his meaning. It was a stupid suggestion. Sloane deserved more than just a warm body and a good time. But that was all he had to offer her.

She tipped her head back and laughed.

He stared at her, baffled.

She stopped laughing as soon as she saw his face. "Oh my God. Are you serious?"

Reece didn't know why this statement put him off so much. He'd never heard a complaint from any of the women he'd dated.

"Why not?"

She raised her index finger. "First of all, you still owe me one more chore. I feel like that would muddy up the waters." She put up another finger. "And second, we don't even get along half the time. You hate me."

He reared back, shocked that she'd come to that conclusion. Reece had never hated Sloane. Not even when she had targeted him with her wrath. "I don't hate you."

"Okay, fine. What I'm trying to say is that we bicker, even on the best of days. Adding *that* to the mix would be a disaster."

"You're probably right. Wouldn't want you getting attached. That might get awkward." He was goading her. He just couldn't seem to stop himself around Sloane.

She leaned into him, her hair brushing against his shoulder. She smelled of roses, mint, and marinara sauce.

Her lips coasted along his ear as she whispered, "I think it'd be the other way around."

His mind conjured up a hundred different fantasies involving her mouth. The way her tongue would feel flicking across the tip of his cock. Sloane's mouth had always been his favorite part of her. Besides her ass. She had a spectacular ass. One that his hands ached to grab. To knead.

The urge to grab her and pull her onto his lap, to devour that wicked mouth of hers again, washed over him. He'd bury himself in her, make her scream his name.

His hands slid to her sides, and she tensed, pulling away.

"Sorry. Did I do something wrong?" From the way her brows scrunched together, it looked like he'd hurt her. He'd been way off when reading the situation.

For the first time that evening, Sloane didn't look sure of herself. "I don't think this is a good idea."

"You're probably right." Even though he didn't think it was a bad idea at all. In fact, the only thing he wanted to do was touch her. He shifted farther away on the couch and cupped his hands to his thighs, pushing past all the parts of Sloane's body he'd like to explore with his mouth.

She looked unsure as her eyes shifted to his. "I'd like you to stay, though."

He nodded. "I'd like that too."

The relief in her face was palpable. Which made him realize he'd been way off base about where this was going. When Sloane had flashed her dating prospect in his face, he'd been under the impression that she was trying to make him jealous. Maybe he'd been wrong. Maybe she was actually interested in the dude.

Wait. Had Reece just been put in the dreaded friend zone? That didn't sit well with him.

This was a first. He had a lot of experience with women, but not when it came to friendship.

"TV?" she asked.

Reece glanced over at her, and she was so beautiful it hurt. Even with her hair pulled into a messy blue bun on top of her head and her Heck yes, I'm a unicorn socks.

He swallowed hard and focused on the TV, which was currently blank because she hadn't turned it on yet. "What are we watching?"

"I've been bingeing on *Supernatural* lately."

He shook his head. "Never seen it." Andie was obsessed with one of the guys on the show, though. Even went to a Comic-Con in town and paid a small fortune to have her photo taken with him. A waste of money if he ever heard one.

"I know we weren't really friends before, but now your chances are definitely blown. It's only the best show ever."

"You sound just like my sister. And you have seen *The Walking Dead*, right? Because that's the best show," Reece said. He eased his back against the couch, and Peaches hopped up between them, settling on the middle cushion.

"Child's play. Come to the dark side." She motioned to the TV.

"Fine. Start it up. Let's see what all the hype is about."

He leaned back into her couch and glanced around her apartment. He'd been in here a couple of times since the auction, but he hadn't gotten a good look those other times. Mostly because he wanted to get out of there as quickly as possible. Now he noticed the mound of blankets on a tufted blue chair, a vase of sunflowers sitting in the window above the kitchen sink. The wood floors were covered in an eclectic mix of rugs that, even though they were crazy patterns, seemed to go together.

Everything about Sloane was chaotic. Nothing like the simple home he'd built himself. His home seemed so . . . vacant compared to this.

"Are you even watching?"

He turned his attention back to the screen. "Yes. Guy has charmed life. Bangin' girlfriend. And now there is some dude sneaking into their house." He'd zoned out for the past ten minutes but got the gist.

"Not just any guy. Dean Freaking Winchester." She let out a small sigh.

He glanced at the rugged-looking dude in the tan work jacket on the screen. Is that the type Sloane was into? "The guy's named after a gun?"

She rolled her eyes. "I shouldn't even watch this with you. You're going to ruin it for me."

She went to grab for the remote, and he stopped her, his fingers wrapping over her bright purple nails. "I'll give it a fair chance."

Sloane sat about a foot away from him. He'd watched movies with her before when they were younger. Being here brought back memories of high school. Something so inconsequential as sitting next to a girl now felt . . . important again. He was noticing things. The way her hair teased at the neckline of her shirt every time she moved. The soft curve of her jaw. Gooseflesh pebbled over her arms as she rubbed at them.

"Cold?"

She nodded. "A bit."

He got up from the couch and grabbed one of the blankets from the pile on the chair.

He unfolded it and saw the pattern and laughed. It read BEST RESCUE MOM EVER, with pictures of dozens of dogs. Some with Sloane hugging them, some where she was crouched next to them.

He laughed. "Awesome blanket."

Her fingers stroked over one of the images of a golden retriever, and she smiled. "Madison made it for me last Christmas."

He could see how much she loved fostering dogs, just from the way she traced her fingers over the pictures on the blanket, a sad smile on her lips. It wasn't right that her apartment had changed their pet policy. She seemed to enjoy them, as evidenced by Peaches curled up next to her on the couch, soundly asleep. Maybe he'd been a prick for not letting the dog up on his own couch. He still drew the line at his bed.

"Nice of her."

She nodded.

"One of my favorite gifts. The dogs tend to like it too."

"How come you never adopted a dog of your own? Why foster them?"

She tucked a stray strand of hair behind her ear. "Well, before the rule in my apartment building changed, fostering was just something I liked doing. I figure then at least it's not long term. But I think I'd like to change that."

"Yeah? That mean you're going to move out of here?"

She looked thoughtful for a moment. "Someday."

"Maybe that Aaron guy will have a house you can keep your gaggle of foster dogs at." He didn't know why he'd said that. But it bothered him that Sloane was going out with him on Friday.

"Maybe."

But even her answer sounded half-hearted. Sloane deserved to be happy. She was one hell of a woman. And even though Reece knew he wasn't the one who could give that to her, it didn't stop the kick to his gut.

Chapter Eighteen

Reece swiped his hand across his sweaty brow and then pushed the "Up" arrow on the treadmill. His feet pounded heavily on the machine, and his legs felt like they would give out at any moment.

"Going for an Olympic record?" Hollywood asked, walking in front of the treadmill. He leaned an elbow on Reece's towel, looking far too comfortable. "Aren't you supposed to be taking it easy?" It'd been a week since the accident, and he'd been cleared for work. Same with Hollywood, who was lucky to have only a few bruised ribs and nothing broken from when he'd been hit by the man's bat.

"Doc said I'm allowed to push myself." More like push out thoughts of Sloane. The way she felt around his fingers. Her delicious lips. He needed to focus on his job because the last thing he needed was to get sloppy. Especially over a woman where all the signs were pointing to "not interested."

"Hold on. Let me get out my phone so I can record you when you wipe out."

Reece lifted a middle finger in response. Well, halfway. His body was tired enough that it could, in fact, give out at any moment. But that was the point. He wanted to be tired enough so that he wouldn't think about his problems.

Reece's feet stumbled, but he caught himself before he could crash and burn. Hollywood held the "Down" button until the treadmill slowed to a walk. "I think you've had enough, man. We're supposed to have to do lifesaving measures on civilians, not our own men."

He was right. It wouldn't do him any good to pass out on the job. With a couple of hours left on his shift, anything could happen. All he wanted to do was make it one shift without being called into the chief's office. Reece grabbed his towel off the side of the treadmill and wiped the sweat off his face.

Jake came into the workout room. "Everything okay?"

"He's trying to kill himself via sprinting," Hollywood said.

He was one to talk. The guy always pushed himself to the limit when it came to working out. Hollywood had even joined a CrossFit gym in town and did competitions during his off time.

"That's a new one."

Reece flipped Jake off and slowed down the treadmill to a full stop, wiping the sweat with the bottom of his shirt. "Have to keep in shape. Unlike you softies."

Jake guffawed while Hollywood rolled his eyes. Just like Reece, they both worked hard to maintain their shape. Had to with their job. But that was how Reece worked best—deflecting.

"Chief wants to see you," Jake said.

Reece threw his towel into his bag with more force than necessary and took a deep breath. His heart rate had returned to normal only to spike again at the mention of the chief.

"Did he look happy?"

Jake let out a dry laugh. "Does Chief ever look happy?"

"Good point." Chief's elation and wrath took the same shape on his face. Just a flat, thin line on his lips. Reece had never seen a spark in his eyes, but Chief was a legend in Portland, known for his heroics in the big paper factory fire twenty years ago. It was said that he single-handedly saved his team and fifteen civilians when the building collapsed. But nowadays, he was a desk jockey, something Reece never wanted to become.

Before he had a chance to shower and meet with Richards, the tones went off. Within a minute, Reece and his men were buckled into their seats in the engine, and he tore out of the engine bay.

Reece turned on his headset and took a right out of the station and made his way to the heart of downtown, passing storefronts peppered with potted plants, flags, and customers.

"Commercial residence fire. Looks like it's the bar on Madison."

"The one with the taco Tuesdays?" Reece asked, taking a right down Eleventh.

Jake nodded. "Yeah."

"Damn. They have good tacos," Hollywood said.

They were the first engine on the scene when Reece pulled up three minutes later. Flames flicked out of a broken window facing the street. The thunder of the burn was a deep rumble that vibrated in his chest. After that shift from hell, he was ready to get back in and do what he was meant to do. He glanced at the crowd forming across the block, some holding up their phones, probably broadcasting live on social media.

The police hadn't arrived yet, and neither had Portland West.

Reece hopped down from the engine and waited for his men to come around to his side.

"Hollywood, go hook us up. I'll go check out the inside and make sure no one is in there." He nodded to Jake, who was grabbing his mask from the engine. Reece adjusted his fire hood and slid his own mask on, making sure everything was secured before he went into the building.

His jagged breathing and the hiss and crackle of flames in the building echoed in his helmet as he entered side by side with Jake. Thick smoke blanketed the air, making for poor visibility, but Reece and Jake pushed farther inside, first clearing the table area and working their way to the bar.

No two fires were ever the same. Sure, they all burned, but some were hotter, some faster. Reece enjoyed the challenge of putting them out. Had a deep respect for them.

No bodies were found in either area, and Hollywood had made his way into the structure, hosing down the flames licking up the walls. More firefighters joined them, and Reece and Jake continued their search for anyone who might be trapped. Sweat slicked the back of his neck and the base of his spine as the room temperature seemed to spike. It was burning hot, much hotter than if it was just an electrical fire. He wasn't an arson investigator, but he'd seen enough fires to know this one had used an accelerant. They moved to the kitchen area, and Reece spotted a woman lying unconscious on the checkered tile. Blood trickled from a wound in her head, but there was no sign of fire in this part of the bar, just the smoke floating in from the front.

A sense of déjà vu hit him, and his head swiveled around to survey the area, looking for a man with a bat.

The type of fire. The way the front was the most severely damaged, even though the kitchen was in the back, screamed of more than just coincidence.

His attention snapped back to the woman. He couldn't check for a pulse without taking his gloves off, but he slung her over his shoulder and left with Jake as soon as more firefighters entered.

He shouldered his way to the front of the building, his breath hissing in his ears, the woman bumping gently against him with each move he made.

He didn't know if the woman from the last fire had made it. And he'd do everything in his power not to lose this one.

Early-evening light streamed through the haze as Reece exited the building. Sweat poured down his face and chest, and he could feel the temperature drop drastically as soon as he moved farther away from the taco joint.

Portland West had an ambulance ready, stretcher sitting at the curb, when Reece passed more firefighters working the perimeter and pouring into the building. He set the woman down on the gurney and tore off his mask while two EMTs fed her oxygen and measured her vitals.

Detective Ross was already on the scene, along with the arson investigator, Emeline Betts. That was fast, even for someone as diligent as Ross.

"You the ones who got the woman out of the fire?" Ross asked.

Reece nodded.

"Did you see anyone leaving the building?"

Jake walked up beside Reece, holding his helmet in his hand.

Reece shook his head and turned to Jake. "Did you see anyone?"

"No," said Jake.

Reece turned to Betts, who wore blue coveralls and a jacket emblazoned with ARSON INSPECTOR on the back. Her curls were pulled back and hung loosely over her shoulders.

"Thinking these two fires are connected?" he asked.

"That's what I'm here to find out. Just last week a church burned down three blocks from here." She frowned, jotting something into her notebook. "We heard this on the scanner and figured it was worth a shot to check out."

The residential fire he'd been at last shift had been ten blocks from here.

Reece nodded and swiped at the sweat beading on his brow, the December air doing nothing to cool his body. "Just like the one we were at last week, this one might have used an accelerator. It's burning hot in the front."

Betts nodded, like she expected that answer. "If I have any more questions, I'll head on over to your side of the station."

"No problem. Happy to help in any way possible."

Hollywood and Station 10 finished hosing down the building, most of the structure still intact. The owner was lucky—if they'd gotten there any later, it'd be gone, along with the woman.

He peered over at the ambulance and saw that the woman was now conscious. He walked over to where she lay on the gurney, an oxygen mask over her nose. Blood streaked her blonde hair, and her eyes were blinking fast.

Lacey, an EMT he'd worked with over the years, greeted him. "Nice work getting her out of there."

Reece shrugged, and the cold sweat that had collected on his shoulder blades drizzled down his back. He was ready to get back to the station and change. "She going to be okay?"

"The hospital will need to do a few tests, but she's responsive, which is a good sign. Knows her name—Sandy—and the date."

The woman tore off the oxygen mask and grabbed Reece's hand. Her skin was sooty, and dirt smeared onto his skin. He smiled down at her, grasping her hand in his. "How are you feeling?"

"Are you the man who saved me?"

He nodded.

"Thank you." Tears welled in her eyes and streaked down her cheeks, creating a path of pale skin between the ash caked on her face.

"Of course." This was what he lived for. To help other people. It made those hard days worth it to know this woman had a second chance at life.

"Do you . . . do you know who did this to me?"

He wished he did. Whoever this was needed to be put away before they burned down half his city. "I think the investigators were hoping you could help them out with that."

Just then, Ross and Betts strolled over.

"This is Detective Ross and Investigator Betts." He motioned to the two. The woman squeezed his hand harder.

"I don't know what happened. One minute I was prepping the bar for tonight, and the next, something hit me hard on the head. And when I woke up, I was here." She motioned to the ambulance.

"We're going to get her to the hospital. If you want to question her, do it there," Lacey said.

Betts nodded. "We'll meet you down there. We're glad you're safe."

Sandy gave a weak smile. "Me too."

Reece saw Jake and Hollywood putting away the gear in the truck. "Take care, Sandy." He gave her hand one last squeeze and watched as Lacey and another EMT finished preparations and closed the ambulance door.

He finished helping Hollywood and Jake with their engine, and then they all loaded up while the Station 10 crew took down their street barricades.

After heading back to the station and showering off, Reece returned to his blues and made his way to the chief's office. He couldn't stop thinking about the woman and how the hell she'd recover from something like this. Although Amber had never tried to have him murdered, he definitely knew what it was like to have his trust annihilated. He wondered if that was what all relationships ended in. Cinders and ashes. One thing he did know—he loved his job. And was glad he was the one to save the woman today. He'd tuck this in the back of his mind, because now that he was back at the station, it was time to see what the chief had wanted earlier.

Chief Richards was in his swivel chair, hands over his paunch. Since he hadn't been out in the field for a while, he'd let his training fall by the wayside. Reece vowed he'd never become this. He'd rather give up firefighting altogether.

The chief didn't even look up from his paperwork as Reece knocked. "Wondering when you'd show up."

"Got called out before I could make it to your office." He took a seat in front of the chief. He'd been here just weeks ago when the chief had threatened his job. Now what?

"Any updates on your Four for Four winner?"

"I've completed a few chores. Still waiting on the last." With any luck, Sloane would end this madness so he wouldn't have to sweat the status of his job.

The chief tapped his pen on the table, regarding Reece. "I haven't heard from Sloane, which probably means you aren't screwing up too bad."

Reece rubbed at a tight muscle in his shoulder. "I'll take that as a glowing review."

"Don't be a smart-ass, Jenkins. That's your problem. You don't respect authority." The vein in the chief's forehead began to throb.

"I respect you plenty." What was up his ass? Reece followed protocol to a T. He made sure his men were taken care of, that they made it home to their families at the end of the day.

"What about this report that you wrote last week?" He chucked it across the table. Several of the sentences were highlighted, a few red pen marks circling things that Reece couldn't see from where he sat.

"Your paperwork sucks. Your grammar needs improvement, and for Christ's sake, learn the proper use of a semicolon."

Reece gritted his teeth. Arguing with the man would prove to be a fruitless effort. There was no reasoning with the devil. Especially when the devil had complete control over his paycheck. "Will do."

"I would hate to see you have to move shifts because of these inadequacies."

And there it was. The chief holding his greatest fear over his head. "Won't be a problem." He'd make sure of it.

He'd buy a grammar book and read through it like it was the Bible if that was what it took to keep the chief happy.

"Good." And with that, he went back to his paperwork. When Reece hadn't moved from his chair, the chief glanced back up at him. "You can go now." His voice was clipped.

Reece pushed up from the seat and strode out of the office.

The rest of his shift crawled by. And by the time C shift was preparing for their day, Reece was ready for another round on the treadmill to try to forget.

Just as he was getting into his Jeep, his phone buzzed in his pocket.

Sloane: **Manage to get through a shift without any injuries today?**

He smiled. Because even though the chief had put a damper on his mood, one text from Sloane could turn it all around.

Chapter Nineteen

Sloane, Erin, and Madison sat at the breakfast bar at Jake's house. Well, technically it was Erin's house too, now, but Sloane hadn't really wrapped her head around that. From across the room, Sloane spotted pictures on the mantel of Jake, Bailey, and Erin. Pictures of the three of them at Bailey's science fairs, robotics competitions. They made a beautiful family.

Sloane pulled out her phone and triple-checked with Aaron that they were still on for tonight. It felt weird going on a date with him after she'd just hung out with Reece the other night at her apartment. There was nothing to feel weird about, though, right? They weren't even friends. More like a weird bond over *Supernatural* and pizza.

Aaron had messaged her earlier today to confirm they were still on. She stared at the message waiting for the other shoe to drop. But two hours before the date and . . . nada. Just as she clicked out of her messenger app, a text came rolling in.

Reece: Peaches made her way onto the couch.

Sloane: Run out of Blake Shelton pictures? Or is she finally immune?

Reece: She chewed through one of them. Now Blake is missing an ear. Also, she says that Sam is obviously the better Winchester brother.

Sloane held back a cackle.

Sloane: You just like him because he is broody just like you.

Reece: I'm not broody. And it's Peaches who thinks so, not me.

Sloane: Whatever you say. Glad you're liking the show.

"What's got you smiling?" Erin asked.

"Just plotting world domination," she said, putting her phone down on the table and opening up the cozy mystery she'd been reading earlier.

"Are you texting my brother again?" Erin didn't buy her answer.

"Oh, are you and Reece an item now?" Madison asked, digging into one of the packages of peanut butter crackers on the counter. A piece broke off and dropped into her curls. Erin leaned across the table, picked it out of her hair, and chucked it into the sink.

"We aren't a thing. But we're slowly building a truce." She didn't tell them about their kiss the other week. Or the way his finger felt inside of her. How it made her toes curl and it took every ounce of strength to pull away from him. If she'd kissed him any longer, she would have ended up in bed with him . . . and that would have been a mistake of epic proportions.

"Well, it's about time." Erin landed a speculative look on Sloane. "And I think it's good because I think you like him."

"Do not." She bristled. Reece was not datable material in the least bit. All he did was owe her some favors. That was it. And if he happened to be an excellent kisser? Well, that was a nice perk, but it did *not* mean she wanted to date the guy. "Plus, I have a date tonight."

Madison looked up from her computer where she was editing photos from a shoot earlier in the day. Erin stopped grading a paper and dropped it on the granite counter.

"When were you going to drop this little truth bomb on us?" Erin asked.

Sloane put her bookmark back in the book, realizing she probably wasn't going to get any more reading done now. "When I figured out it was real and not another false alarm."

"With Reece?" Madison asked.

"What? Why would you say that?"

"Because you haven't been grumbling about him the past couple of days. I thought maybe you two were . . ." Erin drummed her fingers on the countertop, seeming to search for the right words.

"Erin wants to say you're going to Bone Town with her brother," Madison said.

"Bone Town? Madison, you can do better than that."

Madison shrugged. "Hey, it's totally a thing."

Sloane rolled her eyes but smiled. "No, it's with Aaron. I showed you guys his pic last week."

"You mean Khaki Guy?" Erin asked, writing something in her planner.

Madison and Erin had taken to nicknaming the dudes Sloane showed them. Last week there was Crazy Eyes, Bigfoot's Second Cousin, and Guy Who Is Definitely Married. The last one was another nail in the coffin for her faith in men. If they were going to cheat on their wives, at least take a profile picture without the wedding ring.

"Yes. I figure, why not? And, bonus points, he hasn't been shady yet or stood me up."

Aaron, whom her friends had deemed "Khaki Guy" after they looked through his pictures and found that he was wearing this style pants in every single shot, seemed like a safe choice. Someone who wouldn't make her heart feel like it might take flight and blast through her chest cavity. Someone who'd give her tiny butterflies.

"That is a low bar to set, my friend," Madison said.

Sloane frowned and closed down her text with Reece. Maybe it was, but it weeded out 92 percent of the dudes on the dating apps. Which was pretty sad when Sloane thought about it.

"I'm sending over his details. I have his phone number and Facebook profile."

"Did you get his Social too?" Erin mused.

"If I could find it, I totally would." She wondered if guys on the site did this too or if she was just taking it to the extreme.

"Man, do you remember in college when we used to go out with guys and we didn't even know their last names?" Madison said.

She thought back to how she had met Brian in class. He'd asked her to go to his frat party for Heaven and Hell, a Halloween-themed bash they threw every year. Back then, she hadn't been particularly into organized parties. She'd liked to watch reruns of her favorite shows with Madison in their dorm and get drunk off Carlo Rossi. Even almost ten years later, she still preferred to stay home rather than go out. Too bad first dates couldn't just be that.

"This isn't college. It's online dating, and who knows if there are Ted Bundys out there."

"At least we'll know who to call once we find your body in a freezer," Erin said.

She rolled her eyes. "Thank you for that."

"It's going to be just fine. Seriously. Not every guy is going to be an asshole like Brian. You just need to get back on the horse and give dating a shot," said Madison.

"I know. That's why I agreed to drinks and appetizers with him at some fancy French restaurant. And I was really craving Mexican tonight." She frowned and toyed with the cover flap of her book. "You don't think I should bring a roofie test strip, do you?"

"Dear Lord." Erin put her head in her hands. "It's going to be fine. Trust me. And if you don't check in by ten, we'll go into sleuth mode."

"Thanks."

"And promise us you're not going to wear that on the date," Madison added.

She glanced down at her outfit. Jeans and a T-shirt. Nothing out of the ordinary. Nothing truly hideous that could be used for blackmail pics later down the road. "What's wrong with this?"

"I could fit my fist through the holes in your jeans. He's taking you out to a French place. Dress up."

She sighed and wished that she were more excited for this date. "Fine. I'll wear something fancier."

Thirty minutes later, she was back in the confines of her apartment, staring at the contents of her closet. Did a dress say too much? She just wanted a drink. Even if her friends wanted her to get back in the pro-verbial man saddle, she didn't know if she was ready to have someone back between her sheets. Besides, the other night when Reece's hand had been between her thighs, that was the only time in the past year she'd felt ready to crank it up to eleven. She swallowed hard. Drinks and appetizers only tonight.

She decided on a pair of dark jeans—no holes—and a dressy tank top. Cute, but definitely not sending the get-some-tonight signal.

She checked her phone and saw she had twenty minutes till she needed to be there. Before she went out the door, her mind wandered to what Reece was doing. She quickly pushed that thought away and closed the door.

"What do you think, Peaches?" Reece was sitting on the couch with the dog. He'd finally caved and let her up, and now she had made herself at home, taking up an entire sofa cushion. The dog was in high fashion today with a Seahawks jersey. Much more respectable. And if anyone asked, the outfit came with the clothes he'd been handed at the shelter. No need to tell anyone how much he'd spent on Barbie-size clothes.

Peaches stretched even farther across the seat cushion until her paws hit Reece's leg. He didn't even know how that was possible, but he was sequestered at the far end of his side of the couch. He had a bowl of cereal in his hands, while the mutt had a little Greenie beside her. Because the vet said that dental hygiene was of the utmost importance. And still no word from the shelter. Then again, he hadn't bothered to call for a status update either. Not that he'd admit this to Sloane, but he was getting used to having a dog in the house. It was . . . nice. "Football or basketball?"

Peaches let out a bark.

"Football it is." He rubbed her head. "You have pretty good taste for a foo-foo dog."

He had to admit it was nice to have someone to come home to. Someone excited to see him after a shift. He made sure that either Erin or his mom came to take her on a walk when he was on his shift. Maybe he'd find a doggy day care so she could socialize with other dogs.

A knock came from the front door, and he got up. Peaches didn't bark, didn't even move from her spot.

He eyed her and shook his head. "We need to work on your guard-dog ferocity, girl."

He opened the door to find his sister dressed in her teacher clothes. Pencil skirt, a red blouse, and her blonde hair pulled into a messy bun that was drooping.

"Wasn't expecting to see you. What's up?" he asked Erin.

"Is that the warm welcome you give all your guests?" She brushed past him and moved straight for the couch, using baby talk on Peaches. "How's my princess?"

Peaches wagged her tail. Over the past week, she'd appeared to be losing the urge to expel her bowels when people came to the door. He hoped this trend would stick.

"Everything okay? Jake okay?" Erin wasn't usually one to stop by unannounced. She usually called ahead.

"Yeah." Peaches rolled over, giving Erin an open invitation to rub her belly. His sister obliged. "I've actually been sent over here on behalf of Mom."

He hadn't been to the house in more than a week. He'd missed Friday-night dinner because he'd filled in for another firefighter on C shift.

"Does she need me to look at the garbage disposal again? I told her that she needed to get a plumber out there." Reece was good with his hands, but even he could admit that some things required a professional.

"No." She let out a sigh. "It's about Andie. Have you talked to her lately?"

He didn't like lying to his sister, but Andie wanted to keep the college stuff under wraps. It wasn't his place to tell her. "No. Why?"

"She just seems more secretive than normal. Mom—and I—are worried about her."

He would have loved to lessen the burden of carrying this secret, to share with Erin how proud he was that Andie was finally doing something about her future, but he was a man of his word. "I think it's just normal stuff. She's almost twenty. It's probably just a phase. You remember how you were back then."

"I try to forget that sometimes," Erin said absentmindedly. She turned to him and studied him. She had her scheming face on. "What are you doing tonight?"

"Just kicking it with Peaches."

She mashed her lips together. "You know, Sloane is going out on a date tonight."

Yeah. He knew. He'd thought about it more often than he would ever admit. "Why are you telling me this?"

"I just had a feeling that maybe this was information you wanted to know."

He scratched the dog's ears while Erin continued to rub her belly. Peaches had it better than any human he knew. "We're just friends. Not even that, Erin."

Erin put her hands up. "I'm just saying. I think it'd be cute if you asked her out. Before it's too late. Not that I think you have much competition with Khaki Guy."

"Khaki Guy?"

She laughed. "Yeah, that's the only thing he wears."

He wondered if it was the same guy from the profile Sloane had shown him a few days ago. "Sounds like a serial killer," he muttered.

"That's what I said."

"They're meeting at Château Dumont if you, you know, happen to be taking Peaches for a walk later."

"You're reaching."

Plus, he didn't know why his sister was trying to play matchmaker. Erin, of all people, should know just how horrible he and Sloane would be together. They'd fight all the time.

And then he could think of a million different ways to make up. He'd thought about them many times with his hand wrapped around his cock.

She shrugged. "Just sayin'. I'm going back home. And, Reece, you should really add a little bit of color in here. It's pretty drab." She got up from the couch and made her way to the door. "Anyway, gotta go relay the *non*news to Mom."

"I wouldn't worry too much about Andie. And, Erin?"

His sister turned around before she reached for the door handle. "Yeah."

"Thanks for the heads-up about Sloane."

She smiled and left.

He bent down and petted Peaches. "Sorry, girl. I'm going solo tonight." And then he grabbed his jacket and headed to his truck.

Chapter Twenty

Sloane gripped the steering wheel as she sat in the parking lot of Château Dumont, the warmth of the car fading as the clock ticked closer to seven.

She could do this. Maybe. Although going home and bingeing on Netflix shows did seem appealing at the moment. What if he looked nothing like his profile picture? What if he had a machete in his car and was going to take a swing at her when they said good night? Was she supposed to kiss him good night?

Dear Lord. This was a lot to think about.

Just as she reached for the door handle, a text came through.

Reece: Fun fact: Peaches has picked up on sign language. She now knows the sign for beer. Next week I'm going to train her to grab one out of the fridge.

Sloane exhaled a laugh, and the tension flooded from her chest. It was highly unlikely the dog would ever be able to open the fridge when she was barely bigger than the beer itself. Also, it was endearing that Reece had taken to caring about Peaches, even if he didn't outright say it.

Sloane: Keep your cheese somewhere safe. Dogs love that.

Reece: Good to know. Have a good night, Smurfette.

She stared at her phone. *Do it. Ask me out. I'll cancel my date this nanosecond if you do.* She was woman enough to admit that her thundering chest had nothing to do with her scheduled date and everything to do with the prospect of seeing Reece again. She'd much rather spend the night listening to Reece bicker about *Supernatural* than spend it in a stuffy French restaurant.

She pocketed her phone and opened her car door. The damp air chilled her bones, and she wrapped her scarf tighter around her neck. Portland wasn't known for its dry winter. Instead, it was filled with a whole lot of rain. Over the mountain, it was a winter wonderland, but in the valley, they were lucky to get a few snow days. Water sloshed on her boots, peppering the tops of the brown leather with raindrops. She pulled her hood over her hair, hoping that her flatiron job wasn't a total wash.

She opened the door to the restaurant at exactly seven. The restaurant was packed, many of the patrons standing, waiting for their names to be called to be led to tables. She did a quick scan of the waiting area and debated scurrying back to her car.

Nope. You made it here. At least give the guy a chance.

She owed herself that much. Because even if Sloane was perfectly content being single, she'd reached a point where she was ready to share her life with someone. And Aaron with the affinity for khaki pants just might be that person. Who knew?

A man who resembled Aaron's profile picture leaned against the wall nearest the hostess station, staring at his phone. He was cute. Had a dimpled chin, black-rimmed glasses framing blue eyes, sandy-brown hair that was crafted with hair wax, and was wearing a nice button-down that fit against his lithe frame. Everything that would normally send her heart into palpitations. She waited for it. To feel an ounce of *something*. A *Whoa, baby, you need to get on that steed, STAT.*

Nada.

This isn't even close to how you feel when you're around Reece.

She told her inner voice to shove it.

Then again, she still had time to duck out without him noticing.

No. She owed herself this. Sometimes connections took time. It was a possibility that by the end of dinner, she could feel totally different. She took a deep breath and made her way over to him.

"Aaron?"

"Hey, Sloane." He smiled and stuck out his hand.

Oh. Okay. So formal. She took his grip and shook. She hadn't been on a date in years, so maybe this was the new protocol. Also, the fact that she even had to second-guess how to start a date made her feel super old and crotchety. And now she was doing a mental eye roll at herself because she sounded like her parents when they'd chime in with, "When I was your age, I used to walk to dates uphill in the snow, both ways." Her father had grown up in Southern California, and her mother had been raised in Florida. Highly doubtful on both claims.

"I told the hostess to hold our table, even though you're late," Aaron said.

She glanced at her phone because she remembered giving herself a mental pat on the back that she was early when she'd pulled into the parking lot. It was still seven on the dot. "I was right on time."

He shook his head and rolled his eyes. Actually rolled them. It seemed so off compared to Aaron's persona online, where he'd come off as light and breezy. Which was exactly what she needed. Definitely not a broody firefighter who didn't know what he wanted out of life.

She let Aaron's comment slide. Maybe he was one of those nuts who actually liked to show up ten minutes early to everything. The only thing Sloane was on time for was work, and that was out of necessity. Everything else went on her own time frame.

The hostess walked them to a table at the window facing the streets of downtown. The table itself was nice. A large lacquered wooden tabletop complete with a small vase of flowers and votive candles. The waitress filled their crystal stemmed glasses and brought a basket of bread.

"I'm glad I got to meet up with you tonight," he said, looking over his menu. His jaw worked as he chewed a piece of gum, and then he popped a loud bubble.

Sloane flinched. "Yeah. This is actually my first date from online dating."

He quirked a brow, looking over his glasses at her. "Why? You got something wrong with you?"

Whoa there. Sloane was a direct person by nature, but even she knew the difference between that and just plain rude. She dragged her finger through the condensation on her glass and made a heart. "Uh. No. I just wasn't ready." Maybe she still wasn't ready.

She swallowed hard.

He laughed. "I'm just messing with you. But it does seem like a common problem with you ladies."

"Excuse me?" *Oh no.* She thought she'd done her homework, researched the guy's profile. Nothing in it pointed to him being a jerk. He'd passed the three-point background checklist Erin had given her:

1.   Employed/no arrest records
2.   No recent pics of exes
3.   No mansplaining posts

But Sloane supposed a few a-holes could slip through the cracks.

"Sorry. I know it's sometimes hard to understand. But I saw this article online that said that when women are getting old and their eggs are drying up, they become desperate to finally find someone. To, you know, have kids and all." He adjusted his stupid Clark Kent frames, and Sloane had the urge to rip them off his face and chuck them into the fireplace in the corner of the restaurant.

Did he really just casually drop info about a BS article regarding the female reproductive system within five minutes of meeting her? *Oh. Hell. No.*

And Sloane's eggs weren't drying up. She wasn't even over the thirty mark. And she knew she hadn't done this in a long time, but was it socially acceptable to throat-punch on the first date?

"I don't know who you think you're taking out on a date, but let's get one thing clear. You don't get to try to school me about my own gender." She stretched her neck from side to side. *Settle in, Aaron, because it's about to get real up in here.*

Just as she was about to rip into the dude some more and possibly toss her wine in his face, a text buzzed through on her phone.

Reece walked down Twenty-First Avenue, trying to figure out what he wanted to do for dinner. He'd been in a foul mood ever since he'd found out Sloane was going on a date tonight. Damn Erin for planting that seed in his head to go see Sloane. Now he couldn't stop thinking about her sitting across from some schmuck, his hands coasting over her curves.

His curves.

Fine. Not his. But damn it, he wanted that to be true. He was man enough to admit he'd kiss her feet and beg if he needed to. It was more than just the physical attraction. Sloane was easy to talk to. He could tell her things. Something he hadn't been able to do for a long time. And every time she smiled around him now, it wrecked him. That smile made him burn hotter than any fire he'd fought. He'd gladly burn for one chance with her.

So he'd walked to the exact spot where Erin had told him Sloane would be. Why, exactly, he didn't know. What was he really going to do? Wave her down from the street like a lovesick teenager? Not exactly his style. It shouldn't have bothered him, but what did she even know about the dude?

His eyes caught a flash of blue in the restaurant window. And there was Sloane, staring at her wine, frowning. And then the dude said something, and an inferno burned in Sloane's eyes, and if looks could do anything, hers would have incinerated the guy right there in his seat till there was nothing left but ash and embers. He couldn't tell what Sloane was saying, but she was gesticulating wildly with her hands, and a few patrons around her were taking notice. He considered storming into the restaurant and swooping in to save her, but he knew Sloane better than that. She'd resent him because she liked to save herself. He'd respect that even if it went against his every single instinct.

He pulled out his phone.

Reece: Unhappy with your date because you know I'd be a much better conversationalist?

He knew the second his text went through because she stopped midconversation and picked up her phone from the table. A smile spread across her face, and Reece felt like he'd won some victory. His chest tightened. He liked that smile. It'd been years since he'd seen her smile like that . . . because of him.

Sloane: I'm having a fabulous time. We're really hitting it off.

Why did she feel the need to lie to him? Was it just another way for her to try to get under his skin? Whatever it was, he knew that look. And knew when someone was in need of saving.

Reece: Liar. You look miserable.

She looked up from her phone, her gaze tracking everyone in the restaurant.

Reece: Meet me outside in two mins. I'll show you what a real date should be like.

Sloane: Are you crazy?? I can't just leave in the middle of a date.

Reece: Sure you can. You're texting in the middle of one even though your date is sitting there, staring at you. And if you want to experience the best Mexican food in Portland, you have a little over a minute left to get your ass out here, Smurfette.

He couldn't hear what she told the guy, but moments later, she pushed back from her chair and made her way out of the restaurant. This was his one chance, and he wasn't going to blow it.

Chapter Twenty-One

Two minutes ago, she'd been verbally accosting Douchebag of the Year (her new name for Khaki Guy), and now she was breezing out of the restaurant.

The rundown:

Douchebag of the Year: *Blah, blah, blah, why are you on your phone? Hold on while I stroke my hand through my hair because I think it looks cute.*

No self-respecting guy touched his hair that much.

Sloane: *The guy on the phone is much more interesting.*

And yep, the palpitations started.

Douchebag of the Year: *Don't worry. I'll just be doing douchebag things like uploading pics of our pinot to my Insta story and totally mansplaining the way a person should sip wine.*

Sloane: *Date. Over.*

Okay, so it didn't go quite like that, but that was how it went down in her head.

After Sloane grabbed her purse from the back of the chair, she hightailed it out of the restaurant. This had to be a record for shortest date. She considered the guy lucky that Reece had come along because she was ready to lay into him about a little thing called human decency and treating women with respect.

Reece was leaning against a parked car, his hands in the pockets of his tan jacket. Her heart hammered in her chest as she regarded him. The sharp line of his jaw. The scruff of his blond beard. The way his eyes lingered on her like she was an entrée at that fancy French restaurant. How it made her *want* to be devoured by him. She hadn't felt a modicum of this when she'd sat across from Aaron.

"What are you doing here?" Reece didn't deserve any pleasantries. She should have never told him about the date in the first place. And then he had had a front-row view of the worst date in history. How embarrassing.

"I saw you by accident. I was looking for something to eat."

She regarded him, trying to see if he'd known where to find her. His expression remained neutral.

It made sense. Both of their places were close to the heart of downtown. And this area of town did have the best options for food. Still.

"Maybe I should go back in there. I mean, who bails out on a date? Especially one that was getting his ass handed to him."

The muscles in his jaw twitched. "You don't owe him anything. And, besides, if he's that horrible that you were eviscerating him at the table, it's time you lay that one to rest."

"Was not."

He quirked a brow.

"Okay, I was. But still. It seems so wrong not to see it through. I'm not a quitter." Not in work, not in the sports she'd played in high school, and definitely not in dating, even when she'd been in a craptastic relationship for almost a decade. That last one was not something she was proud of. And she definitely wouldn't settle like that in the future.

"There's always a first for something."

Aaron was insufferable. And Reece had swooped in like some shining knight. Well, he'd tried, at least. Sloane was perfectly capable of handling herself.

"Come on. Let's go get something to eat," he said.

"I don't know . . ." She'd been gung ho a moment ago when she'd made her badass exit from that horrible date. But now, she was starting to have second thoughts. She didn't think her pride could take much more of a hit tonight.

"You'd rather sit with someone that makes you bored?" A look she'd never seen before flashed across Reece's face. Was that hurt in his eyes? It spoke of need and desire. Before she could decipher his look any further, his mouth turned into his signature smile.

"C'mon, Smurfette. It's just a meal. Let's drop your car back off at your apartment and eat."

Her gaze raked over him. Under his tan jacket, he wore a flannel button-up. Dark, broken-in jeans fit nicely around his thighs, and his blond hair peeked out beneath his black beanie. "Fine. What is this supposed restaurant that will blow my mind?"

"La Hacienda. Heard of it?"

Had he been tapping her phone when she'd been talking about that same restaurant with Erin and Madison earlier in the week? She'd been wanting to try it out for a while now.

"Sure."

He put his arm around her waist and led her down the street. And for the first time that night, she didn't feel nervous.

Reece stared at Sloane's mouth as she took another bite of chips and salsa. They were red and plump and glossed. Good enough to take a bite. He shook his head. Ever since he had kissed her, it seemed like that was the only thing on his mind.

They were settled into a corner booth at the hole-in-the-wall restaurant a few blocks down from the fancy place where dickwad had met up with Sloane. The best places in Portland were that way. The grimier, the better. Sure, the facade might be in need of a new paint job, the chipped tile tables could use a fresh coat of grout, and they were probably in violation of a couple of health codes. But La Hacienda was the real deal. With handmade tortilla chips, spicy salsa that added hair to your chest, and the sauces slathered on their enchiladas, they were on a whole different level in terms of authentic Mexican food. Like the heavens-parting, angels-singing level of cuisine divinity.

"Is this where you take all your dates?" She toyed with a chip, swirling it around in the black mortar dish of salsa.

Reece tapped his thumb on a pristine yellow tile on the table regarding her. "Just when I steal them from other miserable ones."

Her cheeks bloomed a light shade of pink, trailing down her neck, and disappearing into the top of her pale blue top.

Their eyes met. Hers were soft, the lightest shade of brown, complementing her skin. Everything about Sloane was soft. Her lips, her curves, her glossy hair. Reece would do anything to bury his face into any one of those. For his mouth to explore every inch of her.

Just as she was about to say something, their food arrived, the server using an oven mitt to hold Sloane's fajitas. She then slid Reece's chili *colorado* in front of him.

Sloane loaded her fajita with steak and vegetables and picked up their conversation where they'd left off. "Reece Jenkins, firefighter and savior of women on bad dates."

"It has a certain ring to it." But if he knew one thing, it was that Sloane wasn't a woman who needed saving. He liked that about her. He cut into his food and took a bite. Perfection.

"How are things going with the chief?" She took a bite of her fajitas, and his mouth went dry as he watched her chew.

He grunted. What could he really say? The chief had him under a microscope and was just waiting for him to screw up. Not that he would. He did everything by the book, like always. Sometimes that wasn't enough with a dick for a boss. With the way things were going, he fully expected the chief to find some way to put him on suspension before Christmas.

"That good?"

"Worse."

She frowned. "I'm sorry."

He shrugged. He didn't need a pity party. He definitely didn't need Sloane, of all people, to feel bad for him. Why had he admitted this to her? His job was basically in her hands. Hands that had threatened on many occasions to extricate his manhood from his body.

He decided to change the subject to something safer. "Tell me, were you really going to stay and finish that date even though you were having a bad time?"

She took a deep breath, and the frustration was clear in her eyes. "I feel so stupid. I thought I was ready for this whole dating thing, but obviously I'm total crap at it."

"You're basing that off one date with a dude who cared more about being a dick than getting to know you?"

"Isn't that what you do?"

Did she really think so little of him? Sure, he'd dated a lot. And he'd never really settled down over the years. With anyone. But what was he really going to tell her? No one had made him feel the need to settle down since Amber.

"I'm glad you have such a high opinion of me."

She pointed a finger at him. "I use the facts."

"I guess knowing you since you had brown hair doesn't count for anything." He hadn't seen her natural hair since high school. He liked the colors. It fit Sloane. Would still find her just as hot if she dyed her hair unicorn colors.

"We don't speak of a time before hair dye," she said in a hushed conspiratorial tone.

"I guess we'll also forget that cute chipmunk picture when you got your wisdom teeth out." He remembered that day. He'd driven Erin over to Sloane's house with a pint of Ben and Jerry's. Poor Sloane was draped over her couch, cheeks swollen, looking absolutely miserable. Her face had brightened when she'd seen the ice cream in his hand. He wondered if she was still fond of Chunky Monkey.

"You're such an asshole sometimes." She paused and took a bite of her fajitas. Her face softened when she said, "Thank you for convincing me to bail tonight."

"No problem."

"I mean, it's not every day that the fire department makes personal calls." Her lips twitched.

"I could have carried you out over my shoulder, but I decided that'd be a bit much. Plus, I wouldn't want to make the guy feel too bad. You were already doing a great job of that."

Her lips twitched again. Even a semblance of a smile was a sucker punch to his gut. "Is that what you do to women? Just use brute force and they all swoon?"

"Is that what you like? That I'm a brute?"

"I like my *firefighters* with finesse. You never know when you'll need a delicate touch." Her finger traced across the rim of her plate, and he was thankful for the table covering his thickening cock. He tried to shake images of those bright purple nails wrapped around him, stroking him off.

"I know how to be gentle when needed. Make them squirm under my touch." He took a bite of his chili *colorado*, and Sloane's eyes followed his lips. She swallowed hard. Yeah, he was moving himself out of the friend zone. It was his goddamn mission. "I can get very creative with my fingers. My mouth."

He'd love to show her just what he could do with his mouth. Make her back arch. Cry out his name.

She took a sip of water, her face turning a deeper shade of pink. "We are talking about firefighting, right?"

"Of course. What did you think I was talking about, Smurfette? Get your mind out of the gutter."

"Right." She let out a shuddering breath and shifted in her seat.

Yeah, he was getting out of that friend zone.

♥ ♥ ♥

Twenty minutes later, they finished up their meal, and Reece walked Sloane back to her apartment.

"We good now with the favors?" He didn't actually want to be done with them. He liked having an excuse to see her. But he also would like his job to go back to normal.

"Not a chance. I'm still decorating your apartment. Your act of chivalry was not of my asking."

"I forgot. Smurfette is too good to beg for help."

"I don't beg. Especially for you."

He eyed her. "I bet I could change that."

Their light mood evaporated, and his reaction to her was becoming evident. She swallowed hard, and her eyes widened. And an image of her beneath him—legs wrapped around his waist, begging for him—washed over him.

"I'd like to see you try," she said.

He quirked a brow. "You know what happened the last time you said something like that." He moved closer, his body pressing against her soft curves. "You try to act like I don't affect you, but I can see it in your eyes." He leaned down and lowered his voice. "How bad you want my face between your thighs. I want to lick you until you beg me to stop, until you're riding my face."

She mashed her lips together, pink filling her cheeks.

"That's just me getting started. You play it off like you don't care, Sloane, but I can see how bad you want it. You deserve to be worshipped, and I'd make sure every inch of you is explored. I won't stop until my name comes from your lips."

He pressed his throbbing cock against her stomach, and she let out a whimper.

Fuck. He was getting himself worked up, just imagining exactly what he'd do to her. How her nails would pull at his hair as he rolled his tongue over her.

"Seriously, look what you do to me. How is it one minute you can be so sweet, and the next I want to throttle you?"

He liked the honesty. Made it hotter to know he affected her this way.

"Throttling." He grinned. "I knew you were into the kinky shit."

"Did anyone ever tell you that you have a sharp tongue?"

"Nobody has ever complained about my tongue." He arched a brow, and his nostrils flared.

In an instant, he took a step forward, only a wisp of air between them.

"Look at you, Mr. Badass Firefighter. You think you can intimidate me."

"Will you shut up for just one minute, Sloane?" He leaned down until his forehead touched hers.

"Make me," she breathed.

Challenge accepted.

Once those words slipped out of Sloane's mouth, Reece closed the space between them, his body pressing into her, moving her backward until her shoulders hit the wall. They were still lingering outside her apartment door, right out in the open where anyone in her hall could witness. His fingers combed through her hair, and she was staring up at his eyes. Hungry. Wanting. She bet that the same was reflected back in her own. She tilted her chin up as he leaned down. Their faces were inches apart, and the peppermint from Reece's gum mingled with her breath. He probably tasted like a candy cane. Something so sweet on such a bad mouth seemed so wrong. She wanted to taste him.

Her tongue darted across her lips to wet them, and her pulse hummed in her ears. His eyes searched hers for a moment. Calculating. No. She'd made her own rules.

She closed the gap between them, her lips on his, soft and warm. But nothing about this kiss was soft. Her lips parted, and Reece's followed suit. Her tongue swept into his mouth, and then they were fighting for control. His breath sped up, and the grip of his fingers in her hair tightened, like he was fighting for the last shred of control. Strong hands drifted down, skimming her neck, inching down her curves until they moved to cup her ass. He pulled her up, and she wrapped her legs around his waist, pressing her harder into the wall.

Everything in Sloane went liquid. The space between her thighs throbbed as she moved against Reece. The promises that had just come out of his mouth—she wanted him to keep those. To make her mind go blissfully blank. Everything ached to be closer, needing more. A groan ripped out of him.

She hadn't been kissed like this since . . . well, ever. The way his mouth moved over her, it devoured her. He wasn't gentle. He was demanding. And Lord help her, in that moment, Sloane was willing to cave to anything that Reece asked.

After a long moment, Reece slowly pulled back, eyes hooded, his lips swollen. He was the embodiment of sin. She'd have to do a heck of a lot of Hail Marys to atone for the thoughts going on in her head right now.

Crap. There was no stopping now. Any voice of reason floated away like wishes on a dandelion puff.

She grabbed his face, feverishly kissing him, only pulling away to jam the key in her door and open it.

They spilled into her entryway, Reece's fingers working at the button of her jeans, his other hand slowly lowering the zipper.

He pulled back, breathing hard. "Tell me to slow down, Sloane, and I will."

Was he actually insane? The shuttle to Pound Town had left the station. There was no return ticket. "Why the hell would I do that?"

His lips curved into a wicked grin, and he carried her to the kitchen and set her down on the counter. With her jeans already unzipped, he pulled them off with efficient grace, along with her panties, until she was bared for him on the counter.

"Damn, Sloane." He kissed down her neck, his fingers slipping underneath the straps of her tank top, yanking them down until her breasts were exposed. He pulled back, his eyes raking over her, glazing with lust. That one look sent a wave of heat between her thighs.

His face closed the distance, and his warm tongue swirled around her nipple. "Like I said earlier, I can be very gentle." His teeth lightly grazed her skin, then nipped. Her hips bucked in response. "Or do you need a rougher touch?" He suckled harder, and sparks of pleasure exploded behind her eyes.

A gasp escaped her lips, and she moved closer to him, his tongue and teeth punishing her. "Oh. Wow. Yeah. That." She'd been reduced to one-word answers. She'd never done anything in any place other than a bedroom before. The cold granite bit into her ass. It seemed so forbidden.

He worked his way down her stomach and kneeled on the floor and grabbed her legs, placing them over his shoulders.

"Reece, you don't have to do this if you don't want—"

"Smurfette." He looked up at her with intense hazel eyes that sent a fresh curl of lust blooming under her skin. "Let me get a taste. I've been dying to do this." And with that, his tongue was on her, flicking over her center.

Her head knocked back against the cupboard, and warmth flooded her, her body going hot and tingly. Lord, this was probably a bad decision, but she couldn't find it in herself to really care at this moment. Not with strong hands cupping her thighs and his lips on her skin. His tongue circled her clit, and she cried out, her foot knocking something off the counter. She peered down and saw the bottle of chocolate sauce she'd used on her ice cream last night splattered on the floor.

"I like your idea of dessert," he said. He reached down and picked up the bottle, giving her a wicked smile.

Oh, she liked that smile. It promised hair-pulling, panting, using-the-Lord's-name-in-vain things.

He drizzled the chocolate down her stomach, down farther until the cool liquid trickled onto the space between her thighs. Reece moved to her stomach, lapping at her with long, languid strokes while his fingers tweaked at her nipples.

Slowly, he worked down her body, sweeping up the chocolate with his tongue. The heat of his tongue trailing across her skin made her nipples pucker. Warmth bloomed at her core as his mouth hovered over her, and then his tongue was on her, relentless. The familiar climb toward bliss created an ache, one that Reece was about to fix. His hands skimmed down her body until a finger slid between her thighs and entered her. His other hand gripped her hip, pulling her closer, his tongue hitting a spot that sent her past the point of no return.

"Oh God. Reece." She grabbed at his hair, and he looked up at her, his eyes crinkled in pure delight. And then she spiraled, her eyes scrunching shut, stars sparking behind them. She rode out the wave of ecstasy, grinding shamelessly against Reece, and he groaned in response.

She was left breathless, panting on the counter when Reece stood. He pressed a kiss to her neck, to her cheek, and then her lips. If his hand wasn't on her thigh right now, she might float away.

"And that's how a good date should end. Let me know when your next date is so I can crash that one too," he whispered into her ear.

She smacked his chest. But she was too tired to argue. He'd more than kept his promise. And now that she knew how good it could be, she didn't want to go back to the way things used to be between them.

"Do you . . . uh . . ." She was trying to find out if he wanted anything in return. That was how it had worked with previous relationships. Expectations and all.

"No way. Seeing you fall apart because of me was more than enough." He pulled her into a kiss, and she could still taste herself on his lips. The thought made her flush. "I'm going to head home. I have to take Peaches out."

He grabbed her hand, and she hopped down from the counter, pulling on her pants. She walked him to the door, still feeling like she was having an out-of-body experience, her limbs languid.

He turned to her. "I know you don't need saving, Sloane. But it's okay to show people you're vulnerable."

And with that, he turned and made his way to the elevator.

Sloane closed the door and threw herself on the couch, blowing out a shuddering breath. Her fingers found their way to her lips, and she smiled. What the heck was that?

Reece made it back to his apartment in record time. He needed to take a cold shower, stat. He hadn't been expecting the night to end this way. When Erin had come over earlier to tell him about Sloane's date, he thought maybe he could catch her afterward, give her a hard time. But when her lips touched his, something sparked in his blood, setting fire running up his veins.

Peaches greeted him, and he had a towel ready by the door to catch the pee that flew toward his shoes. *Ha.* It was getting easier, and he did like the little pooch around. The towel came up dry. "You're learning, girl." A swell of pride puffed in his chest.

He gave her a scratch behind the ears. He most likely had only a few more days left with her, and that didn't sit well with him. They'd gotten into a routine, and if there was one thing he hated, it was breaking up a good schedule.

After taking her out for a bathroom break, he unleashed her and tore off his beanie and shirt. His pants and boxers followed quickly after as he made his way to the shower.

It was smart that he'd left when he had. The trust that he had in himself wavered around her. He could have continued, taken her to the bedroom, and given her what they both wanted, but she deserved better than that. More. He just wasn't sure he was ready for that jump. Just weeks ago, they hadn't even been on speaking terms.

He started the water and stared at himself in the mirror. His eyes were wider than normal. His face was flushed. He attributed that last one to the fact that it was freezing outside. When the hot water had steamed up the mirror, he put his head under the water, closing his eyes as he put his head under the spray. He reached for the soap and lathered up his hands, staring at his fingers. They'd been inside her not even thirty minutes ago. He groaned. He could still hear her voice crying out his name as his tongue flicked over her.

His fingers found their way to his throbbing cock. He thought about Sloane. How her hands had roamed over him. How she'd writhed on the kitchen counter, crying out his name as he licked her clean. He'd never been so hard in his life. His soaped hand wrapped around his cock, and he groaned as his grip tightened, and he pulled from shaft to head.

She'd been so tight around his finger. That sweet pussy would wreck his cock. That, and her pretty purple nails would be the end of him. She had delicate hands, ones that were steady enough to fix his injuries, but he didn't doubt for a second they'd be firm, punishing while wrapped around him. He knocked his head against the tile, slicking his hand up and down.

He'd give anything for her to be here right now. If he hadn't kicked himself out, maybe they'd be doing this right now.

"Shit," he ground out.

Everything about Sloane did it for him. The way her wicked tongue threw out insults. How he knew she cared for him under all that bluster. The way her blue hair framed her gorgeous face. Those luscious curves. They were mouthwatering. He liked that she wasn't rail thin. The way her hips filled out her yoga pants. How his hands itched to grab her gorgeously round ass. He couldn't get her out of his mind.

He stroked harder, everything growing tighter.

He finally released and sucked in a jagged breath as the warm water began to turn cold.

This woman was trouble. And he was heading full force into a train wreck.

Chapter Twenty-Two

Reece had a rule when it came to women. One night and that was it. No more texting. No calls. No emails.

He was breaking all that and more today and didn't care. It'd been less than twelve hours since he'd seen Sloane, and he was already going through withdrawal. He pulled out his phone and tapped out a message to her.

Reece: How's it going?

Sloane: I'm still cleaning chocolate sauce out of my grout.

A smile twitched at Reece's lips, remembering how it had spilled everywhere when Sloane had knocked it from the counter.

Reece: It was delicious. And so were you. In fact, I can't think of anything I'd rather eat right now.

His pulse thundered in his temples as soon as he hit "Send." It'd been a long time since he'd done this. Wanted something more. Given himself the chance to *hope*. When she didn't respond for a couple of minutes, he was kicking himself for being too forward. Damn it, how had he gone from never wanting anything past a night with a woman to sweating over a text? Sloane had driven him absolutely mad.

Just as he was about to apologize, a text came through.

Sloane: I'd like that.

Sloane: But I have other plans for you today.

Reece: Such as?

Sloane: Time to decorate your apartment.

Reece groaned. But a promise was a promise. And he wouldn't pass up more time with her.

Reece: Fine. Do your worst.

Two hours later, he picked her up from her apartment, and they ended up at a place downtown that Sloane swore by. It was the type of place that had throw pillows and candleholders in the shape of giraffes. A store that Reece would never set foot in of his own accord.

They were currently in aisle three, arguing over his bedroom decor. Or lack thereof, according to Sloane. "I'm not getting a goose-feather comforter. What's wrong with the one I have?" he said.

"It's cozy." She hugged it to her chest. "Perfect for snuggling. You do like snuggling, yes?"

If it involved Sloane, then yes. Bring on the snuggles.

She tilted her head, and Reece had a hard time concentrating on the task at hand. Her hair was pulled back into a braid that hung over one shoulder, and she wore a white beanie that was both cute and sexy at the same time. He debated taking her to a deserted aisle and showing her all the other things he'd rather be doing right now.

She sighed. "This isn't going to work if you stick your nose up at everything."

"I'm willing to try." After these past couple of weeks, he realized he was willing to try in a lot of aspects of his life. He pressed her against the shelving unit and swept her into a kiss, lingering, savoring the taste of her lips. By now, he'd kissed her several times. Each one was better than the last. Sloane's lips were by far the best thing he'd ever tasted.

He pulled away slowly and watched as her eyes fluttered open.

"Just because you kiss me like that does *not* get you off the hook. C'mon. Goose. Down," she said, like this was enough to sway anyone.

He caved. She could upsell him on a lemon of a used car right now, and he wouldn't be able to resist. "Fine."

Her lips pulled into a smile, and his chest swelled. He'd do anything to keep this feeling.

Two hours later and they ended up with three large bags and were on their way back to his apartment.

Sloane stared at the blank palette she had to work with, a.k.a. Reece's apartment. While he prepared dinner, she'd taken it upon herself to start decorating. The apartment in itself had great bones. High ceilings, turn-of-the-century charm in glass doorknobs, and a breakfast nook. It was a building she'd been eyeing when she'd first started her apartment search in the city. Alas, in this part of town, she'd have better luck winning the Hunger Games than finding another apartment to rent.

She grabbed the throw pillows and the small area rug from the shopping bag and positioned the pillows on the couch and the rug on the floor.

Next, she added a few decorative frames to the entertainment system and worked her way to the kitchen. There might have even been a few rose-colored embellishments—she'd snuck those into the cart when Reece wasn't looking. An hour later, Sloane admired her work. Creamy drapes that fell just above the baseboards. A new curved glass lamp sitting on a distressed wood table. Tufted seat cushions lining the previously bare dining room chairs. Luscious rugs covering hardwood floors. Everything came together in an elegant, understated grown-ass-man-lives-here kind of way. One who still lived on Frank's hot sauce. For someone who knew how to work a grocery store, he didn't keep anything stocked in his fridge, except for the groceries they'd just picked up on their way back to his apartment.

Just as she was putting the finishing touches on the bedroom with the goose-feather comforter, new drapes, and lamp on his bedside table, Reece called out that dinner was ready.

She made her way to the kitchen and found Peaches scooped up in Reece's big arms. He leaned down and gave the dog a kiss, then set her on the floor. "Go ahead and get comfy, girl. I'll get your dinner in a bit."

He didn't notice Sloane there. That much was obvious since he was talking to Peaches in a cutesy voice saved for small animals. Sloane cleared her throat, and his eyes darted to hers. He stiffened and resumed stirring the minestrone soup, the savory smell making Sloane's mouth water.

"Smells amazing. But before we start, I want to show you what your awesome apartment looks like now."

She led him out of the kitchen and opened her arms Vanna White–style. "Tada. Do you want a tour of your newly updated apartment?"

His face pinched as his gaze bounced around the room. The two little lines between his forehead deepened when he took in the pillows and the framed abstract art on the wall.

"Wow. It's something, Sloane."

Her stomach dropped. "You don't like it?" This was her thing. Well, besides helping keep people alive. Madison worked her magic with photography, Erin worked her magic with being the Mary Poppins of teachers, and Sloane pulled a room together like she was on HGTV. And now Reece looked like he was going to lose his dinner over the new rug she'd bought.

"It's not that. I'm just not used to seeing this place look like . . ."

"A place." Which was what she'd been going for.

"Exactly." His voice was quiet. Maybe she'd misread the situation. Was there a reason he wanted to live in complete minimalism?

An ache built in her chest. It shouldn't matter what Reece thought. His opinion shouldn't matter. And yet, the look on his face sent an unexpected spear of sadness through her.

"Sloane, I didn't mean to make you upset. I like it. I really do. Look, Peaches is already at home."

The dog was snuggled inside a blanket propped on the couch. At least someone would enjoy it.

He paced the length of the hallway and then paused. "There's actually something I wanted to ask you. Something that's been on my mind all day."

She swallowed down her pride and forced herself to smile. Because even if he couldn't appreciate her work, it was still a job well done, and now he didn't have blank walls. "What?"

"I want to take you out. On a real date."

"That was a statement, not a question."

He leaned down, his lips brushing against the fleshy part of her ear. "I know how much you like to be bossed around."

She shivered, folded her arms, and didn't bother to argue. Because, in fact, she had liked it when Reece took charge.

"How about I pick you up at eight on Thursday?"

"Is this about last night? Because you shouldn't feel obligated just because you did . . ." She trailed off. Why was she arguing against a date? Was she an idiot?

He strode over to her, and she moved until her back hit the wall. Being this close to him, the heat of his chest against her aching breasts, made her whole body hyperaware to each touch. The pad of his thumb climbing up her side. The way his thick thigh pushed at the space between her thighs. A dull throb pulsed there, practically begging for a redo of the other night. His lips were on hers, his tongue slipping into her mouth. The taste of mint tangled with a hint of soup. Her fingers found their way to his broad chest, raking over the hard muscles, and Sloane realized she'd require a lot more time to explore. Reece had a lot of real estate, and she needed to make a thorough property evaluation.

He pulled back, and she was left leaning against the wall, completely out of breath.

"What I did has nothing to do with why I want to take you out. Although I'm definitely not against doing it again. I like you, Sloane. And even though you drive me up the wall seventy percent of the time and decorate my apartment with throw pillows and goose-feather comforters and all that pink crap, which I'm pretty sure I told you to put back at the store, I realize there's no one I'd rather go out with."

A grin split across her face. "You drive me crazy too."

Chapter Twenty-Three

Four days later, and Reece was sweating his Thursday-night plans. His shift had just started, and they'd just finished up their morning meeting and quick brushup on intubation procedures. It was a good thing Reece knew how to intubate a person quickly and efficiently because he'd completely zoned out on what Hollywood had said in the meeting. Instead, he was focused on where to take Sloane for their date.

In the fifteen years Reece had been legally considered an adult, he'd never once planned a date. First, because going out to a fancy restaurant to try to get someone into bed seemed financially reckless. He usually stuck to cooking dinner at home. Add in a couple beers, and then they'd be good to go. Sometimes he'd go to happy hour with them. Yes, now he realized how much of an asshole this made him. The women he'd dated—if you could even classify it as that—had deserved much better.

But now he wanted to take Sloane on an honest-to-goodness real date, and he was way out of his depth.

It'd been half a week, and he still couldn't figure out where to take her. Which was how he found himself in the engine bay, checking supplies and asking someone as equally unqualified.

"You do realize that my idea of a date is starting out on the dining room table before we make our way to the bedroom? Don't even get that far some of the time," Hollywood chuckled. "Shit, man. What did Sloane do to you?"

It wasn't what she did. It was what she made him feel. When he'd dated in high school, he used to get the sweatiest palms right before he asked a girl out. Just the thought of Sloane, the thought of her smile, the delicate curve of her neck as she threw her head back to laugh, was enough to send him over the edge.

"I knew I shouldn't have asked you." He shoved the airway bag back in the engine and reached for the blood kit.

Hollywood marked something on the clipboard. "No, no. I just never thought I'd hear this from you."

Reece focused on his checklist, thinking about the best way to erase the last few minutes. "Yeah, laugh it up, asshole."

"I am going to enjoy every second of this. Coming to the youngest one for dating advice. Why not ask Jake? He's the one that's living like a *Brady Bunch* movie."

"Because he'll make a big deal about this. Which is exactly what I didn't want. And exactly what you're doing."

"Sorry, man. It's just a shock to the system is all."

Was Reece that far into bachelorhood that no one thought he'd ever go on a date?

"This conversation is ending now."

"Sorry. Okay, I'll be serious. What does Sloane like? Usually you cater the date to what you think they'd be into."

"She likes those Pusheen things," Reece said, thinking back to all those pillows on her couch.

Hollywood screwed his face. "What the hell is a Pusheen?"

Reece continued looking through the med supplies, making a note that they'd need to stock up soon on more insulin. He waved his hand flippantly. "It's this cat cartoon thing. Apparently people collect it."

"You said she likes to decorate stuff, right?"

"Yeah, turned my apartment into a Pottery Barn ad." It had been jarring at first, but the more he was in his apartment, the more he liked it. Peaches had staked claim on the new blankets Sloane had picked out.

Hollywood shrugged and continued to stare at his list. "Then appeal to that."

Reece nodded. *Okay.* He could work with that. Portland had a lot of options when it came to the arts.

"I think I've got it." He clapped Hollywood on the back. "Thanks." Now he just had to make a few calls.

Before they finished their morning checks, Detective Ross and Investigator Betts appeared in the engine bay.

They moved toward the doors and entered the firehouse.

"Everything going okay with you guys?"

"Just investigating a new fire yesterday. Another church. Another body. Didn't get to her in time." Ross frowned.

"Have any leads on who's doing this?" Reece asked.

Betts shook her head. "This guy's careful. Keep your eyes peeled for any calls like this today. His time between arsons is shrinking."

"Sure thing."

Once they disappeared through the doors, Hollywood turned to Reece and said, "Who was that?"

"New arson investigator." Reece realized that Hollywood had either been injured or not on the scene when Reece had spoken with her the two previous times.

Hollywood glanced at the door and gripped the side of the engine. "Damn," he mumbled. And Reece didn't think he'd ever seen Hollywood look at a woman with such intensity.

He was about to heckle his friend when the tones rang.

When Reece knocked on Sloane's door, promptly at eight, she took one last glance in the hallway mirror, let out a nervous breath, and opened the door. Reece wore a dark green flannel shirt that brought out the flecks of green in his hazel eyes, and dark jeans that hugged his thighs. Sloane had thought she'd been nervous for her date with Aaron, but nothing prepared her for the squall of epic proportions going on in her stomach.

He stood in her doorway, looking, for the first time since she'd known him, unsure. This was the man who had an answer for everything. Had enough ego for ten men. And he seemed . . . nervous. He licked his lips and leaned on the doorframe. "Listen, I know this is kind of weird because we've known each other pretty much our whole lives."

"It is weird." He frowned, and lines creased in his forehead. She quickly added, "But I'm glad we're doing it."

The dent between his brows disappeared. "I—uh—have something for you."

"You . . . got me something? You didn't have to do that." Reece, of all people, got her something? The man who, up until last week, didn't have a knickknack to his name. Had they somehow landed in an alternate dimension?

The muscles in his jaw feathered, and he said, "I wanted to." He pulled a tiny figurine of a dog out of his pocket and placed it in her hand. It was a tan dog that looked like Peaches. It even had a blue sweater.

"I saw it, and it made me think of you. I know that you can't foster dogs here, but this one will keep you company."

Sloane had never been much of a crier. Her emotions were more along the lines of cold cyborg, but even this warmed her robot heart. She cradled the tiny figurine to her chest and smiled. "That's really sweet, Reece. Thank you. Let me put this down in the apartment, and then we can get going."

She placed the dog on her nightstand in her bedroom, grabbed her coat and hat, and then locked the door behind her.

"Are you going to tell me where you're taking me now?" She tugged on her hat and slid her arms into her coat as they headed toward the stairwell.

"It's a surprise."

Reece had been mysteriously cryptic about their date tonight. Honestly, she was surprised he'd asked her out in the first place. It went against his MO. Then again, everything they'd done went against what he normally did. Sloane kind of liked this side of him. As if he was back to the old Reece. The one she enjoyed being around.

She just hoped he didn't take her to one of those upscale restaurants like Aaron had. Everything about that screamed uptight and suffocating.

Fifteen minutes later, they were in the heart of downtown, and Reece parked his Jeep on a side street. This corner had specialty restaurants, ones with delicious smells wafting from open storefront doors.

She looked up at a sign. **CLUB DIY**. The letters were made out of recycled parts and tools. The windows were tinted enough so that Sloane couldn't see in them at this time of night. Was he bringing her to . . . a hardware store?

"I've never been here. What is it?" There were always new stores cropping up in the area, and Sloane could never keep up with the latest buzz.

He shot her a smile, one that made his entire face light up. She didn't think she'd ever seen him so excited over something.

"Let's head in and find out."

Banging and clanging rang out when Reece opened the door for Sloane. The shop was tiny, with cement floors and wood beams crisscrossing along the ceiling.

Several people sat at canvas-covered worktables, pounding nails into boards. Some were painting; others were stringing together beads on thin black strings.

A woman with large gauges in her ears and bright red curls pulled back in a bandanna greeted them from behind the main counter. "Welcome to Club DIY, where you can make your own special project. Do you have reservations?"

Reece nodded. "Should be under Jenkins, party of two."

The woman's long red fingernail tapped against the screen as she scanned her iPad. "Yep. Looks like we have you down. If you look at the sheet here, you can pick a project that you're interested in. They go by difficulty level and time it'll take to complete."

"Thanks," he said, and he pulled Sloane closer. She liked how she fit under Reece's arm. Secure. Safe. Wanted. All things she'd craved but didn't expect to experience so soon.

The woman set down the iPad and grabbed her knitting needles and yellow yarn, and she started in on what Sloane assumed was a scarf. "Just let me know when you've decided, and I'll get you set up."

Sloane glanced around again, eyeing the rainbow array of paints in one corner, the bins of tools in another. "This is a really cool place."

"I thought you might like it." He practically puffed up with pride.

"Don't look so smug. It's unbecoming." Okay, she totally loved this. She could make a new piece to add to her collection.

His lips twitched. He was obviously pleased with his choice. And he should be, because this place was exactly what Sloane would pick. She scanned the list of items to make. She went back and forth between the painted piece of barnyard wood that could spell out any phrase she chose and the nail and yarn sign. Either one would be perfect to hang in her apartment.

After a few more moments of scanning the options, she asked, "What are you going for?" She was surprised Reece had picked something like this, since she knew of his inclination for bare walls.

He pointed to the list and said, "The nail yarn one."

"I think I'm going to paint."

Reece waved the employee over, and she helped get them set up at the table. It was a tough, weathered canvas table with long reams of construction paper draped over it for protection. Lacquered wooden benches were on either side of the table. Each one could hold at least eight people, and there were six more tables like it in the shop. All the other tables were taken. There were a few groups of women, a pair of couples, and the far corner was filled with a bridal party wearing BRIDE SQUAD sashes.

Sloane took off her hat and coat and laid them over her purse on the bench. With all the bodies in the tiny space, the shop was warm and cozy, and it had the calming scent of paint and sawdust. It reminded her of her parents with their home improvement projects, spending lazy Sundays in the garage, working with their hands.

After the woman gave them their instruction packets, Sloane and Reece made their way to the bar in the corner of the shop. The bar top was made from recycled wood, and the barstools were pieced together with an array of little pieces of metal.

"IPA good for you?"

"Yeah." She liked this. That he already knew her drink of choice. In some ways, there was no guesswork when it came to Reece. The part where she knew his likes, his dislikes. And then there was this whole new side of him that she was still figuring out. The one with the wicked tongue who saved her from bad dates and took her to places like this. "How did you think of this place?"

He ordered the two beers and carried them back to the table.

"Heard about it from one of my friends."

"Your friend has good taste."

He took a long pull from his beer and set it down, his thumb streaking down the condensation of the glass. "Listen, I'm kind of new to this. The whole going-on-a-date thing. But I'm glad I'm doing it with you."

Sloane's lips pulled into a grin that hurt her cheeks. She could give him a hard time, say something that would be a jab, but that didn't feel right. Not after they'd been getting along so well lately. "Me too. Besides the date with Aaron, this is the first one I've been on since I broke it off with Brian."

His lips curled like he didn't even enjoy the mention of her ex. "He was an idiot."

Sloane nodded. "He was. But hey, not everyone can be as awesome as us." She lifted up her beer, and he clinked her glass.

"To not being idiots," he said.

They both took a sip.

Something about this felt so odd, like she'd rolled out of bed using the left side instead of the right. And yet, it was like she'd been dating him for years, and going to swanky art places and drinking good beer was a normal thing they did. She kind of wanted it to be.

After deciding on a slogan she wanted to put on her piece of wood, she looked at the paint options on the floor-to-ceiling shelving unit on the other side of the shop. After picking out indigos, blues, and greens, she carried the jars and brushes back to the table.

"What are you making?"

"I think I'm going to paint 'Home Is Wherever the Hell You Want It to Be.'"

He laughed, and his dimples appeared. Her heart sputtered in her chest. Reece was flat-out gorgeous when he dropped the grumpy facade. "It has a certain ring to it."

She glanced over at his design. "You're making a dog?" From what she could tell of the template, it was a smaller dog, his tail sticking straight up in the air.

"Peaches will love it. Although I might add a little puddle under the dog to make it more realistic."

She giggled. "I'm glad you two are getting along so well."

"A lot has changed lately, that's for sure." He glanced over to her, his eyes searching hers.

Sloane couldn't help but feel like he wasn't just talking about the dog.

Reece was sweating. His hands were clammy, which didn't help with the hammering. He was forty nails into his seemingly endless project. He didn't think he'd be nervous taking Sloane out. He'd purposefully picked a place that didn't feel like a date. He knew Sloane would appreciate that. She'd said as much when she had mentioned that the French restaurant was stuffy. With the luck she'd had on dating sites, he just wanted her to have a good experience. And for him not to be lumped into the same categories as those guys. He didn't even know why this felt important, but it did.

"How's it going at the hospital?" *Come on, man. That's the best you can do?*

He was running out of things to talk about. And was it over a hundred degrees in this place? He tugged at the collar of his shirt and took another sip of beer.

"The hospital?" She gave him an odd look. "I guess it's fine." She set down her paintbrush and turned to him. "Reece."

He swallowed hard. He deserved to deck himself in the face for making this awkward. But it was like civilians at a fire. They couldn't help but stare in horror while the whole building went up in flames. And here he was holding the Zippo. "Yeah."

She let out a deep breath that ruffled the blue yarn he'd set between them on the table. "I'm nervous."

He caught her glance out of the corner of his eye. "Yeah?"

"I don't usually do small talk. I like that we know each other. I already know the little annoying things about you." She continued swirling her brush on her canvas, the sky in her painting a deep blue.

"I think you meant to say amazing."

She rolled her eyes at this.

He continued. "I'm nervous too. I'm sweating all over this stupid hammer."

She giggled, and the sound pulsed deep in his gut. He liked to see her smile. Gave him the same adrenaline kick that happened every time he was dispatched to a fire. Maybe even more so.

"There. See." She pointed the paintbrush at him. "You can make a joke out of anything. I like that about you. So let's save the 'Oh crap, I've run out of things to talk about' stuff for another time."

"You're right. There's really no need to be nervous when we both know I'm going to make the better art project."

She scoffed and made another stroke across her canvas. "Says the person who draws stick figures."

"Hey, at least they're anatomically correct."

She shook her head, and they fell into an easy rhythm, one where Reece didn't feel the need to bring up small talk for the rest of the evening. Instead, they created a happy balance of goading and comfortable silence. Just being next to Sloane, breathing in her rose scent, put him at ease. Watching her hands work across the canvas, her tongue peeking past her lips as she concentrated on each stroke, squeezed something in his chest. He could watch her do this all night. And, in between hammering and wrapping yarn around nails, he did.

Two hours later, they held up their pieces of art.

His was a dog that closely resembled Peaches. And he had, in fact, added a tiny blue puddle underneath. "I have to admit, this came out better than I was expecting," he said.

"You're just really good at nailing things, huh?"

He raised a brow. She really just walked into that one. "I haven't had any complaints yet."

She rolled her eyes but smiled. "On that note, I think I'm ready to hang this up in my apartment. Care to help me?"

Chapter Twenty-Four

Sloane slid her key into the lock of her apartment, not quite ready for this night to be over. Reece held on to her painting while she shucked off her coat and hat and hung them on the coatrack.

"I think I want to put it above my bed."

Yep, she was leading him straight to her bedroom. If she were psychoanalyzing the reasons behind this, she might come up with something like:

- She wanted to know what all the fuss was about.
- He was good with his tongue. She wanted to see what the rest of him could do.
- She might have been catching the f-word. The nondirty one.

Feelings.

She swallowed hard and led him to the narrow hallway that ended at her bedroom.

Reece blew out a low whistle behind her, his breath ruffling the hair against her neck. "Your room's so . . . colorful."

She took a look around. To her, it was home. All the blues and purples of the paintings, the vases and books stacked by color instead of by author. She had a rainbow in her room. "See? I told you I went easy on your apartment."

"My mom loves what you've done, by the way. Although I still get shit for having throw pillows from the guys."

"They're just jealous. Plus, I know for a fact Erin will put all sorts of decorations in Jake's house whenever they decide to tie the knot."

"Hey, what's this?" Reece strode over to her nightstand. He lifted up the pamphlet from the firefighter auction.

She didn't want to admit the truth about why she'd kept it. At first, it'd been a nice reminder of how she had Reece just where she wanted him. And now, it was because this was what had brought them together.

"That?" She snatched the pamphlet. "Oh, nothing. Guess I forgot to throw it away." She set it down on her dresser.

"A month after the fact?"

She sighed. "Fine. I keep mementos, okay?"

"Nothing wrong with having something that reminds you of me in your bedroom. I can think of other things, though."

She swallowed hard. Oh yes. She'd like that. She'd been thinking about it all night.

"The painting." He lifted it. "Jeez, what did you think I meant? Get your mind out of the gutter, and stop objectifying me, Sloane." He gave her a wicked grin. One that promised everything she'd been desiring for the past week. She wanted his lips on her again. Everywhere.

Ass. "Not even dignifying that with an answer."

He jutted his chin to the painting he still held. "Do you have a hammer and a couple nails?"

"Yeah, they're in the hall closet." She left Reece in her room while she disappeared into the hallway to grab the supplies. She held the hammer in her hand and took a deep, shaky breath.

What are you doing?

Did she really just invite Reece into her bedroom to hang a painting? Even to her untrained dating eyes she could see how desperate this looked. But at the moment, she didn't care.

She came back into the bedroom and found Reece sitting on her bed. His bottom lip was hooked between his teeth, and he clasped his hands between his spread legs. The painting was set next to him. Both were nice additions to the room.

She cleared her throat, and he immediately shot up, looking as if he'd been doing something wrong by being there. She wondered if he had ever just lain in a woman's bed and *not* screwed around. According to the women in her nursing unit . . . no.

That thought was a cold splash of water to the desire coursing through her veins. He'd been with her friends. The people she worked with. And treated them as nothing more than passing mile markers on the interstate. Would he . . . do the same to her? She tried to shove that thought out of her head and handed him the hammer and nails.

He kicked off his shoes and stood on the bed, grabbing the painting with one hand and the hammer with the other while biting a nail between his teeth.

Five minutes later, there were two new holes in the wall above her bed and a freshly dried painting. "How does it look?" he asked, straightening the frame.

"Good." But all she could look at was the way his thick legs fit in his jeans. The sliver of exposed skin on his back where his shirt rode up as he reached for the top of the painting. She wanted to glide her hands over his skin, for her fingers to trail around to the front of his jeans. She wanted her fingers to slip underneath them, to his boxers, until they met the one part of Reece she'd never seen before.

"I can feel your objectifying eyes on me again." He turned around and found her staring at him.

"That would require me to be interested enough to objectify you." Okay, she totally was.

"Yeah, I'm calling bullshit on that one. It's okay to stare. I know I'm a lot of man to handle." He grinned.

"Full of yourself much?" She was so far out of her depth here. Because, really, she was debating the proper protocol for begging for great oral sex again. That was where her mind was headed. And there came the nerves again. She thought she'd been nervous at Club DIY, but right now, her hands were shaking, and her heart was pounding enough that she seriously questioned if she was going into a cardiac episode. "I think I'm going to need some wine. Do you want any?"

"Sure." He followed her out to the kitchen, and she grabbed a bottle of wine out of the fridge and a corkscrew from the silverware drawer.

Her fingers fumbled to open the bottle of wine, but she managed to get the cork out without breaking it.

Just wine. Just Reece. No need to freak out.

She took a deep, calming breath. *In, out. In, out.* Then her thoughts went in a completely different direction because even her inner monologue wasn't safe from her teenage-boy mind.

As she reached to pour the wine into the glasses, her sleeve caught the bottle, and it bounced on its side on the counter, splashing Reece. Huge red drops went everywhere. On his shirt, his stomach, even a few on his pants.

"Oh no. I'm sorry." She raced for a towel and dabbed the front of his shirt, but the fabric was blooming red with the wine. "Crap, that's going to stain."

He shrugged. "It's just a shirt."

"Take it off. I'll throw it in the wash real quick." She motioned to him to hurry. She'd had enough wine spills over the years to know that the quicker something was washed, the more promising the outcome.

"Is this all part of your master plan to get me naked? I promise you just have to ask."

"I'd kick you out, but I don't think your head will fit through my door."

"Guess that means you're stuck with me." Playful hazel eyes looked up at her, followed by a smirk. He unfastened his shirt, making quick work of the buttons, and then handed it to Sloane. Her mouth went dry. As a nurse, Sloane saw all kinds of bodies. Small ones, larger ones, skinny ones, muscular ones. And in her seven years she'd never seen a chest that made her want to salivate.

He stood in front of her, his bare chest inches from her touch. His pecs were dusted with sandy-blond hair. More hair started at the bottom of his navel and disappeared into the band of his dark jeans.

She grabbed his shirt and moved out of the kitchen to the laundry closet and shoved it in the washer, giving her hands something to do.

Reece had found a spot on the couch when Sloane got back to the living room. He looked so large on the sofa that comfortably fit her and her two friends. The muscles in his broad shoulders bunched as he propped his arms on the back of her couch. Her gaze laser-focused on his biceps and sinewy forearms corded with veins.

She stopped, barely able to breathe. A low hum coursed through her veins, heading straight to the space between her thighs. It throbbed in a rhythm akin to an SOS message: *Must. Mount. Sexy. Firefighter.*

She hadn't been with a man in more than a year. Hadn't even thought the possibility was near, not by a long shot.

"Something you see pique your interest?"

If someone had looked at her with *her* shirt off, she'd try to cover up every inch of exposed skin. Reece was sitting there, welcoming the stare. "It seems like it's pretty run-of-the-mill firefighter stuff. I mean, aren't you all loaded with muscles?"

Of course this was a lie. Reece was gorgeous. The type who would make women do a double take on the street and say, *Dayum.* With a body completely covered in tattoos from shoulder to elbows, collarbone to pecs, that wasn't a surprise. Her eyes and hands would be busy for days exploring. Her eyes flicked to the disjointed scorpion with the fading red scar. The wound she'd stitched.

"I think we both know you're lying. You know how I know?" He put out his hand, an invitation to sit next to him. She took it, and he led her down to the spot next to him. The wine had gotten to her. Even if she'd had only three sips, and a beer a couple of hours ago, it still must be the alcohol.

"How?"

"You have a tell. Do yourself a favor and never play poker."

"What's my tell?"

"Right here." He looked at her for a long moment and then leaned in. The scent of his shampoo and body wash enveloped her, putting her into an even deeper fog. His lips moved to the corner of her lips. Just a light graze. Every inch of her skin lit up, waiting for more. "You tip your lip down when you're lying." He dragged his bottom lip across the skin of her cheek line. "And your cheeks turn a delicious shade of red."

"They do not."

But she didn't doubt it. Her body felt flush. With something that she felt acutely between her thighs. It pulsed there, almost painfully.

"Sloane, if you want it, I'll strip off every single stitch of clothing from your body and make you forget your own name."

"I—I can't."

His mouth turned into a wicked grin. "You say one thing, but your eyes say something completely different."

"And what do they say?"

His mouth moved to her ear, his warm breath caressing, sending a shiver down her spine. "That you want me. That you'd beg for me. To fill you." He pressed against her harder. "To bury myself deep inside you until you scream my name."

And she felt the evidence of what he could do, thick and swollen against her. She fought back a shudder.

"I can't." Because she couldn't. She couldn't give him what he wanted because that was what every other woman in her unit had done, and they'd ended up as one-night stands. Sloane didn't work that way.

"I'm patient. I'll wait." He pulled away, not pressuring her. If he had, she might have caved.

Damn it. Why did he have to be such a good guy? It'd make it a lot easier to kick him out of her apartment. Every single cell screamed to take her refusal back. But she was choking. It was like those horrible instant replays of a football game where a player missed a game-changing pass, the ball slipping through his fingers. Her body was the bewildered fans in the stands yelling, *What the crap, lady? You had a perfect pass thrown to you. Take it to the end zone.* Even if her body was completely ready for him to make good on his promise, her brain just wasn't on the same wavelength. Yet. And she wanted every part of her to be ready for Reece. Because she knew Reece would be worth it. The good guy who'd been protective of her and Erin as kids. That guy she once knew had been gone for more than a decade, dating around. Now, it was like the fog had lifted, and the old Reece shone through.

"I'm feeling kinda tired." *Ugh.* Would Reece think she was a total loon if she smacked herself right now? She was such a chicken. And she wanted to take it back as soon as the words popped out of her mouth.

"No problem. You know where to find me." He smiled that knee-buckling grin and made his way to the coatrack and pulled on his jacket without a shirt underneath. He gave her one lingering kiss that curled her toes, and then he left.

As soon as she locked the dead bolt, she let out a groan. *Idiot.* She was so completely stupid.

She pressed her head against the door. Seriously, what was wrong with her? Right now she could be well on her way to O-Town, and instead, she'd kicked him out because of his past indiscretions. It was for the best, though. She didn't want to be someone's one-night stand. Didn't think her heart could handle it. That was Reece's MO. So she did what she always had. Shut it down before it could become an issue.

A couple hours later, Sloane moved to her bedroom and flopped down on her bed. She turned over and pulled out her phone and pulled up a picture of Reece from his profile. One of him at North Fork River with Jake. He had his shirt off, and water droplets were beading down his chest. A huge grin was plastered across his face. Sloane's heart lurched.

She needed to get laid so bad it physically hurt now.

Her fingers slid down and under her panties. She continued to look at the picture of Reece. Of what the powerful body would feel like over her own. How it'd crush her. How it'd completely fill her.

Her index finger found the spot that always promised release and glided over the slickness. She could still hear Reece's words in her head. The promise of filling her, teasing her until she didn't even know her name. She didn't doubt it.

No matter where her fingers went, she couldn't find release. What was this fresh hell? She'd never had an issue before. Maybe Reece had broken her. Filled her with so much need that not even her honed skills would allow her a release. Of course he'd ruin this for her. He ruined everything. Like how she now wanted the one person who just a few short weeks ago she claimed to have hated with every fiber of her being.

No. He was not going to ruin this for her. And damn it. She wanted him. It was time to stop being scared of taking it to the next level. She threw on her clothes and boots and went out the door, ready to chase the Holy Grail: the Reece Promised Land.

Reece took a deep breath as soon as he made it out of Sloane's apartment. It'd been one of the harder things he'd had to do in the past few weeks. He'd always respect a woman. There were no ifs, ands, or buts about that. Still, now he needed a cold shower. He walked down the block and made it to his apartment. Back to the apartment that had become more of a home since Sloane had come busting into his life.

Once inside, he stood in the doorway and gave Peaches a rub on the head. His keys clanked on the counter as he threw them aside to riffle through his mail. Anything to keep his mind off Sloane. But everywhere he looked was a reminder of her. From the stupid throw pillows he liked but would never admit to his friends, to the new rug that Peaches was rolling on. He had a damn hard-on staring at a carpet. Something was obviously wrong with him.

He looked around the room to find anything that would distract him.

TV. That was a smart choice. If he drowned out his thoughts with *SportsCenter*, even better. He could focus on stats. That was easy enough.

Each second dragged for the next few hours, and he kept staring at his phone, thinking that maybe Sloane would text him. The only person who messaged him was his mom, asking him to come over to help with fixing the barbecue. By midnight, his keyed-up body had finally calmed down.

"Ready to go to bed, girl?" He'd already taken Peaches out to go to the bathroom, and she was now cuddled in his lap. A month ago, he'd get a hernia from laughing so hard if someone told him he'd be the foster parent to an incontinent dog while sitting in a fully decorated apartment. Now, he couldn't picture his life any other way.

Reece had just drifted off to sleep when a knock came from the door. Not gentle taps, but full-on pounding. He glanced at his clock and saw that it was one in the morning. More pounding came, and he was worried about what he might find on the other side of the door. It was never a good sign when someone came to the door that late.

"I'm coming!" he shouted. If anything, he didn't want the person to wake the other tenants on his floor.

He made his way out of bed, stumbling through the hallway. Peaches hadn't even gotten out of her doggy bed near the door of his bedroom. She sucked as a guard dog.

Just as another round of knocks came, he unlocked the door and swung it open.

Sloane stood on the other side, rosy-cheeked from the cold, out of breath.

"What are you doing here?" Was this a dream? He had just been dreaming about her, so it could be a possibility that this was just an extension of the dream. Except he could smell the pomegranate from her lip balm. And the shea butter from her lotion. Both scents he was never able to replicate without her presence.

"I can't stay away from you anymore," she said. "I want you so bad that I throb. Everywhere. I know you don't want anything serious, and I'm not looking for anything light, but damn it, I need you." Her voice was laced with need that sparked something in him.

It'd been a lie that he didn't want anything serious. A lie to Sloane, and one to himself. He just had a hard time admitting this aloud. Instead, he said, "You want me to fix that for you? Just say the word, and I'll do anything you want."

Her eyes were wild, unfocused. Like she really was at war with herself. He'd seen her earlier, how she didn't want to give in. He wanted to see all of her. Needed to devour her. Worship.

"Yes. Please, I need you, Reece."

Everything in him flexed. He was in boxer briefs, and it did nothing to hide his reaction to her words.

"Well, I hoped you'd show up sooner or later." He'd wanted that, at least. He thought that she might text him back, until he finally gave up checking his phone a little after midnight. He groaned at the thought that he'd turned into the guy who stared at his text messages. Sloane had flipped a switch in his brain.

"I'm here. What do you plan to do with me?"

"Everything." His mouth was on her as he guided her inside and closed the door behind her. "And you're sure you're fine with this?"

She looked at him, and this time there was no hesitation in her gaze as she said, "Yes."

That was all he needed. He'd show Sloane just how much he wanted her. For so damn long.

He grabbed her and pulled her to him.

Reece's hands found their way to Sloane's hair. The pounding on the door had woken him out of a dead sleep. A dream where he was on Sloane. In Sloane. He still didn't know if this was a dream. She looked up at him, eyes full of want and need, and he didn't care if this was real or not. He wanted to live in this dreamworld forever.

His hands moved down her body, skimming over her curves. She was soaked, her jacket plastered to her. He moved to unzip it, and it fell to the floor with a small *thud*. She looked beautiful, her hair matted to her face like she'd just stepped out of the shower.

Her fingers found their way to his chest, smoothing over him, raking down his stomach, down to cup his cock.

He bit back a groan as she stroked him. Strong, bold strokes that set off a fireworks display behind his lids. He hissed a breath through his teeth.

They were standing in the middle of the living room. He'd take her right here, he wanted her so bad, but Sloane deserved better. He gripped her hips and, in one fluid motion, threw her over his shoulder, her legs kicking in front of him.

"Oh my God, you're such a barbarian," she said, but there was a lightness in her voice that indicated she didn't mind.

"They don't call it a fireman carry for nothing." He smacked her ass. "And I know you like it, so don't even try denying it."

Her silence confirmed his suspicion.

"You're mine for tonight, Sloane. I plan to devour every inch of your skin." He gently placed her on his bed and hovered above her.

She gazed up at him, eyes registering both desire and panic. That was how he was feeling at the moment. Because if she got up and left, he'd be devastated. He'd let her go, of course. But he wanted this. Wanted to taste every inch of her skin more than anything.

After a long moment, she said, "Okay." She let out a deep breath. "Only if I get to do the same."

"I'm nothing if not fair."

She rolled her eyes, but this time she didn't look so scared.

His hand slid under her shirt, grabbing the hem. Her stomach dipped, but she didn't tell him to stop like she'd done before. He caught her gaze and raised a brow. She nodded.

He pulled the shirt over her head and threw it to the floor. Tattoos bracketed each hip, one of a rose and one of a shooting star. The ink disappeared under her jeans, and Reece was desperate for more. He'd never felt this urgency before, like his next breath depended on what lay beneath, to see every inch of Sloane's skin.

Patience. He had all night. He'd devour her. But he'd take his time, show her exactly what she deserved.

He looked at her lace bra, her breasts spilling over the cups with every deep breath. His fingers found the clasp and unhooked it, sliding her arms out of the straps and tossing the bra on top of her shirt.

His mouth moved down the column of her throat, down her chest, to one of her pebbled nipples. He took it in his mouth, and she writhed beneath him. Her eyes scrunched shut, and her mouth parted. The sounds that came out of Sloane's mouth were the sexiest thing he'd ever heard. Made him rock-hard.

He moved lower, kissing down her stomach, moving his lips over every dip and swell. Sloane had curves for days. Perfectly soft curves that he could bury himself in.

"I need you." Her fingers raked down his back, urgent and needy. "Right now."

And so he obliged.

Chapter Twenty-Five

Sloane fought to keep her breathing at a somewhat normal level as Reece hovered between her thighs.

"Please, Reece." She'd resorted to begging. One more lick from him and she'd be a goner. But she wanted more than this. She ached for him to be inside of her, to feel the fullness that he'd provide. It'd been over a year, and she wanted to be properly bedded, to end this dry spell.

He moved up the bed until he was on his elbows, taking her bottom lip between his teeth.

"Tell me what you want. I'll give it to you."

Was it bad that she didn't know exactly what she wanted? Just that she wanted Reece in her. Pronto. Half of her body screamed, *This is a bad idea! Abort mission!* And the other half said, *Bitch, that other half's brain is rotted from not enough action.* True story: she hadn't had sex in more than a year and quite possibly had cobwebs for a vagina. In fact, spooky crypt-opening sounds might actually happen if she spread her legs wide enough.

She shifted her gaze to the nightstand next to his bed and shuddered at the picture of Blake Shelton staring back at her. "Can we, uh, put the pictures away for a little while?"

Reece chuckled. "Yeah." He shoved the photos into his nightstand and pulled out a condom.

His Adam's apple slid down the column of his throat as he regarded her with such intensity that Sloane's whole body flushed.

"Smurfette, I can't wait any longer." Their gazes met, him asking silent permission.

She nodded.

He ripped open the foil and rolled on the condom. Just a year ago, she'd wished him to do the very same thing. Had begged him, even. And she was so glad that he'd turned her down then. Because she had been too drunk to savor this moment. The look in his eyes as he lowered himself to press against her entrance.

"You don't know how long I've wanted this," he said. He pushed inside her, filling her. "Shit," he growled.

His jaw tensed, and he stilled above her. He looked down at her with adoring eyes.

"Sloane, I've thought about this since high school. When I shouldn't have been thinking about you. I've wanted you for a long time."

He plunged deeper into her, and her head knocked back into the pillow. So good. Every inch of him sent a wave of ecstasy through her.

"You're the sexiest thing I've ever seen." He grabbed her legs and pulled them over his shoulders and slid all the way to the base of his cock.

It was too much. So many sensations. Sloane screwed her eyes shut, fighting for control.

"Open your eyes, Smurfette. I want you to watch me while I'm inside you."

Dear Lord. She might combust. She was ready to even before he set his hands on her. Now he was looking at her with that intense gaze that made her want to melt into the mattress.

Her legs shook as he quickened his pace.

And then his hand slid down her leg, and the pad of his thumb moved to stroke her clit. Sloane nearly levitated off the bed, and a moan escaped her lips. She was climbing higher toward release.

His gaze caught hers, and there was something in his eyes that told her that this was not like his previous relationships. There was trust there.

"So perfect." His mouth was on her, and her whole body quaked as she went over the edge, her world bottoming out. Reece followed shortly after, her name on his lips.

Thirty minutes later, they'd gone a second time, and Sloane was officially too tired to move.

Reece had it wrong. Sloane was far from perfect. But as she lay on his chest drifting off to sleep, she decided this moment was perfection.

Sloane woke up the next morning to the smell of bacon and pancakes. She opened one eye and found Reece's side of the bed empty. She smiled at the thought that Reece was checking off so many of her goals for next year before Christmas even rolled around.

She pulled on his flannel shirt and smiled at the fact that it went clear down to her knees.

Reece was in the kitchen, shirtless, flipping pancakes while Peaches stood on her hind legs, trying to get to the food on the counter. He eyed Sloane as she came in and sat on the kitchen counter, his pupils dilating, nostrils flaring. "Come out here looking like that, and breakfast won't get finished."

She rolled her eyes but smiled.

"I've been thinking," he said.

She snagged a piece of bacon off the counter and took a bite. "Does your brain hurt now?"

He flicked a glob of batter at her, and it landed on her calf. "Smart-ass. Are you going to let me say what I was thinking?"

She motioned for him to continue.

"I'm not one to go with official names or classification. I think I missed that whole lecture in eighth-grade science. But what I do know is that I don't want to stop doing this."

"I feel the same." She grabbed a paper towel from the dispenser on the counter and wiped off her leg before Peaches could get to it first.

"Also, did that end my auction obligations to you? Because I feel like I might have earned it with that last one. Plus, you have only a few more days until your last chore expires."

Sloane bit off a piece of bacon. "We'll see."

The sun streaked in through the window above the sink, casting a glow around Reece. After what he'd done to her last night, it wasn't a far stretch to claim he was otherworldly. She glanced behind him to the sunny weather outside. Much brighter than her normal 6:00 a.m. wake-up. "Crap. What time is it?" she asked.

He glanced at his watch. "Nine thirty. Why?"

She'd slept in longer than she had in a long time. Probably because they hadn't actually gone to bed until a little after three. Even still, she felt completely rested, her body sated. "I need to get ready for work, and then I have to pack for my girls' trip this weekend." Normally she was fine with packing thirty minutes before taking off for a trip, but Erin had put her on chocolate-and-entertainment duty. Which meant that she needed to swing by her parents' house and pick up some board games.

"Where are you going?" Reece flipped a pancake, and Sloane couldn't help but stare at the sinewy muscles that corded up his forearms. The scar on his shoulder.

"We're going to the coast. Usually we go down to Shasta, but since Erin's living in town now, we don't need to travel so far." All she knew was that Erin had booked them a little cottage at Cannon Beach. And after last night, she wasn't as excited as she had been to get away from it all. She wanted to jump back into bed and burrow under the covers, memorize the smell of Reece's pillow.

His lips found the sensitive flesh behind her ear and gave it a light kiss. Her eyes fluttered shut. She could get used to this. "When are you coming back?"

"Aw, it's so cute how you're already missing me, and I'm not even gone yet." She had to admit that it was nice how normal this felt. Brian had never once made breakfast for her in the ten years they'd been together. She'd never needed to be taken care of. Prided herself on that. But when it came to Reece, she liked that he went the extra step. It made her feel . . . special.

"You know, that mouth of yours is going to get you into trouble." He gave her ass a swat with the spatula, and she proceeded to smear batter on his bare chest. Which then led to showering off together and breakfast being very burned.

Sloane could have stayed there all day, but she needed to head back to her apartment and change before her shift at noon. She stood on her tippy-toes, and Reece's hands smoothed down her sides as he bent down for a kiss.

She pulled back and fought the shiver shimmying up her spine. Decidedly, it would never get old tasting him. "Thanks for breakfast. And . . . you know, last night and everything."

He grinned down at her. "I'll see you when you get back."

Chapter Twenty-Six

Since Reece had the day off, he decided to make his way to his mother's house. He hadn't made an appearance in more than a week and figured his mom would start worrying if he stayed away any longer. With her turn-of-the-century bungalow, the to-do list to keep the property functioning was never-ending. She'd seemed to ease up on the tasks since Erin had come home. Something about all three of the siblings in the same town had quieted her need to tend to home projects.

He pulled into the driveway and cut the engine, staring at the peeling yellow paint. It had seen better days, and Reece made a mental note to get exterior paint once the weather let up.

Finding the key on his key ring, he opened the door to find his mother bustling around the kitchen.

She wiped a rubber-gloved hand over her forehead and smiled. "How are you, sweetheart?"

He strode into the kitchen and put an arm around his mom, giving her a kiss on the top of her head.

"Good. Just running a few errands." He had to pick up some more dog food for Peaches and wanted to grab baking supplies so he could coax Sloane into making her peanut butter oatmeal cookies when she got back into town.

"You seem happier today. Something happen?"

"Same shit, different day." Though that wasn't the truth. He hadn't felt like this since high school. The hope that love was still real and fresh. That hope had been extinguished for years. And he was fine with that. He'd resigned himself to the fact that he probably would never find *the one*. That the thought of that was an illusion only fools dreamed up.

"Is that why you have so much pep in your step?"

Reece shook his head. *Nope.* Not even his mother's needling would get to him today.

"If you must know, I met someone."

"Sloane." His mom shrugged, like this was old news. He hadn't told *anyone* about last night. How was this even possible?

"What? How did you know that?"

"First, do you expect anyone in this family to keep their mouth shut when it comes to someone's love life? Second, because the last time you were together in a room, you wanted to murder each other. And Erin claimed that you asked her for date ideas." She smacked Reece on the arm. "I may be getting older, but my eyes work just fine. Plus, this makes for great fodder online."

"Don't you dare post anything. And remind me to never tell Erin anything anymore."

"Fine. You're no fun." She playfully tugged at the shell of his ear, something she'd been doing since before he could walk. "But it brings me so much joy that you're so happy."

He shrugged, trying to play it off cool. If anything, he was about as cool as his middle-school self when he'd decided bleached tips were a good idea. "It might not be anything."

"Is that what you really think?"

He took a moment to consider his mom's question. "I don't know." And he didn't. It was so new that he didn't even want to breathe a word about it because it seemed like such a fragile thing. Something that might crumble in his hands if he mentioned it.

"I know I asked you to help with the barbecue, but will you help me with this light bulb? It went out in the mudroom."

He went to the pantry, grabbed a light bulb, and headed toward the mudroom in the back of the house.

"Maybe you should invite her over for dinner. Maybe we could all go out as a family."

"Mom." He loved her. Fiercely. But the way she meddled made him almost regret that he'd said anything at all.

She held up her hands. "Just saying. Sloane comes over anyway. It wouldn't be a big deal."

"I'll think about it." That seemed to appease his mother because she smiled and started back into the kitchen. "And you should start thinking about a Christmas gift. Not that she's your girlfriend or anything," she called over her shoulder.

His fingers fumbled with the light bulb, and he caught it before it could crash to the floor. *Damn it.* Christmas was in a week. He hadn't even thought about that. Did people who didn't classify their relationship need to get gifts for each other? Then again, this wasn't a normal person he'd just met on a dating site. This was Sloane. He'd known her his whole life.

"I don't think it's gotten to that stage yet. Don't you think that's a bit sudden?" he called after her.

His mom poked her head back into the room and gave him a perfectly arched brow.

Well, okay, then. What did he know, anyway? He hadn't dated seriously for more than a decade, which meant that he was probably a little rusty.

"Fine. I'll look into it."

Maybe.

He didn't like all these expectations that came from a relationship. Which was why he'd kept things casual for years. Was it really worth all the hassle if he had to deal with stuff like this?

For Sloane, he didn't even have to think about the answer. It was a resounding yes.

Before he made his way out of the house, he peeked into Andie's room. She was lying on her bed, earbuds in, probably listening to more terrible music. He knocked on the doorframe, and she bolted upright, tearing out an earbud.

"I just got back from the shelter. Mark says hi."

Reece smiled. He'd never had a doubt his sister could get back into college, but this was a big step toward. He liked to see her initiative. "Did you hear anything back from"—he peered over his shoulder to make sure his mom wasn't listening—"you know?"

"Not yet. Although I heard of one person posting online that they've already heard back from colleges, and they submitted at the same time." She frowned.

"It'll happen. Keep a little faith."

Andie's eyes bugged. "Was that in your fortune cookie or something?"

He shrugged. "I'm trying out the whole optimism thing."

"Oh, not you too." She groaned and flopped back down on her bed.

If this was what being with the right person felt like, then he never wanted it to end.

Sloane pulled up her social media app and scrolled through the noise of people shouting into the void. As a rule, she often took breaks from all her accounts because she tended to get worn out by all the horrible news each day. She dealt with enough sadness at the hospital. She even saw recently that there was a term for this. Normally people had a fear of missing out, or FOMO, but now with all the shitstorms in the media, people were retreating into their safe havens and enjoying some much needed JOMO—joy of missing out.

She noticed a new post from Erin and Reece's mom @ hotmamajenkins:

> Just want to say that my son has been acting WEIRD lately. I don't know what's up with him, but I think there is a new lady in his life.
>
> It all started last night. He was humming while helping set the dinner table. HUMMING, people. I don't think I've heard him sing a song since he was in high school.
>
> And then, this morning, he swung by before his shift and brought me doughnuts from my favorite bakery. Something is up with him, and I'm going to get to the bottom of it.

This thread was from last week. There was another one from today. @hotmamajenkins:

> Found out what's going on with my son. GUYS. He has a girlfriend (title unconfirmed, but I am making it official), and he is like something out of a "Walking on Sunshine" music video.

Sloane's lips twitched. Oh, Mama Jenkins, you have no clue. Then again, neither did Sloane. It was one thing to throw barbs at each other. It was another to want to spend time with him. For him to make her smile. Which was happening with alarming frequency. A day away from Reece and she was already feeling the withdrawal symptoms.

She made her way to the bathroom, finished straightening her hair, and pulled her sweater over her head. After checking her suitcase two more times, she zipped it up, wheeled it to the door, and grabbed her keys. Figuring out whatever this was would have to wait because it was officially girls' weekend.

"Am I going to have to drag you away from Portland?" Erin looked up at Sloane like she was ready to tear her suitcase out of her hands and chuck it in the back of her car.

"I'm ready." What was this voodoo magic? She was reluctant to go on a girls' weekend retreat because she wanted to spend another night with Reece? Yeah, her pathetic meter was in the red.

"I have handcuffs if you need them," Madison offered, chucking her bag in the back of Erin's Prius.

Erin did a double take at Madison. "Do I even want to know why you have handcuffs on hand?"

Madison shrugged. "Just had a cop-themed photo shoot."

"Right." Sloane shook her head. "Let's stick to that."

Sloane slid into the front seat while Madison took the back, right behind her. "Did anyone check the traffic?" Madison asked.

"Already on it," Erin said. She pulled the GPS up on her phone, which was already set to their cabin destination. Sloane hid her smile, because of course her friend had checked ahead of time. "I'm ready for some beach time," she said.

"I'm surprised you're actually going to brave the water this time of year, California girl," said Sloane.

Erin held up a hand. "No one said anything about stepping foot into the water. I'm going to admire the majestic beauty from the comfort of my window." She pulled out onto the coastal highway.

Sloane was missing her parents right before the holidays, and a couple of days of hearing the ocean's waves would do her heart some good. As a kid, her parents had taken her to Newport every summer.

They'd load up on saltwater taffy, walk down the main street, and splash around in the water. After a bowl of clam chowder, they'd head home, and Sloane would fall asleep in the car before they even got out of the city.

Sloane slid her phone out of her purse and texted Reece that they were on their way, and she'd see him on Monday. It was an odd feeling. Knowing that just a month ago she couldn't stand to be in the same room with him. Now all she wanted was to be in his arms.

Reece: Drive safe. Have a good weekend.

She smiled. Damn it, she had that goofy grin on her face again.

"What's got you so happy?" Erin asked, glancing over as she shifted gears.

"Er—it's nothing." She clicked her phone so the screen turned off.

"Did the date go well with that dude? You never texted us about it. In fact, you've been MIA for almost a week, missy," said Madison.

"It went horrible. Worst date I think I've ever been on," she admitted. The date after that had been one for the record books, though.

"Then who's putting that smile on your face?"

Sloane didn't even hesitate. "Reece."

Erin let out a cackle, and Madison doubled over in the back seat.

"What's so funny?" Sloane looked at the two of them.

"We had a bet going for how long it'd take you two to get together. Better pay up, Madison." Erin reached her hand back toward her friend.

Madison sighed in the back and then scrounged up a ten and smacked it in Erin's palm.

She looked from Erin to Madison. "You bet actual money on me?"

"Of course. And I said a month from the firefighter auction. Madison said two."

"But—" Sloane started.

"How did we know? Because you two are more alike than you'd like to think."

She thought about Reece, his dedication to his job, the kindness he showed to patients, and the volunteering he did.

"Yeah, I guess things changed." She stared out the window at the flat farmland, the wineries and hops trellises, the pastures with cows and horses. Soon the terrain would change to the mountain range and then give way to the salt and brine of the coast.

"What changed?" Madison asked.

She toyed with her phone in her lap. "I realized he wasn't completely worthy of the wrath." Sure, he still drove her nuts, but that was Reece. That part of him was just one of the many things she was starting to find endearing.

Erin clutched the steering wheel and cackled. "Madison, hold me. The I-told-you-so is coming in strong."

Madison scoffed. "If you're not going to say it, I will. *Told. You. So.*"

Sloane shook her head but smiled. "Yeah, you're both jerks."

By early afternoon, they'd made it to Cannon Beach. It was one of those unicorn days at the coast, where the wind was nonexistent and the salt air was warm. The sun was out, shining on Sloane's face as Erin parked her car in front of their rental cabin. It was a tiny blue cottage with wind-distressed white shutters. A gravel path led from the driveway to the cheery yellow front door. From the picture on the site, it had beach access, which was always a plus.

Sloane stepped out of the car and let the salt air tangle in her senses. She breathed deeply, enjoying the scent of the ocean. A group of seagulls flew overhead, cawing, and even though she couldn't currently see it, the waves rolling over the shore played like a loop in the background. Her parents had traded the Oregon coast for warm sandy beaches on the East Coast, but she didn't think anything beat a sunny day here.

Sloane opened the trunk and extracted her suitcase. "Ready to get set up?"

"Heck yes. I'm starving," Madison said.

"Dude. Didn't you just eat before we came?" Erin asked.

She'd seen the remnants of this morning's granola on Madison's shirt. She was the type to eat a bunch of small meals throughout the day. She said it helped with her metabolism.

"Would you rather have Madison hangry?" Sloane asked. Their best friend was one of the sweetest people Sloane had ever known. A bleeding heart. Until she got hungry. Then she turned into one of those Snickers commercials. And it was a toss-up between being pathetically whiny or slipping into Hulk-smash mode.

"Good point," Erin said.

They each grabbed grocery bags filled with snacks from the back seat, and Sloane retrieved the key that the owner had left in a potted plant next to the doormat.

Sloane pushed the door open with her foot and grabbed her bag at her feet. She smiled when she took in the cute tiled entryway. The main room had two couches, a TV, and a large wooden coffee table made out of driftwood. Their shoes slapped against the floor as they wheeled their luggage deeper into the house.

There were three bedrooms in this cabin, each one with its own theme. They scanned the rooms—one nautical, one with seashells, and one that reminded her of a forest. The walls were hunter green and adorned with wood carvings and frames made out of twigs, pine cones, and acorns.

"I'll take this room if that's okay with you guys," Sloane said, pointing to the forest-themed room.

Erin and Madison shrugged, and each took one of the other rooms.

Once they set their bags down, they unpacked chargers and Kindles. A few minutes later, they made their way down the road to the local brewery that they'd seen on their way to the cabin. When they opened the door to Peg Leg Jim's, rock music that could easily be the score to a *Pirates of the Caribbean* movie blasted through the speakers.

Once they were seated, Erin started in. She pulled out a sparkly green planner from her purse and flipped to an earmarked page. "I figured we'd first start with a walk down the beach. Then I saw online there was a wine shop less than a mile from our house. Maybe we can find something for tonight's dinner."

They went through this every. Single. Trip. No fail. Erin just needed a little nudge in the right direction. "Slow down there, Speed Racer. We are on vacation, right?" Sloane said. She liked doing things at her own pace on a trip.

Erin tapped her pen to her planner and worried her lip. "Well, yeah."

"How about we figure out what we want to do after the food gets here," Sloane suggested. She expected Madison to pipe in, but she was uncharacteristically quiet.

There was nothing she loved more than spending time with her girls. They'd been there for her through everything.

Erin closed her notebook and put it back in her purse. "Fine. Madison, what are you ordering?"

Madison was staring at the menu. Or more accurately, she was staring *through* the menu. Sloane worried that Madison had passed into what they'd deemed the no-coming-back zone.

"Is she too far gone?" Erin said.

"I think we can salvage this." Sloane grabbed a packet of saltine crackers from the container in the corner of the booth. "Here, eat these."

Madison grumbled, but she grabbed the package and inhaled the crackers. Ten more packages and Madison was starting to look human again. They even managed to get her to order when the server appeared.

Sloane rubbed Madison's back. "Welcome back to the living."

"Sorry. I obviously have not been getting enough to eat lately. Work has been so erratic, and I've been eating way too many of those protein bars."

The waitress came over and refilled their drinks and brought their meals. Sloane dug into her clam chowder and sighed. It was perfect, like usual.

The three of them lazed about the cabin for the remainder of the day. They'd made their way to the deck overlooking the Pacific. Erin had picked up a merlot from the wine shop and poured them each a glass.

Erin took a sip of wine. "It's weird not going to Shasta."

"No need to travel that far since you're home now."

"It feels good to be home," Erin said. "Even if Jake and I are still ships passing in the night lately."

Sloane kicked off her shoes and propped her feet on the balcony. "Maybe things will settle down after the holidays."

"Yeah. Plus, he's up to something. Twice now I've come into the kitchen, and he and Bailey stopped talking."

"Maybe it's a surprise," said Sloane.

Madison drained the rest of her glass and set it down on the weathered table. "Agreed. It has to be something good if he has Bailey involved. Maybe . . . something shiny and small that fits on a certain finger?"

Sloane would put money on it happening before the end of the year.

"It's possible, I guess. Or maybe they're both planning on the best way to dump me."

"He's not going to dump you," Sloane and Madison said in unison.

Busy schedules or not, there was no way Jake would be having second thoughts. They were gaga for each other. "You know what this calls for? Some extra wine. A preemptive celebration for when Madison and I can claim we told you so." Sloane grabbed the bottle and filled the three glasses back to an appropriate level for girls' weekend. "To nobody leaving town for years at a time. That includes you too, Madison."

Madison grabbed her full glass and cradled it in her palms. "Not a chance. You know I could never leave."

"To being stuck in Portland for the rest of our lives," Sloane said.

They all clinked their glasses together and said cheers. Each of them settled into their Adirondack chairs, enjoying the heat of the outdoor fireplace. The sun had set over the Pacific, and they were now left with a patchwork of stars blanketing the sky.

They were all quiet, and she didn't know what her friends were thinking about, but thoughts of Reece kept floating in and out of her mind, like the tide along the shore. Flashes of places she wanted to take him. Skiing at Hoodoo, paddleboarding in Bend, checking out new restaurants popping up in the city. Heck, she could make a list of activities for each season.

"Think we'll all still be doing this when we're ninety?" Madison asked.

Sloane didn't even have to think about it. These two had been with her through everything. If they could make it through zits and maxi pads, then adult diapers and hemorrhoids should be a breeze. "Um, is there really any question? I mean, if Erin doesn't give herself a heart attack by then."

"At least I have a nurse friend who can bring me back to health," Erin said, patting Sloane's thigh.

"We'll be like the Golden Girls," Madison said as she unwrapped a Hershey's Kiss and popped it into her mouth.

"I'd be Blanche," Sloane said.

Erin snorted. "No, you're definitely a Dorothy."

"Am not." Was she? Maybe she'd been that way for the past few years, but right now, the way she felt was light. Less snarky. Maybe that was what good sex did to you. It changed the wiring in a person's brain. She'd heard about cases in her clinical psychology stint where major life events could change certain synapses. Maybe Reece had bumped a few of those loose.

"Plus, I'm Blanche, and Erin is Rose," Madison said.

"Am not," Erin said.

Both Sloane and Madison exchanged glances. "Totally are," said Sloane. "And ninety seems like so far away."

Erin nodded. "Yeah. Feels like a whole lifetime."

"I want to travel the world by then," Madison said. "There is this cruise that goes down the Nile River. I want to do that and then see all the pyramids."

"I want to be retired and be a tester for planner supply products," Erin said. She let out a contented sigh.

Madison and Erin turned to her, waiting for Sloane to proclaim what she wanted to accomplish by then. "I want to fall in love by the time I'm ninety."

"Oh, honey. I think that's coming sooner than you think," Erin said.

Maybe. For the first time in a year, she gave herself permission to hope.

They all drank from their glasses and stared out at the ocean. The breeze was cool as it floated into their cozy cluster on the porch. The outdoor fireplace flickered, and Sloane fed it another log.

Maybe they were right. Reece had shown her that she didn't need to have her guard up around all men. That there were decent ones out there, ones who would make her feel wanted. Sexy. Things she hadn't felt in years.

Suddenly, Sloane felt the effect of all the wine she'd drunk tonight, her world going fuzzy around the edges, more topsy-turvy than she usually allowed. "I think I'm going to turn in for the night."

Erin yawned. "Me too. Just need to give Jake a call."

Sloane slipped inside her room and shut the door behind her with a soft click. She pulled out her phone and saw that she'd missed a few texts from Reece.

Reece: Where are you? I need to discuss the turn of events in Supernatural. Also, why did you pick a show with so many seasons?

Reece: Seriously, why are these brothers complete idiots when it comes to each other?

Reece: Miss you.

The last one made Sloane's lips curve into a smile.

Sloane: Didn't you know that people do really stupid things for the people that they love?

It was late—almost a quarter till midnight. She didn't expect Reece to answer. He usually fell asleep before eleven when he wasn't on his shift. It was strange thinking that she had picked up so many little tidbits about him over the past couple of weeks.

When she saw the three dots pop up onto her screen signifying that he was typing, her pulse raced under her skin.

Reece: Sam is a whiny bitch boy.

Sloane: I'm going to ignore that you just said that about my man.

Reece: Didn't know you were already claimed. Guess I should back off.

Sloane: Well, I guess I have been seeing this one guy. He's pretty accident prone, though.

Reece: Does this guy at least have someone to stitch him up? I know a nurse. She has horrible bedside manner. Takes way too much pleasure poking people with needles.

Sloane: Sounds like my kind of gal.

Reece: Me too.

She turned over in bed, resting her head on the pillow. The bed was too big for one person. Even starfished across the middle, her arms couldn't touch the sides.

Sloane: Wish you could be here.

Reece: And what would you do with me if I was?

Sloane giggled. And then hiccupped. She'd never sexted before. Usually if the person she was dating was in the mood, he'd say something like, "Hey, want to come over for some fun?" That was the end of that. Nothing romantic or sexy about it, but it did get the job done. Reece made her feel things. She wanted to be sexy. For him.

Sloane: If I wasn't two drinks past proper brain function, I'd think of something sexy to say.

Reece: Get some sleep, Smurfette. Can't wait to C U when you get back.

She had someone to come back to. A warmth settled over her.

Sloane: I relinquish you from your last task. Score is settled.

Reece: Don't worry. I can think of other favors that'll make up for it.

Sloane pulled up her laptop. Reece was done with the tasks she'd given him. She could have emailed his chief a couple weeks ago, but honestly, she wanted more time with him. And a secret part of her was worried that as soon as she gave him a glowing recommendation, whatever was between them would vanish. Obviously that was ridiculous. But as she was learning, relationships were anything but rational.

She clicked on the email tab and loaded up a message. Might as well start the draft. The room was swirling, but she was suddenly too amped-up to sleep. A draft pulled up onto the screen, and she typed in a few words.

Dear Chief Richards,

I'm happy to report that Reece Jenkins has fulfilled his duty as my humble manservant for the past month. It was very, very hard. Just like certain parts of his body. But he knows just what he's doing. Especially with his tongue. God, that sucker is amazing. Anyway, I know you're probably busy fighting fires or something, so I won't take up too

much of your time. Reece is amazing. Everything
about him. I know it was unintended, but this
brought us together, and I have you to thank for
that.

xo
Sloane Garcia

Sloane giggled and closed down the computer. Obviously that
email would never see the light of day, but it was fun to write it out. She
could just imagine that grumpy old man's eyes bugging while reading it.
She'd write Reece a real email when she got back into town. One that
was professional and gave him a glowing review. Because if his boss was
a hard-ass like Reece claimed, then he needed some help. She nestled
under the cool covers and fell into a deep, dreamless sleep.

Sloane woke up the next morning to seagulls, ocean waves, and the
throbbing pain of a hangover. Too much wine. She vaguely remembered kicking back a few glasses last night, but nothing out of the
ordinary.

She squinted her eyes and managed to pull herself out of bed and
make her way to her purse out in the main room to grab a bottle of
aspirin.

"Rough night?"

Erin was in the living room, reading a book. Madison was on the
couch, watching an episode of *Real Housewives*. They both looked like
they were completely unfazed by a night of drinking.

"How do you two look so good? I feel like death warmed over."
Double that. Like twice-baked potatoes.

"Did you drink water before bed?" Erin asked.

Sloane scrubbed her hands over her face. Her mouth was dry and her breath could possibly knock out anyone in a five-mile radius. "I knew I was forgetting something."

"Rookie mistake. Breakfast is on the stove," Madison said.

She glanced to the stove, where a pan with french toast and sausage sat. Bless her friends. She grabbed a glass from the kitchen and filled it with tap water. After swallowing a couple of aspirin, she filled a plate with food and went over to the couch and sat next to Madison.

"I'm glad I have you guys."

Madison tore her attention away from the show. "Because we always fix your hangovers?"

"That, and because you're the best." She shoved a piece of french toast in her mouth.

Erin flipped through her planner and tapped her pen to the page. "I was thinking after breakfast we could—"

"No," Madison and Sloane said in unison.

Erin held up her hands in surrender. "Fine. We'll see where the day takes us. Sheesh." She closed her planner.

Sloane leaned back against the couch and raked the tines of her fork through the syrup on her plate. Some of the women were getting into it on the show, one of them pouring a drink into the other's hair.

"Oh, girl. You are so brutal," Madison squeaked, covering her mouth with her hands. "Take Bianca down."

"Too bad you didn't get a chance to go on that reality show. I think you'd be the silent, plotting type."

Madison swatted her. "Would not."

The three of them settled into easy conversation as they continued to watch the show. After breakfast, they spent the rest of the morning on the beach and arrived back into town that evening. She couldn't wait to see Reece tomorrow.

Chapter Twenty-Seven

Reece walked through the entrance of the station and set down his backpack in the sleep area. The past few shifts had been eventful during the night, and Reece had almost decided against bringing anything to sleep in.

Jake and Hollywood were already sitting at the table across from the kitchen, playing paper football, waiting for the morning meeting to start.

The chief was still in his office, which gave Reece at least a few minutes without the guy breathing down his neck.

The chief breezed out of his office, wearing a gruff expression on his face. He looked more pissed off than normal. This close to retirement, Reece didn't blame him. Most of the guys who were close to checking out weren't there mentally.

"Busy day today," Chief Richards said. "We have the Toys for Tots drive ending soon. Need one of you to drive the gifts over to the receiving center."

"I'll do it at the end of my shift tomorrow." Reece hated kissing ass, but if it got him in the chief's good graces, he wasn't above doing backflips at this point.

Chief nodded, his sour expression not changing. "Cole, go ahead with the lesson for today."

With that, Hollywood flipped to the tabbed sheet of paper in the medical binder. "Figured we could go over neck-injury procedures."

Reece listened to the information and nodded along, comparing his prior knowledge to the info Hollywood relayed. After the lesson, they decided to go wash the truck, since A shift had left it a mess the night prior during all the storms. Mud caked the rear steps of the engine, clear up to the ladder-stowage deck. Tree debris was caught in the wheel wells. It looked like they'd taken Engine 11 for a little off-roading expedition. In actuality, they'd had to help with the mudslide on 84 early last evening. Reece had kept by his phone just in case they needed more men on the scene.

Reece grabbed a couple of buckets and the soap while Jake untangled the hose from the station bay.

"What's got you smiling today?" Jake asked.

"Sloane gets home today. I get to see her tomorrow after our shift ends." He'd turned into one of those cheeseball Hallmark cards and had zero qualms if anyone noticed.

"Seems like you two are getting along lately. Something change?"

Everything had changed. In a matter of weeks, they'd gone from wanting to strangle each other to sharing a bed. The thought gave him whiplash. And now he was one of those schmucks who had a stupid grin plastered on his face. For the first time in a while, he was happy.

"You know, Christmas is this week."

Yeah, he still needed to get presents for his family. He'd go with his typical gift card for his sisters and something for the food truck for his mom. Last year he'd bought her a new mixer so she could retire the one that'd been in use since before Reece had been born.

"You trying to hint that you want me to get you something? I figured I didn't have to dress up, now that Erin's in your life."

Jake gave him a quick spray with the hose. "Sloane will be over at the house on Christmas. Erin already set it up since Sloane's parents are in Florida."

The last time he'd had a woman over for a holiday, he'd given Amber a promise ring. And that was how he learned the hard way that promise rings were complete crap. But Sloane wasn't Amber. She wasn't the type to screw him over. The shredded remnants of his heart clung on to that, to the fact that he could trust her.

"Do I need to get something for her? Mom says to, but we haven't been seeing each other that long."

Jake shrugged, then went on to spray the soap off the engine. "Depends."

"On what?" Reece continued scrubbing at the dirty wheel well.

"Do you want to keep that relationship?"

"You mean a gift is expected?" This was why he didn't do relationships. He didn't like the expectations. He didn't think that Sloane would expect that of him. She knew him. Knew that he would rather show his appreciation for her in other ways. Like the ones he planned to do when he was off shift in the morning.

Hollywood came around the corner and soaked his sponge in the soapy water. "Cheap-ass Reece complaining about buying a Christmas present for his new lady? Don't drop the ball, man."

"I'm not dropping the ball. There is no need to do presents this early in a relationship." Although his opinion was starting to waver, with Jake and Hollywood staring at him.

"I know you're a cheap ass, but if you care about someone, you get them a little something for Christmas," said Jake.

"I dressed up as Santa one year. That was enough of a present," Hollywood said, waggling his brows.

"Yeah, and how well did that relationship turn out?" Reece said.

"Doesn't have to break the bank. Just has to show her that you care," Jake said. "I'm getting Erin a few packs of washi tape and new pens for her planner because I know that's how she gets her rocks off."

Reece knew Sloane. Had known her for years. He knew what she liked. What she hated. There had to be something he could find her.

"You could always get her a movie. Chicks dig those Lifetime flicks," Hollywood said, taking a towel to the engine.

"Sloane thinks they're lame. Says there's not enough kissing in them or something."

Hollywood's brows shot up. "Sounds like you're really into her."

Yeah, he was surprised too. Just a few weeks ago, he was worried that she'd poison his food.

Before his friends could bust his chops, the chief busted through the engine-bay door, the handle smacking against the wall with a loud clang.

The chief looked directly at Reece, his face red, the vein in his forehead visible, even from a distance. "Jenkins, in my office now."

Chapter Twenty-Eight

The chief's tone made the hair on the back of Reece's neck stand up. Chief Richards channeled grumpy asshole better than anyone Reece knew, but this took it to the next level.

Hollywood clapped him on the back as Reece passed him, and he caught the door before it slammed shut.

He trailed behind the chief, and it brought him back to his middle-school days when he'd be sent to the principal's office with Jake. He followed the chief into the office and shut the door behind him.

"I got a disturbing email from a Ms. Sloane Garcia last night." The vein in his head was still throbbing. Not a good sign. He hadn't seen him this mad in . . . ever.

Reece's mind raced. It'd been a great night. They'd texted until he fell asleep. What the hell could have gone wrong between then and now?

"What did it say, sir?" he said cautiously.

Richards waved his hand dismissively. "As an employee of the city, it is important for us to uphold a certain image."

"I'd say I've done my part in that." What was he getting at? What was in that email?

The chief's hands were clasped on the desk, and he leveled Reece with a look of disgust.

"Did you have inappropriate relations with a contest winner?"

Shit. Why would Sloane send an email like that to the chief, of all people? "To be fair, I have known Sloane my entire life. She's my little sister's best friend."

"And someone who could ruin our image as a station. You do realize we are under a hiring freeze, and extreme budget cuts are heading our way. Between that and a serial arsonist on our hands, we have reporters up our asses trying to find their own connections. Do you really think people are going to want to make donations if they think we're screwing around when we're supposed to be working?"

Anger flashed hot in Reece's blood. He'd always taken his job seriously. He took pride in his work. And he knew Sloane. She wouldn't say something like that. This had to be a misunderstanding.

"I don't know what was in that email, but I can assure you that what I do in my off time has nothing to do with my performance on the job."

"I'd like to believe that. But with your actions over the past month, two injuries sending you to the hospital, I find that hard to believe."

Reece stared at the chief, his fingers digging into the chipped plastic handles of the swivel chair. This was unbelievable. He knew the guy had it out for him, but what happened on calls wasn't completely in his control. "What are you trying to say?"

"I'm saying that I'll have no choice but to bring you to the ethics board." He paused and gave him a hard look. "Unless you start looking for a place to transfer in the New Year. Then this can all just go away. I hear there's an opening at Mount Halo."

No.

It'd be a death sentence.

His anger washed away and was replaced with a wave of panic sliding over his skin. What was in this email? There had to be something he could do to fix this. "Sir, you can't do that."

The chief slammed his palms down on the table. "I can. And I will. I don't want this rubbing off on the rest of your team. I've disliked how you've performed ever since I transferred to this station, and this is the final straw. Your days are numbered here."

Reece's temper flared. How could this be happening? Things with Sloane were great, which made this the absolute betrayal. She knew how much this job meant to him. There'd be no way she'd jeopardize this for him. He needed details from her. And fast. "This is insane. I've done everything by the books."

"See if the district cares. They don't want a scandal. And everything about this is controversial." The chief smiled. Actually smiled. And Reece lost it.

"Fuck it. I'm out of here."

The chief's face turned a deeper shade of red. Reece might find it comical if he wasn't the central focus of his wrath. "You will not. You still have twenty minutes left of your shift."

He leveled the chief with as much disdain as he could muster. "According to you, I'm one to break the rules. So watch me."

And with that, he shoved up out of the chair and stormed out of the room.

He strode past the meeting area, past the kitchen, and went to grab his backpack from his locker. Jake came around the corner just as Reece made his way to exit the station. "Hey, what's going on? We still need to check the engine, prep it for C shift." He blocked Reece's way, putting his hand on his shoulder.

"No. I'm not. Get out of my way." He shouldered past Jake.

Jake threw up his palms. "What's going on?"

He shrugged off Jake's second attempt to try to stop him. "Ask Sloane. But I'm finished here. Seems I'm going to be transferring soon. To Mount Halo." He'd need to contact his union rep to see what could be done, but from where Reece was sitting, it didn't look good.

Jake's face paled. He knew exactly what transferring there would mean. A career ender. "Shit. What did Sloane do?"

Reece was already out the door, ignoring his friend. He needed answers. He needed this to all be a horrible misunderstanding. "I'm about to find out." He'd give her a chance to explain. But he doubted anything she could say would make this better.

Sloane sat huddled under two blankets, bingeing on another episode of *The Great British Bake Off* when three loud knocks came from the door.

They were ominous knocks. Ones that meant business. Her stomach bottomed out as she tried to think of who it could possibly be. She bolted off the couch and opened the door to find Reece. His cheeks were red, his lips tilted into a grimace. The sight sent a chill creeping down her spine.

"What's going on?" she asked.

"Did you send an email to my chief?" He was breathing hard, regarding her with an intensity that made her want to shrink into herself.

"I was just typing it up. A glowing recommendation. You're welcome, by the way." Sheesh. She'd had nothing but praise for him. Starting with how he'd completed all his tasks, was a perfect gentleman, and a great, upstanding member of society.

"Did you also mention how I've had inappropriate relations with a contest winner?" His tone was venomous.

Sloane found herself immediately going on the defensive. She didn't like how he was talking to her, like she was in the wrong. "Excuse me? I haven't even sent it yet. Why are you so worried?" Sure, the previous draft may have contained some X-rated content, but she'd been smart enough to delete that the night at the beach.

He let out a humorless laugh. "Oh, but you did."

"Reece. I'm sure I didn't." But now she was starting to question herself. Had she deleted the email? She was sure she had.

"Apparently you told my boss something. And now I'm going to be transferred to another station."

"I did not." She pulled out her phone and clicked on the email in her drafts. "Here, take a look for yourself."

Reece's brows furrowed as his eyes scanned her phone. He thumbed down, and then his frown deepened. "What about the one in your sent folder?"

She took the phone and scanned it. Right there in her sent messages was the original email. The one she'd written while drunk.

Oh my God. Had she really clicked "Send" instead of "Delete"?

Especially with his tongue. God, that sucker is amazing. "Oh my God." Hot tears pricked behind her eyes. "Oh my God. I'm so sorry."

He blew out a long sigh and shoved his hand through his hair. After a moment, he nodded to himself. "I'm going to need some time."

No. They'd make this right. *She'd* make this right.

This was bad. So bad. To the point where even the best intentions might not be able to fix this.

"You have to know this was an accident." He had to believe that. After all they'd gone through, she wouldn't screw him over like this.

His eyes were cold as he regarded her. "Was it, Sloane? We have been at each other for so long. Are you sure this wasn't just a ploy to get back at me?"

What an asshole. Did he really think that little of her that he thought she'd fake this whole thing just to ruin his life? "I wouldn't do that to you. I mean, yes, at the start, it was fun making your life hell, but I would never ruin your job. I'm not evil."

He just shook his head, clearly not buying anything she had to say. Heat washed over her face, and her chest ached at what he'd implied. That he really did think it was possible she'd do this.

"Well, it's been done. Nothing I can do about it now. But I was serious about the break. I don't think I can do this anymore. Not until I figure this out," he said.

She'd never thought she'd ever have to fight for a guy, especially Reece. But the panic rose in her throat. She'd finally found someone she could count on, and she'd hurt him in the worst way. This job meant everything to him. "Reece, please. You have to believe me." Her voice cracked. Tears stung her eyes. She'd messed this up for him. It was her fault that he was losing something that he loved so much. "I'm so sorry."

A heavy weight pulsed through her chest. If someone had asked Sloane a month ago if she'd care if Reece lost his job, she would have laughed. Told them that karma had probably caught up with him. But at the moment, devastation ripped through her. She'd hurt him. Someone she cared deeply for. And now she'd lost him, and there was nothing she could do about it.

"I'll see you around." He gave a curt nod and then walked down the hallway toward the elevator.

"Reece," she called after him. *Oh God.* She was such an idiot.

He ignored her and went into the empty elevator. She debated sprinting after him, like some maniac. But what was she going to say? She'd already ruined his career. No need to add insult to injury. She closed the door and slid down the wall. Tears streamed down her face.

She had to make this right.

Chapter Twenty-Nine

"Come on. You've been moping for days," Erin said. "Christmas is in forty-two hours. Let's get out of the house and get you some fresh air."

Reece was spread across his couch in his boxers and a shirt he hadn't bothered changing since he'd last seen Sloane. He'd only moved from this spot for one shift at the station, where he'd managed to avoid the chief.

Peaches lay against him, and he stroked her fur and closed his eyes. "I don't need it." It was just him and Peaches now. He'd called up Kurt from the shelter this morning and finalized the adoption. At least something good had come out of this whole debacle. Peaches may not have been a huge dog, and they definitely needed to work out a happy medium of acceptable outfits, but she made Reece happy, and right now he could use a little bit of that.

He hadn't bothered to return the house decorations yet. It was the last reminder he had of her, and he wasn't quite ready to let go of it.

"You did hear the part where she apologized. For the millionth time," Erin said, repositioning herself on the chair across from him. Sloane's chair. Yep, he'd have to get rid of that too. The whole apartment would be bare bones by the time he stripped away everything that reminded him of her. He'd go back to the shell of an existence he'd been living before the auction. Before everything went sideways. He'd called his union rep yesterday, who'd said he'd try to work something out, but it wasn't looking promising.

"Doesn't matter. You do realize that I'm losing my place at the station because of it."

"And that's devastating. Trust me. I know what it's like to lose a job." She squeezed his hand. "But what good is it going to do you by carrying this around? I've never seen either of you so happy before—you're really going to give that up?"

"She cost me my job." Anything else. Sloane could have picked anything else to screw with, and he could have laughed it off. But not this.

"That asshole chief of yours was looking for anything to put the nail in your coffin."

He thought about the chief, whom he could never seem to please. Everything rubbed the chief the wrong way. And Reece had come to terms with the fact that he would never be in his good graces, especially after what had happened. *Thank you, Sloane.*

"What does that matter now?"

His sister sighed. "Tell me. You're willing to give up a great thing just because of a mistake?"

"Yes." *Maybe.* He wasn't sure anymore. This was all too confusing. Which was why he didn't do relationships in the first place, because things just got too complicated. "I get what you're trying to do, but honestly, nothing you say is going to change my mind."

"You can be such a stubborn ass. You really want to go back to the way things were before? Look at your apartment. Look at what you've become in the past month. I haven't seen you this happy since high school. Since—"

"Don't bring her up." He didn't want to hear about his ex. Another person who did something that he just couldn't forgive. He'd had enough introspection. He'd done enough dwelling. "If you're done, I'm going to take a shower and head off to bed. Appreciate the concern, but I'm fine."

Erin got up from the chair and made her way to the door. "I love you. You know that, right? And you're coming to Christmas, yes?"

"I'll be there." His mother would send out special ops to retrieve him if he didn't come to Christmas. "Love you too."

He'd been thinking about that word a lot lately. *Love.* Now he didn't know what to think.

Erin shut the door behind her. Reece was left in his empty apartment, everything around him reminding him of Sloane.

He sat down on the couch and tossed the throw pillow aside. *Damn throw pillow.* Peaches hopped up and settled in his lap. The pup let out a sad sigh and laid her head down on his thigh. A paw jabbed into him, and she let out another sigh.

"Don't you give me attitude too. What is this? A girl gang-up?"

Peaches just looked at him with those dark chocolate eyes.

A heavy weight settled in his chest. He didn't know if this would ever go away. He ran a thumb across the dog's cheek. "I know. I miss her too, girl."

Sloane didn't know what the heck had come over her. One minute she was pacing the length of her apartment, and the next, she was standing in front of the chief's door, palms sweating.

She knocked. There was no turning back now.

The chief looked up from his paperwork and frowned. "Ah, Miss Blue Hair. Sloane, is it?"

She nodded.

He held up a hand, motioning her to the chair. "Come in."

"Sir, I won't take up a lot of your time, but I wanted to talk to you about something." She swallowed hard. This grumpy old man just stared at her over the bridge of his glasses, looking like he had zero patience for a second more of her time. She'd make it quick, then.

"I think you've more than said your piece," he said. "And I did get the fourteen emails you sent, by the way."

"Yes, well, my parents always taught me persistence pays off." She smoothed her clammy hands on her pants. Normally she didn't have a problem telling people how she felt. But she needed to tread carefully because she'd already screwed this up enough for Reece.

She stared at the grooves in his face, the way his cheeks had sunk into jowls. He looked like one of those mean, old junkyard dogs. "Go on. Tell me what brings you in that fourteen emails couldn't convey."

"The original email"—she took a deep breath—"I sent that when I was in a . . . not-so-excellent state of mind. That email should have never been sent."

"Okay." He didn't look convinced. She couldn't imagine working for this guy. She'd been lucky and had warm, supportive supervisors who listened to her concerns. Ones who would always give her the benefit of the doubt.

"So I wanted to tell you exactly why Reece Jenkins should stay at your station. The station that is one of the best in the district."

He didn't stop her, so she took that as the green light to open the floodgates. She told him everything. "I know he can come off like an ass sometimes. Believe me. I know. But I don't think you're giving him a fair chance. Everyone who deals with him loves him. I've seen the patients brought in to the hospital."

He had a way with people. He may have had that grumpy outer coating, but inside, Reece was as soft as they came. He was loving and generous and kind. And holy unicorns surfing on a rainbow, Sloane was falling for him, so hard that she might not recover from the impact. And she'd screwed this up beyond repair. So she did the only thing she could think of doing, and kept talking, telling the chief about all the sweet things Sloane had witnessed. From his volunteering at the homeless shelter on Twenty-Seventh Street to taking in a rescue dog to being professional on every level when he was on the job.

"So, as you see, he's never done anything to compromise his job while he's on shift. What we do outside of that is, quite frankly, none of your business, and I'm sorry that email was sent in the first place."

He nodded. "I see."

His expression hadn't changed. He was like a statue sitting there judging her. And she realized in that moment, she didn't think she could fix this. And she didn't know if she was more devastated by the thought that Reece wouldn't be here after the New Year or the fact that he wouldn't want to be with her at all.

"Does that mean you'll give him another chance?"

He drummed his fingers along the barren desk. "I'll take it into consideration."

That last shred of hope deflated. She didn't think it possible, but she felt worse than when she'd first knocked on his door.

She nodded. She knew when to raise the white flag, and right now was one of those times. "Thank you for your time."

She stood and gave him one last hopeful glance and then made her way out of his office.

Holiday music blared over the speaker system at the station on Christmas Eve as Reece cooked chicken for the guys. Everyone was in a festive mood, especially Jake and Hollywood, who were stoked to have the holiday off for the first time in three years. Reece, on the other hand, was debating taking on another shift. Anything to take his mind off the past few days.

"Jenkins, get in my office," Chief said as soon as he rounded the corner to the kitchen.

Jake took over with the cooking while Reece wiped off his hands and walked toward the chief's office. He was not in the mood to talk to the chief. Not that he ever was, but he definitely wasn't now that he had a target on his back and he'd be transferred by the end of the month. Mere months before the chief was set to retire.

He stood in the doorway and looked at the chief sitting at his chair. It was like Groundhog Day all over again. What else could he take away this time? Put him back to rookie status? Make him stay in from calls?

"Sit." He motioned to the chair across from him.

Reece shut the office door and took a seat.

"Your girlfriend stopped by while you were out on a call today."

Reece cocked his head. If this was just another tactic to get under his skin, it was working. He pressed his teeth together, fighting for calm. After three nights of nonexistent sleep, he wasn't in the mood to screw around. "I don't know what you're talking about."

"The one with the blue hair." He waved his hand, seeming to conjure her name in the air. "Sloane or whatever. Unless you have more than one girlfriend."

"I don't have any girlfriend, sir. We broke up." They were never officially together, but that technicality didn't make it any less painful.

The hurt on her face still flashed across his lids whenever he closed his eyes. Didn't matter, though. He'd had fun while it lasted, but this was exactly why he didn't have attachments—it messed with his life.

"That's not how I saw it." He shook his head. "Anyway, she's a scary little thing. But she did make some good points."

Reece swore on all things holy that if she screwed this up any more, he'd do everyone a favor and take an extended vacation down to the Florida Keys before a brain aneurysm hit.

"What kind of points?"

"That you're better off here than at another station. Your men look up to you. It'd be bad morale to switch that up. Plus, they all put in a request to transfer to wherever you went."

"Bennett and Gibson did that?"

Chief nodded.

He loved his friends.

"I don't need that many lateral transfers in the district. Looks bad on our station. Especially with the arson investigations." He waved his hand dismissively.

His mind reeled. Seemed like he had a lot of people on his side.

He allowed himself a moment of hope. To really understand what the chief was trying to say. "Does this mean I'm staying here?"

"I won't have to put up with you much longer since I'm retiring in a couple of months, so, yes. You're here. Let the next chief deal with you."

Wow. The chief's change of heart completely floored him. "Thank you, sir."

"Don't look at me like you want to hug me. Now get out of my office before I change my mind."

Reece didn't like the man, but at the moment, he actually would consider hugging him. Maybe he'd been touched by the holiday spirit.

Instead, he pushed out of the chair with a newfound lightness. He wasn't completely screwed over. Well, besides the whole thing with Sloane, but he'd push that to the corners of his mind for now.

Jake and Hollywood were in the kitchen when Reece came out of the chief's office. Hollywood was spreading Miracle Whip across a toasted hoagie roll while Jake diced up the cooked chicken.

"Chief bend you over his desk and give you twenty lashings with a ruler?" Jake asked.

Hollywood licked the remnants of Miracle Whip off the knife and tossed it into the sink. "From the look on his face, I think he went with an open palm."

"Yeah, he does have that afterglow to him," Jake said.

Reece leaned against the fridge, still floored by the turn of events. From what the chief had told him. "You assholes really put in for a lateral transfer?"

Jake nodded. "No use splitting up a good team."

Reece's throat tightened. What had he done to deserve friends like this? And Sloane . . . she'd gone to bat for him even when he'd turned her away and ignored her calls.

"Thanks," he said, his voice strained.

"Don't leave us hanging here. What did he say?" Hollywood asked.

"I have my job back. He's canceled the transfer."

Hollywood clapped him on the back. "Good to have your grumpy ass back."

"I think this calls for some celebratory beers after Christmas," Jake said.

Reece nodded. He'd need more than one.

"Did he say what changed his mind?" Jake asked.

"Your threats, and I guess Sloane scared him into submission."

Hollywood took a bite of his sandwich. "She does do that good crazy eye. I bet she pulled that on him."

The workings of a smile twitched at his lips. Anyone who knew her would know it was all a front. But the thought of her here, fighting for his job, made something in his chest shift. He shouldn't have yelled at her.

Everything in him screamed to take the easy way out and shoot her a quick text that said thank you. But that was cheap. She at least deserved to talk face-to-face.

He pulled out his phone.

Reece: Do you have time to talk tomorrow?

Sloane: Yeah. Let me know when you get off shift, and I'll head over.

He closed his phone. This was a disaster in the making, but a disaster worth fighting for.

Chapter Thirty

Erin: OMG, GUYS. I HAVE NEWS.

Sloane's heart went into overdrive. She'd been staring at her phone all morning, waiting for Reece to text that he was ready to talk. Once she pushed past the initial disappointment of the message not being from him, she opened up the group chat with Erin and Madison.

Madison: Okay . . . care to share?

Erin: LOOK.

A picture came through of a sparkly solitaire diamond ring surrounded by dozens of tiny diamonds. Happiness welled in her chest to think that her best friend was going to spend the rest of her life with the man she loved.

Sloane: OMGGGGGGGGGGG!

Madison: Ah! Congrats <3

Madison: Also, we told you so.

Sloane: Totally did. So happy for you, sweetie.

Sloane's heart swelled. Just as she suspected, an engagement before the New Year. She couldn't wait to see the ring in person. To give her best friend a hug, to share that bit of happiness. She needed it after the crappy past couple of days.

Erin: Get on over here so we can all celebrate together.

Madison: Will be over soon.

Sloane: Same.

As soon as she heard from Reece.

Sloane wrung her fingers as she waited for Reece to text her back, that he was ready to talk. She'd never been one to lament, or stare at her phone, wondering when a boy would call. Then again, she'd never felt this way about a man before. Or shamelessly begged a boyfriend's boss to reconsider their transfer request. She didn't even know if it had done any good.

For the first time in her life, it didn't feel like Christmas. Besides Erin's epically good news. Even so, she didn't feel like spreading her holiday Scroogeness.

Her phone buzzed on her table, and she jumped, grabbing it and opening the text.

Reece: I'm ready.

In warp speed, Sloane grabbed her keys from the counter and went to open her door. And immediately came face-to-face with Reece. Or, more accurately, face-to-chest. Her first instinct was to crumple into him, for his strong arms to wrap her in a hug. To press her nose into his shirt and inhale his scent. A lump formed in her throat at the thought that this might never happen again. And she wouldn't blame him.

"I think I still see the dust you kicked up from sprinting to the door."

She planted her hands on her hips. "Did you come here to mock me?" Because that would be so Reece. Find a way to rub salt in the wound. This time it was one that he'd left. All because of her stupid actions.

His gaze softened. "No. I came to talk to you."

"I'm so sorry, Reece." She didn't know if it'd worked or not, talking to his boss, but she figured she couldn't have made it any worse. She'd do anything to get his job back. Jump through flaming hoops, hike the Pacific Crest Trail in nothing but Birkenstocks and her birthday suit, sit through fifty million horrible dinners with all the Aarons of the world. Tears threatened to spill over, but she blinked them back.

"I know you are. And I shouldn't have freaked out on you."

"You had every right to. I ruined your job. Now you're going to be split up from Jake and Cole, and it's all my fault."

That was what she regretted most. Losing him was devastating, but to think of him unhappy going to work with people he didn't know, the man who loved routine, made her heart clench.

"I'm not going to be transferred. It seemed a very determined blue-haired woman had a talk with my chief and convinced him to let me stay. Do you know anyone who fits that description?"

"They obviously have a great choice in hair color."

He shook his head, his brows pinching together. "Why did you do that for me?"

She swallowed past the dryness in her mouth. How could he even ask that? After she'd screwed things up for him so badly. "Reece." Her voice cracked. "I'd do anything for you." It was in that moment she realized how true that statement rang.

"I know. And I should have let it go earlier. I'm sorry for being a complete asshole." He let out a long, drawn-out sigh. "I just can't seem to do anything right when it comes to you."

"You do. I've been too hard on you. You wouldn't have even been in this predicament if I hadn't bid on you at the auction."

He shook his head. "It's the best thing you could have done." He smoothed a finger down her cheek. "It brought us together."

"I promise to never send drunk emails to your boss again."

He chuckled. "I'd like that. And now I think it's time to celebrate."

"Celebrate what?"

"Christmas." He motioned to the decorations on her door as if to say, *Duh*. "My whole family is waiting for you."

She nodded. "I'd love that."

He grabbed her hips and pulled her to him, his mouth a soft caress over her jaw, planting light kisses along her skin. "Sloane?"

"Yeah?"

"I love you."

She smiled against his chest. "I love you too."

One year later . . .

"Open the present!" Reece said.

Sloane snuggled against Reece in the Jenkinses' living room. Peaches was curled up at Sloane's feet, gnawing on a piece of wrapping paper. Jake and Erin were cuddled up on the couch, talking with Reece's mom about their upcoming nuptials in May. Madison sat on the floor with Bailey and Andie, talking tech stuff and Andie's first few months at PSU. Later that day, Sloane and Reece would be boarding a plane to visit her parents in Florida and staying there until the New Year.

Reece handed her the last present under the tree, a large package that squished under her touch.

"What is it?" she asked.

He shook his head and smiled. "Just open it."

She tore at the package and unfolded a soft blanket with a picture of Sloane, Reece, and Peaches on the front. The top read BEST FOSTER DOG FAMILY.

Family. She liked the sound of that.

Over the past year, she and Reece had grown closer, and she'd moved into his apartment. They were moving next month into the house on Mississippi. The one with the purple door and the heart-engraved shutters.

She turned the blanket over and found a huge picture of Blake Shelton.

Peaches scurried away, hiding behind Madison.

"You pick a side, depending on if we want her up on the couch or not," he said.

"This is perfect for the new house." They'd bought the Craftsman last month, and the sale had gone off without a hitch.

She turned the blanket over and called Peaches back.

"You know what would be even more perfect?" he asked, whispering in her ear. She shivered, thinking of all that his deep voice promised.

She scooted around to face him. "What?"

"If you'd be my wife." He pulled a box out of his back pocket and opened it up, revealing a princess-cut diamond ring with deep sapphires lining the band. It was perfect. "You are the absolute best thing to ever happen to me. You're my best friend."

"Hey, I thought *I* was your best friend," Jake said.

Erin smacked Jake on the chest. "Let the man propose."

Reece shook his head and smiled. "Please make me the luckiest man in the world. I want to live the rest of my life with you."

She nodded, tears streaming down her face. "Yes."

He slid the ring on her finger, and it fit perfectly. "I love you."

His lips met hers in a warm, languid kiss. "I love you too," she said.

Erin, Andie, Bailey, Madison, and Mrs. Jenkins all swarmed around her, looking at the ring and pulling her into a hug.

Life may have a few curveballs in store, but she'd be ready for them. Especially since she'd have Reece by her side.

ACKNOWLEDGMENTS

First, I'd like to thank my fantastic editor, Maria Gomez. I will forever be grateful for you and your support. A huge thank-you to Andrea Hurst, who always manages to push my writing to the next level. Eternal gratitude to Colleen, Devan, Elise, Brittany, Gabby, and the rest of the team for making the whole publishing process so smooth.

Thank you to my readers. You are the reason I sit down at my computer each day.

A huge thank-you to firefighters Brian Mintie and Andrew Burg for answering my questions. Any mistakes are completely my own.

Chanel, Lia, and AJ—I may not get half the pop culture references you throw around, but thanks for putting up with my Rose ways. I'd be lost without you three.

Danielle—thank you for being a great PA and friend.

And to my family—I love you. Thank you for always supporting me.

ABOUT THE AUTHOR

Photo © 2012 Leahana Byrd

Jennifer Blackwood is the *USA Today* bestselling author of the contemporary romance series The Rule Breakers, Snowpocalypse, and Flirting with Fire. Jennifer writes funny and warm novels, as well as sizzlingly sexy romances. When she's not writing, you can find her hanging out at coffee shops and in the planner aisle of Michaels.

Jennifer lives in Oregon with her son, a husband who reminds her that happily ever afters do happen in real life, and an adorable (but poorly behaved) black Lab. For more information on Jennifer and her books, visit her website at www.JenniferBlackwood.com, or follow her on Twitter (@Jen_Blackwood) and Facebook (@AuthorJenniferBlackwood).